146807

D1713280

Texas Horsetrading Co.

Skull Creek

Also by Gene Shelton
in Large Print:

Tascosa Gun
Texas Horsetrading Co.
Hangtree Pass

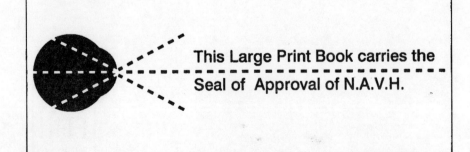

This Large Print Book carries the
Seal of Approval of N.A.V.H.

Texas Horsetrading Co.

Skull Creek

GENE SHELTON

G.K. Hall & Co. • Thorndike, Maine

Published in 1998 by arrangement with The Berkley Publishing Group, a member of Penguin Putnam, Inc.

G.K. Hall Large Print Western Series.

The text of this Large Print edition is unabridged.
Other aspects of the book may vary from the original edition.

Set in 16 pt. Plantin.

Printed in the United States on permanent paper.

Library of Congress Cataloging in Publication Data

Shelton, Gene.
    Skull Creek : Texas Horsetrading Co. / Gene Shelton.
        p.   cm.
    ISBN 0-7838-0137-8 (lg. print : hc : alk. paper)
    1. Large type books. I. Title.
[PS3569.H39364S58   1998]
813′.54—dc21   98-5794

Texas Horsetrading Co.

Skull Creek

ONE

Brubs McCallan had had worse mornings.

He was sure he had. He just couldn't remember when.

For that matter, he couldn't remember exactly why he was waking up today in the Laredo jail with only one arm —

The thought jarred him fully alert in a quick blast of panic before he finally realized his left arm was still attached. He couldn't feel it because it was numb, tucked back beneath his head so that the circulation was cut off. The arm wasn't missing. It was only asleep.

Brubs pried the arm from beneath his head with his free hand. It was like picking up a tree limb. There was no feeling in the flesh. He massaged the arm for a few minutes, then winced as the numbness gave way to tingling needle pricks, as if little four-inch-high Apaches were slapping his arm with prickly pear pads. He swung his legs over the edge of the splintery wooden cot, sat up, and groaned aloud. More of the little red savages were at work on the back of his neck, whapping away at the base of his skull with dull tomahawks. And those were just the beginnings of his assorted aches and pains.

Brubs forced puffy eyes open wider and

glanced around the small cell. He had the place all to himself. At least, he moaned inwardly, he could die in peace. He had a hard time figuring how so many bruises, scrapes, bumps, and sprains could fit in his five-foot-seven frame that carried 160 pounds. He figured he might weigh a tad less than that now, considering the amount of skin he'd lost somewhere. He couldn't recall exactly where he'd lost it.

He became aware of the coarse stiffness in the thick, sand-colored mustache that bristled across his upper lip. He lifted a cautious hand and rubbed the matted hairs. The hand came away dusted with flecks of dried blood. Brubs touched his fingers to his skewed nose and yelped aloud at the quick, sharp stab of white pain.

"Dammit," he muttered to himself through swollen, split lips, "I done went and got my beak busted again. Three times in four years. That there's enough to plumb scorch a man's drawers." He ground his teeth and blinked against the tears as he pushed the squashed cartilage back into the remote semblance of a nose. It started bleeding again. Brubs tilted his head back, pulled the soiled bandanna from around his neck, and pressed the cloth against his nostrils.

From that angle he stared at the cell's only light source. A small paneless window crossed by iron straps showed the gray, weak light of the overcast late February sky outside. Brubs studied the window for a moment. The iron straps were sunk in the middle of an adobe wall at least three feet thick. Not even a team of good draft horses could rip out those bars. The cell door was made of similar thick iron straps, riveted to a heavy metal frame buried deep into the stuccoed adobe interior wall.

Brubs decided he would just be wasting his time trying to break out of the Laredo lockup. And at the moment, he was suffering too much to even try.

The seepage from his nose finally stopped. The little Apaches had sent out for reinforcements. Another war party clubbed rifle butts against his temples and their squaws gouged at his eyes with flint-tipped spears. A housefly buzzed past his mustache. Brubs swatted at the insect, missed, and whapped his fingers against his tender snout. His eyes started watering again.

"Good morning, sunshine."

Brubs turned toward the cell door. Dave Willoughby stood outside the jail cell, a slash of white teeth marking his grin. Willoughby looked fresh as a daisy — clean clothes, boots polished, even his hat brushed. Brubs figured Willoughby probably would smell like bay rum, if Brubs could smell through the busted beak. Willoughby had an aversion to good old honest dirt and whiskers. It seemed to Brubs that Willoughby wasted a hell of a lot of time on baths and razors. Brubs figured bathwater and razors weren't among life's necessaries if there wasn't a woman around. Not even then if the woman wasn't overly persnickety.

Brubs groaned aloud. "You don't have to yell,

dammit. Anybody get hurt in the wreck?"

Willoughby lifted a quizzical eyebrow. "What wreck?"

"Them two Union Pacific trains that hit head-on between my ears. Couldn't nothin' else cause a man this much hurt."

"Well," Willoughby said, "that teamster you decided to whip was about the size of a UP locomotive, now that you mention it."

Brubs sighed. "That what got me throwed in here?"

"Along with a few other assorted violations of the law. Misdemeanor sins, mostly, with a few bordering on felony charges." Willoughby leaned against the iron straps of the cell door, his neatly combed brown hair almost touching the split log rafters of the jail ceiling. Willoughby took up a lot of space top to bottom at six foot two, but not much side to side. He didn't outweigh Brubs by more than ten pounds. Brubs got his build from the badger clan. Willoughby ran more toward the mountain lion breed.

"You don't look so sprightly this morning, partner," Willoughby said cheerfully.

"When you get tired of smirkin' about it," Brubs grumped, "you can tell me how come I'm in here, dyin' a little piece at a time, and you're out there without no scratch a-showin'. Seems damned unpartner-like to me. Man's friends ought to suffer with 'im."

The smile faded from Willoughby's face. "You honestly don't remember?"

"Wouldn'ta asked if I did."

"It's a long story. I'll be right back." Willoughby stepped away from the cell, clattered around out of sight for a few minutes, and came back carrying two heavy china mugs. He nudged the cell door open with the toe of a boot.

"How'd you do that?" Brubs said.

"Do what?"

"Just kick that door open thataway."

"Oh," Willoughby said. "It wasn't locked."

"You mean I coulda just walked out?"

Willoughby shrugged. "Night deputy said he didn't see any reason to lock it. You obviously weren't going anywhere last night. I borrowed some of the deputy's coffee. I thought you could probably use some to get your heart started this morning."

Brubs sighed. "I'd shoot damn near anybody for a cup right now." He reached for the mug.

Willoughby put his own mug on the end of the cot, pulled a small bottle from his hip pocket, uncorked it, and added a generous splash of whiskey to Brubs's coffee. "Doctor Willoughby's Patented Elixir for Banishment of Sins of Evenings Past," he said. "No charge to regular patients."

Brubs sipped at the steaming liquid and sighed. "Mother's milk to a starvin' babe," he said. "Now that I got an outside chance to live, what happened and how come you ain't in here with me?"

Willoughby folded himself onto the cot across from Brubs. "We came into Laredo looking for some horses —"

11

"I recollect that much," Brubs interrupted. "Get to the other part."

The slight grin played at the corners of Willoughby's mouth again. "Well, we didn't find any horses for sale, but of course you found the cantina. Along about ten o'clock you started growing whiskey hair and pawing the ground over a pretty young Mexican girl."

"Angelita," Brubs said wistfully. "Her, I remember. I ain't that near dead."

"Anyhow, it seems you and this teamster had the same plans for Angelita. It started out as a minor rutting season contest, like a couple of thick-necked mule deer bucks rattling antlers against tree trunks, and escalated from there. The first thing I knew, you and the teamster were thumping each other severely about the head and torso."

"Who won?"

"I honestly couldn't say, Brubs."

Brubs lowered a puffy-browed stare at Willoughby. "You still ain't said how come you ain't beat up and hurtin' like me."

Willoughby sipped at his coffee. "At the time, it appeared that you had things under control and didn't need any assistance. So I asked myself, 'What would my friend, mentor, business partner, and genuine Texan Brubs McCallan do in a situation such as this?' And the answer came to me like the clarion call of a reveille bugle. Angelita and I went upstairs while you and the teamster finished wrecking the cantina."

Brubs glared directly at Willoughby for several heartbeats. Finally, his mouth twitched. A slight grin tugged at the corners of his swollen lips. "I'll be double damned for an egg-suckin' hound," he said. "For a Yankee college boy, you're learnin' Texan ways sure enough. Glad to hear it weren't like you quit your partner for nothin'. How long you stay upstairs?"

"All night. I must admit I'm a bit tired this morning. A rather demanding girl, Angelita. Most resilient young woman." Willoughby took a hefty swallow of coffee and heaved himself to his feet. "Drink up, Brubs," he said. "As you've pointed out to me many times, half the day's gone and not a lick of work's been done yet."

Brubs downed a swallow. "What's a mentore?"

"What?"

"You said somethin' about a men-tore a minute ago."

"Oh, that. A mentor is a teacher, Brubs. Someone to look up to."

Brubs grunted. "There for a minute I thought you was callin' me one of them half-bull, half-man critters in them books you keep wastin' our hard-earned money on."

"That's a Minotaur. A creature of Greek legend, confined in a labyrinth built by Daedalus —"

Brubs interrupted with a wave of his hand. "Don't go wastin' my time with none of your fancy yarns, Dave. My head hurts enough as 'tis." He held out his cup. "Gimme another slug of that magical elixir. I'm startin' to feel near human again." He paused for a sip of the refilled mug and licked his lips. "Was she worth ten bucks?"

"What?"

"Angelita. She said it'd cost me ten. I never had no woman cost more than five dollars a set-to. She worth it?"

"Oh." Willoughby shrugged. "She would have been, I suppose. She never mentioned money. I didn't know she charged for services rendered."

Brubs stared in disbelief. "You mean to set there and tell me she let you have it for *free?*" At Willoughby's answering nod, the Texan sighed heavily. "I'll never figger out how come females get knee troubles ever' time you show up, Dave Willoughby."

"Knee troubles?"

"Yeah. They can't keep 'em together. It just ain't fair that I work so hard for women and you come by 'em so easy. Can't figger that out at all." He downed another swallow of Willoughby's magic elixir, this one almost pure whiskey, and let the warm glow from his belly charge the little Apaches. Some of the savages fled. He held out the cup again.

Willoughby shook his head. "A little hair of the wolf that bit you should suffice, Brubs." His tone was almost apologetic. "No need to consume the entire animal. We still have work to do."

Brubs sighed in disappointment and drained the last few drops from the mug. "Pains me to say it, partner, but I reckon you're right." He stood,

14

his knees a bit wobbly, and reached for his sweat-stained, almost shapeless hat. The four-inch-tall Apaches seemed to be getting tired of tormenting him; the throbbing in his temples had eased a bit. His broken nose still stung like fury and whistled when he tried to breathe through it, but compared to a half hour ago he felt downright chipper. He clapped his hat on his head and sucked at a skinned knuckle.

"How much it cost to bail me out?"

"Not as much as usual," Willoughby said. "Fifteen dollars for damages to the cantina. Plus a five-dollar bribe to the deputy and a promise we'd get out of Laredo and stay out for a while. I think the deputy mentioned something like thirty years. Starting this morning. I have the horses saddled and waiting out front."

Brubs shrugged. "What the hell. I been run out of better towns than Laredo." He followed his partner to the small office in the front of the jail building. Willoughby handed Brubs his gun belt and battered old Henry .44 rimfire rifle. The Texan strapped the pistol belt around his waist and shouldered the Henry.

The two men strode from the jail into the flat, shadowless gray light of the Laredo town square. Brubs had to tug his hat down against the stiff north wind. Dust eddied across the almost deserted quadrangle. The breeze still held a bit of a bite, the legacy of a winter that had been wet and cold even this far south. The gray clouds overhead made for a gloomy day, but the fresh air helped roust a few more little Apaches from his head.

Brubs's sorrel, Squirrel, and Willoughby's black — which Dave had never bothered to name — waited patiently at the hitch rail. Bedrolls, jackets, and oilskin slickers were tied behind each saddle. The possibles sack was strapped to Willoughby's rig; they were traveling light this trip, carrying only a minimum of supplies and without pack animals.

Brubs stepped up beside Squirrel, shoved his rifle into the boot, and untied his jacket. He glanced at the possibles sack as he slipped into the flannel-lined denim garment. "Got any whiskey in there, partner?"

Willoughby unhitched his black and stepped into the saddle. "Another pint, which I purchased despite my misgivings. I know what happens when you and whiskey get together, my friend, and the results are usually fraught with danger, mayhem, and pestilence."

"A measly little pint," Brubs said with a frown of disappointment. "You should have got at least a quart. Son, there ain't no way I can promote you from temporary Texan to full-growed one if you don't start gettin' your necessaries straight." He swung aboard the sorrel and reined Squirrel toward the westbound street at the end of the town square. The gelding backed his ears and humped his back.

"Damn you, Squirrel, don't you even think it," Brubs growled at the horse. "You pitch with me the shape I'm in this mornin' and you'll be pullin' a plow on a Missouri farm come spring."

The sorrel seemed to understand the threat. He fluttered his nostrils, then lifted his ears, lowered his back, and moved out in a smooth, fast walk.

Willoughby touched spurs to the black and trotted up alongside Brubs. "Well, since we've been summarily tossed out of Laredo, where do we go from here?"

"I'm a-studyin' on that, partner." Brubs rode in silence until the cluster of buildings dropped from view behind the first of a series of rolling, rocky hills studded with ocotillo, mesquite, prickly pear, and a few stunted cedars. Then he pulled Squirrel to a stop. He sat in the saddle for a moment, studying the northern sky, then turned to Willoughby. "How many horses we got back at LaQuesta now, accordin' to your tally?"

"Just over two hundred and fifty," Willoughby said, "if somebody hasn't stolen them while we've been gone."

"Hell, partner, there ain't no horse thieves even know where LaQuesta's at unless they was born there," Brubs said.

"We know."

"I meant real down and dirty, unethical horse thieves. Not us. The Texas Horsetradin' Company never swiped no animals from poor or honest folks." He shrugged. "Don't fret about our horses none. With Old Man Fernandez watchin' the place, them ponies'll be all right." Brubs twisted his head and spat. "All of which means we still need nigh onto fifty head more, and spring's comin' up quick. Be time to head 'em north when the grass greens up."

Willoughby's frown deepened. "I still contend this horse drive idea of yours obviously came from the bottom of a bottle of cheap whiskey. Trail three hundred head of horses, most of them stolen, across three or more states? Through flooded rivers, Indian country, and bandit gangs? It has to be the most absurd proposal I've ever heard."

Brubs ignored the protest. "Gonna rain tonight. Tomorrow mornin' for sure."

Willoughby cast a sharp glance at the stocky Texan. "What's that got to do with this conversation?"

"Good, steady rain'd cover horse tracks right good. Thought we might swing a tad west on the way back —"

"Wait a minute," Willoughby interrupted. "You aren't thinking about raiding the Fishhook again!"

"Don't see why not. Man's gonna pick a mess of peas, he's got to go to the biggest pea patch. Old Man Turbyfill's got the biggest pea patch around when a man needs horses. Course, they ain't all good ones, but they got hooves and hair. Bring a fair price up Kansas way."

Willoughby's face reddened. "Dammit, Brubs, we hit that ranch not more than a month ago. It was just pure blind luck that we got away then. Turbyfill will hang us from the nearest tree."

Brubs winced. "Damned old skinflint'd probably use an old scratchy, wore-out rope, too, 'stead of a nice, comfortable new one." The frown faded. "Now, Dave, don't you go gettin' on the prod on me. Turbyfill won't figger we're dumb enough to raid his remuda again so quick, which makes us smarter'n he is. And it ain't like we'd be swipin' horses from an honest man. Turbyfill's stole more stock in his time than we ever will. Why, I bet he don't own more'n ten horses out of them two hundred head he owns."

"Quit trying your skewed logic on me, Brubs McCallan," Willoughby snapped. "This is not a question of ethics. It's a question of getting dead."

Brubs's grin spread. "You fixin' to start yelpin' again about how I been tryin' to get you killed? I swear, it's a pure puzzlement to me where you got that idea. Ain't I the one sprung you out of that San 'Tone jail and took you under my wing, teachin' you how to be a real genuine Texan and all?"

A muscle twitched in Willoughby's jaw. "In the first place, it wasn't my fault we wound up in jail. I wasn't the one who started the brawl in the saloon. You were. But since you mention it, in the few short months I've ridden with you, I've been shot at many times and actually shot once. I've been chased by Texas Rangers, trampled by horses, almost drowned, and barely escaped emasculation at the hands of irate fathers and cuckolded husbands." Willoughby paused for a breath. "I have become a thief, a killer, a barroom

19

brawler, and a wanted man with a price on my head —"

"Twenty-five dollars!" Brubs snorted the words through still-swollen nostrils. "Most insultin' thing I ever heard of. Hell, partner, you and me ought to be worth at least a hundred apiece. Besides, that weren't even our fault."

Willoughby ignored the interruption. "And so far, I haven't yet reminded you that we have barely escaped the hangman's noose on several occasions."

"Yep," Brubs said cheerfully, "we've had us a passel of fun at that." He picked up the slack in the reins. "Now that you got that hair ball coughed up, partner, let's go gather us some ponies." He touched spurs to Squirrel.

Willoughby snorted in disgust as he kneed the black into a trot. "Of all the people in the world I could have teamed up with, I pick a snake oil salesman. I'll never understand how I let you talk me into these things, Brubs McCallan. *'On ne meurt qu'une fois, et c'est pour si longtemps.'*"

Brubs cocked a bruised eyebrow at his partner. "I swear, I never knowed a man jabbered that Roman stuff ever', time he got a little put out. Talk American."

"It isn't Roman," Willoughby said. "It's Molière, a Frenchman. It translates as, 'One dies only once, and it's for such a long time.'"

Brubs pondered the translation for a moment, then granted. "Reckon that feller had a point at that. Never figgered a Frenchman looked much past his next bait of snails." He flashed a quick grin. "Knowed a frog myself once. Fancy little brunette down to New Orleans, fresh off the boat from Paris. She didn't speak no American, but we figgered each other's wants out anyhow. I tell you, that was some kinda woman —"

"Brubs," Willoughby interrupted, "I'm not saying your amorous escapades aren't interesting, but how about concentrating your devious skills on the problem of getting us onto and off of Turbyfill's ranch without us winding up lynched?"

Brubs sighed and glanced at him. "Dave, sometimes you get just plumb et up with sour. Find a big chunk of gold, you'd fret that maybe there was a bug under it. You just relax, partner, and leave it to old Uncle Brubs. Ain't gonna be nothin' to it."

Willoughby tugged the oilskin slicker tighter about his neck, tried to ignore the chill wind and steady drizzle, and squinted through the weak light of dawn attempting to poke its way through leaden skies.

He couldn't shrug off the cold lump in his gut; it was time for some serious fretting when Brubs McCallan's ideas went according to plan. The raid on the Fishhook had been simplicity itself. More than thirty horses, appearing to be little more than black lumps against the deepening darkness and growing rain, had been scattered in small groups over the south valley of Turbyfill's

21

ranch — and not a herdsman or guard in sight. Not a yell raised or a shot fired. It just didn't seem normal for a McCallan project, Willoughby grumbled to himself.

They had ridden through the black night in a driving rain that hammered the sandy soil, soaking horses and riders but obliterating all tracks within an hour of the stolen remuda's passage. Brubs rode point, trusting Squirrel to lead them back to LaQuesta without walking over the edge of a cliff or into a box canyon. Willoughby rode drag. He wasn't sure why. It wasn't as if he could have seen a horse wander away in the inky blackness. Brubs's sorrel had done his job. Willoughby figured they had covered a good thirty miles, possibly more, since the Fishhook raid.

He glanced up as Brubs trotted Squirrel back to the drag post.

"Might as well let 'em rest for a spell, case we have to make a run for it later. Fair grazin' in that little meadow up ahead," Brubs said. Water dripped from the front brim of his battered hat, now all but shapeless after the pounding rain. "Rain's lettin' up and it's gettin' light. I reckon we can spare a couple hours. Ain't seen nothin' on the back trail yet."

"What do you mean, 'run for it' and 'yet'?"

"Old Man Turbyfill's gonna be madder'n a wet cat," Brubs said calmly. "Take 'em a while to cut sign on us, but they'll be along. That half-Injun tracker of Turbyfill's is damn good."

Willoughby's shoulders sagged further. "I knew

this was going too easy."

"There you go again," Brubs said. "Always lookin' for lightnin' in ever' little cloud." He reined Squirrel about. "Let's go see what kinda ponies we got, partner. It was a tad dark last night. Then we'll get us some coffee, if we can rustle up some dry wood."

The horses, Willoughby thought, seemed decent enough, considering the Fishhook's habit of stealing sorry saddle stock. Turbyfill must have gotten lucky on this bunch. A majority of them had the look of a Morgan-mustang cross, a mix that usually produced fair ranch horses.

Brubs suddenly reined in and stared at three rangy horses at the edge of the remuda. "I'll be damned. Old Man Turbyfill must be dumber'n I figgered."

Willoughby squinted at the animals for a moment, trying to determine what had piqued Brubs's interest. Then one of the leggy mounts turned; the *U.S.* brand showed clearly on its rain-slicked hip. "Cavalry mounts?"

Brubs nodded. "Turbyfill musta planned to sell 'em down in Mexico. Too chancy tryin' to peddle Army horses on this side of the Rio Grande. Man can get hisself in a heap o' trouble doin' that."

Willoughby's eyes narrowed. "So what do we do with them? Besides get sent to the penitentiary if we get caught with them."

"Can't change the brands," Brubs said thoughtfully. "No way to run a *U.S.* into our

23

Horseshoe brand. We'll cut 'em out and booger 'em north when we hit the Fort Davis road. Lots of Army patrols around there. They'll find 'em." He touched spurs to the sorrel. "Let's see what else we got."

The two rode in silence through the stolen remuda for a couple of minutes before Willoughby reined up. "Looks like we've gathered an old friend along the way." He pointed toward a long-headed, cow-hocked, pigeon-toed coyote dun gelding. The gelding backed his ears and nipped at the neck of a big brown.

"I'll be double damned. Old Ugly's back. Wonder how he got here from Round Rock?"

Willoughby shook his head. "There's no telling. That horse has been stolen more often than the ace of spades at a cowboy poker game. He's got two new brands on him since we sold him the last time."

"That sorry plug," Brubs said, disgusted. "Can't find good horses and can't get rid of the crow baits. No reason we can't sell him again, I reckon. There's a fool borned ever' couple days in Texas." He reined Squirrel around. "I reckon we got some fair to middlin' broomtails here. Let's see if we can stir up some dry wood. I ain't real good company till I get my mornin' coffee."

Dawn had grown into a flat gray light by the time Willoughby had a small fire going beside an ocotillo patch that opened onto the small meadow where the horses dozed or grazed. The

24

rain had stopped, but the wind was still a bit raw. Mud squished under Willoughby's boot and he added a handful of coffee grounds to the pot.

"Coffee'll be ready in a few minutes —"

Brubs cut him off with a wave of his hand. "Heard somethin' out there." He swept his slicker back to expose the worn grips of the Colt .45 holstered at his hip. "We're fixin' to have company, partner. Better grab some iron."

Willoughby stepped to the black. He had his Winchester halfway out of the saddle scabbard when the call came:

"You men at camp! Pull those weapons and we'll cut you down where you stand!"

Willoughby turned — and found himself staring into the bores of a half dozen Springfield .45-70 carbines in the hands of surly-looking U.S. Army troopers. A cavalry officer sat his saddle in the midst of the half circle of blue-clad soldiers. One of the soldiers wasn't holding a rifle; his face was pale and pain-lined beneath the stubble on his cheeks. His right arm was in a sling. Willoughby stepped away from the saddle scabbard and raised his hands.

"What's goin' on here?" Brubs said. "What right you soldier boys got to come waltzin' in here and stick them carbines in our faces?"

The officer cocked the revolver. "I have every right in the world, mister. I am Lieutenant Jubal Storm, Able Company, Fort Davis. You men are under arrest." The officer's black eyes glittered in anger.

"What for? We didn't do nothin'," Brubs protested.

"The ambush slaying of two cavalry troopers, the wounding of a third, and theft of Army property amounts to a bit more than nothing." Storm's tone was cold and hard. "You have three of our stolen remounts in your possession. The penalty for murder of an Army trooper is death by firing squad. We can do it here or at the fort. The choice is yours."

TWO

Brubs McCallan had never figured a hole weighed much.

But the black holes of the bores of the .45-70's laid a mighty hefty weight against his belly. The damn things looked like stovepipes.

Brubs forced a bluster past the nervous yips in his gut and squared his shoulders. He glared into the black eyes of the man in blue. "I'm gettin' a tad peeved havin' guns stuck in my face ever' time I turn around, 'specially by a bunch of blue-leg Yankee soldiers when there ain't no war left."

Lt. Jubal Storm's expression didn't change. "I'm waiting for your decision, mister. Either pull that weapon or get your hand off it. You have the option of being placed under arrest or being shot where you stand."

Brubs let his hand drop away from the handgun. "Since you put it that way, General, I reckon I'll play along. But you boys done treed the wrong coons on this hunt." He chanced a quick glance at his partner. Willoughby's face was the color of flour gravy.

"Lieutenant," Willoughby said, his voice a bit shaky, "my friend and I had nothing to do with the deaths of your men."

Storm's gaze flicked from Brubs to Willoughby.

There was ice in the black eyes. "And I suppose you don't have three of our remounts among your horses, either?"

"Get them damn saddle cannons outta our faces," Brubs said, "and we'll fuss that matter out. My partner's right, General. We didn't shoot no soldiers, and we didn't steal no Army horses."

"We'll know soon enough. Private Richards," Storm called over his shoulder, "come forward."

The soldier with his arm in a sling nudged his horse closer. Brubs saw the dark smear of blood on the trooper's uniform. The soldier's jaw was set, his face pale. Brubs could tell the man was hurting hard.

"Richards, do you recognize either of these men as being with the bandits who ambushed your detail?"

Richards stared into Brubs's face for several seconds, then into Willoughby's. "No, sir, I don't remember seeing these two. I didn't get a look at all the men who attacked us, but the ones I did see were much older."

"Well, General, there you got it," Brubs said. "Your own man says it weren't us. You can move them carbines out from under our noses now."

Storm shook his head. "Not just yet. He merely said he didn't remember seeing you two. That doesn't mean you couldn't have been there. Richards, are those horses over there from your remount string?"

"Yes, sir. I know these horses quite well."

"Then at least we have a theft charge," Storm

28

said. "Unbuckle your gun belts. Sergeant, fetch the irons."

Brubs raised a hand. "Wait a minute here, General," he said. "I got a notion as to how them animals come to be in our remuda. It ain't gonna strain your milk none to hear us out. We might even just be able to help you some."

Storm nodded, but the expression in his eyes was even colder. "I'll let you have your say, then I'll make up my mind whether to have you shot here or back at the fort."

Sweat beaded on Brubs's forehead. "No need it comin' to that." He had to work even harder to keep the bluster in his words. "My partner and me'd just as soon not have to kill these here troopers if we don't have to."

"I'll grant you one thing, mister," Storm said. "You've got nerve to even think about pulling a handgun against an Army patrol holding cocked carbines."

Brubs snorted. "That ain't nothin' special to worry about. You Yanks never could shoot for squat. I figger you ain't got better since Bull Run."

"You don't want to test that theory," Storm said. "Tell me why I should believe I've 'treed the wrong coons,' as you phrased it."

"Because we ain't that dumb, dammit," Brubs said, "but I reckon Old Man Turbyfill might be."

Storm stared at him for a moment. "I have no idea what you are talking about. Why don't you start from the front of this story? Start with your names, so I'll know what to put on the headstones if I decide to shoot you."

"Don't know why," Brubs grumbled, "but you Yankee officers is the most suspiciouses critters I done ever met. I'm Brubs McCallan. This here's Dave Willoughby. We're partners in the Texas Horsetradin' Company. We're puttin' us a big remuda together, pickin' up a few head here, few there. Gonna trail 'em north to Kansas. We figger to do right well by it. There ought to be a big horse market up on the Plains —"

"McCallan," Storm broke in, "I could hardly care less about the demand for horses in Kansas. Or about your business ventures, unless dead soldiers and stolen Army mounts are involved. Get back to the story."

"Can I ask Richards here somethin'?"

"If it's pertinent," Storm said.

Brubs lifted an eyebrow at the wounded trooper. "Richards, you said these men you seen was older'n Dave and me. Was one of 'em short, like me? Rode sort of hunched over like he had him a bad back? One shoulder drooped down and missin' one ear? Maybe ridin' a tall, blaze-face bay?"

Richards looked surprised. "Yes. As a matter of fact, that's an accurate description of the man who shot me."

"That's what I figgered," Brubs said solemnly. "Old Man Turbyfill. Him and his Fishhook boys. Biggest damn horse thieves in the Big Bend, that bunch. That explains how come them Army

30

grinned at Willoughby. "Well, partner," he said, "I reckon comin' up agin a soldier patrol just might keep ol' Turbyfill too busy to fret much about chasin' us. Mighty nice of the Yankee Army to cover our retreat."

Willoughby lifted his coffee cup in salute. "A toast," he said, "to the most devious, convoluted criminal mind it has been my frequent misfortune to observe in action."

The stocky Texan inclined his head. "Why, thankee, partner. I reckon that's the nicest thing you done ever said to me. Now, drink up and let's move us some ponies. I got me a sudden urge to get back home right quick-like."

Brubs had never felt the reassuring warmth and relaxed comfort that wrapped itself around a man when he came home. Until now.

Maybe most people wouldn't consider it much of a home, he figured, but the three-room adobe shack in the middle of nowhere was the first real home he'd ever had, the first place he could call his own.

Brubs had lost track of the years he had spent drifting. It seemed he had been in the saddle most of his life, wandering from one cow camp or hunter's dugout to another, one saloon after another, until the tracks he'd left behind covered most of settled Texas and a lot of it that was still raw frontier.

He had never had a birthright home as such. He bore no ill will toward the whore in

The lieutenant studied Willoughby. "Your name is Willoughby? Did you perhaps serve with the First Ohio?"

The tall man nodded. "That was my regiment."

Storm's expression softened. "I thought I'd seen the name of a Lieutenant Dave Willoughby on a list. The roster of Congressional Medal of Honor winners. Are you that man?"

"Yes, sir."

"Then I'm inclined to accept your version of what might have happened. Besides, it would be most unseemly to execute a Union war hero without irrefutable proof of guilt."

"Damn sure wouldn't earn you no promotion, shootin' innocent civilians," Brubs said.

Storm glared at him for several heartbeats. "I have serious doubts that you are innocent of anything, McCallan. But if Lieutenant Willoughby vouches for you, that's enough for now." Storm glanced over his shoulder at the silent, glowering troopers. "Lower the hammers, men, but stay alert. If either of these two gentlemen makes an attempt to pull a weapon, shoot them."

Brubs's chest heaved in a sigh of relief as the troopers eased the hammers of the carbines. He shifted his gaze to the wounded trooper. "Where'd them bandits hit you, son?" he asked.

"A couple of days ride northeast, on the road from Fort Inge to Fort Davis. They left me for dead. If Lieutenant Storm hadn't happened by on patrol, I would have bled to death."

Nacogdoches who had birthed him or to her unknown customer who had fathered him. He didn't even resent his mother for having given him up at birth to a farm couple outside Nacogdoches and disappearing from his life. Brubs had always figured that being born a bastard beat hell out of never being born at all.

All told, he mused, his childhood had been better than Dave Willoughby's. At least Brubs had been happy. Hungry sometimes. Cold sometimes. But usually as happy as a rooster in a full corncrib.

Willoughby had been born to a rich and powerful family in a big house in Cincinnati. But he hadn't been happy. Every time he turned around, his father or brother had been telling him what to do and when to do it. Brubs wouldn't have traded places with him for anything. He figured the smartest thing Willoughby ever did was when he finally chucked the whole thing after the war and rode off on his own. He had never gone back to Cincinnati.

Brubs had his own idea about why he had been happy and Willoughby hadn't. It was called freedom.

The sorrel between Brubs's knees broke into a trot, as eager to be home as was his rider. Brubs pulled Squirrel back to a walk, ignored the sorrel's irritated flutter of nostrils and shake of head, and savored his homecoming.

The Texas Horsetrading Company's headquarters nestled in a surprisingly lush valley a couple of miles north of the village of LaQuesta, population twelve. The valley was well watered. A spring-fed creek ran the length of the valley year round. Even in dry times the grass was rich and green for most of the year, nourished by the water table only a few feet beneath the valley floor.

The valley itself was more like the floor of a canyon. Steep, rocky walls flanked the two sections of land, with fences of rock or peeled logs closing the whole spread into one big pasture. Behind the house stood a solid barn and corrals. Both house and corrals had their own water wells. On the slope of a hill behind the house was a small grave plot. It was there that the old *mesteñero*, Stump Hankins, now rested, beside his wife and son. Hankins had willed the two young would-be mustangers the ranch and brand — an inverted horseshoe — only days before the shoot-out with Gilberto Delgado's gang at Mustang Mesa left the old man riddled with bullets.

Brubs, riding point, glanced over his shoulder at the remuda of stolen horses and sighed in contentment. With the Fishhook mounts and a handful of others picked up on the way north from the Fishhook, the Texas Horsetrading Company now had almost three hundred horses. That was enough to start the drive to Kansas as soon as the country began to green. Which had to be soon, Brubs knew. Even the rich grass of the valley couldn't take the grazing pressure from three hundred horses for very long.

He rode past the house, waved a greeting to the

stooped Mexican standing on the front porch, and dismounted at the peeled log fence that closed off the south end of the pasture. He wrestled the heavy gate open and stepped aside as the first of the new remuda passed through the opening into their new home range.

Brubs stood with a foot propped on a log rail as Willoughby pushed the last few head through the gate and swung down from the coyote dun Brubs called Ugly. The two manhandled the gate back into place.

"Right fair couple of weeks' work, partner," Brubs said. "We got us a mighty good remuda now. Some prime stock in there along with the crow baits."

"We are, as a matter of fact, horse-poor," Willoughby said. "And if you should happen to be wrong about these animals bringing top dollar in Kansas, we are simply poor."

Brubs clapped him playfully on the shoulder. "Hell, son, it ain't the money. It's the fun of doin' it that's got my anxious up. Speakin' of which, I been itchin' to go see Kat the last few days. And I done worked up an awful thirst."

"Barley Symms's whiskey and wife can wait a bit longer, Brubs," Willoughby said. "First things first. We've some work to do here and some heavy planning to be done. Such as, where are we going to get some help, how are we going to pay them if we find them, and what will we need in the way of supplies? It is, in case you've forgotten, a rather long way from here to Kansas."

37

Brubs sighed. "Dave, you just plumb take the world too serious. Man's gotta have some fun once in a while, just like he's gotta have biscuits and gravy." He dodged a kick from Willoughby's coyote dun and climbed back into the saddle. "You fret too much, partner. Give yourself a case of the vapors over next to nothin'. I got it all worked out except where we're gonna get the help. We'll find it. Just got to trust our patron saint of horse thieves."

Willoughby mounted and reined the dun toward the house. "I just hope Saint Augustine hasn't gone off duty. We're going to need all the help we can get."

Brubs's eyes twinkled in anticipation. "Meantime, I reckon a few snorts of Barley Symms's Old Gutripper and a trip upstairs with Kat might ease your frets, partner. Maybe ward off that case of the vapors you're tryin' to get."

"Perhaps you're right to some extent. As Horace wrote, *'Misce stultitiam consiliis breven: Dulce est despere in loco.'* "

"Talk American."

"It means, 'Mix a little foolishness with your serious plans: It's lovely to be silly at the right moment.' "

Brubs nodded and grinned. "I reckon this Horace feller mighta made a fair Texan at that. Least he got his necessaries straight."

Francisco Fernandez was waiting when the two hitched their mounts to the rail outside the three-room adobe.

"*¿Dificultad, Señor Fernandez?*" Dave asked.

The aging Mexican shrugged and jabbered a mouthful of rapid-fire Spanish.

"What'd he say?" Brubs asked, brow furrowed.

"He said there were no problems," Willoughby said, "except that the big cat — one of the mountain lions that range through here sometimes, I suppose — proved a bit bothersome, but it's gone now."

Brubs snorted. "I got a feelin' this old tamale-eater talks better American than I do. He's just tryin' to aggravate me. And you ain't helpin' much, yammerin' that Mex lingo back and forth at ever' pepper gut we come across."

"After you almost got us both cut open by a mad Mexican down in Tres Perros, it was apparent that someone in this outfit needed to learn Spanish," Willoughby said.

"Dave, you know I never meant no insult to that big greaser."

"Telling him his wife had small, sagging breasts was no way to make friends in a strange land. Anyway, if we're going to live in this part of the country, one of us has to know the language beyond 'beer' and 'whore.' "

"I reckon you got a point." Brubs stared for a moment at the old Mexican. "You know, Fernandez here may be older'n dirt, but he ain't a bad hand. Ask him if he'd hire on to help us trail them horses to Kansas."

Willoughby and Fernandez traded Spanish for a moment. Then Dave nodded.

"What'd he say?"

"Basically the same thing I've been saying all along. That you are about a quart shy of a full bucket between the ears, that this is a cockeyed scheme in which a man could become extremely dead very quickly, and that only fools and idiots would attempt such a project." He shrugged. "I toned it down a little, but that's about what he said."

Brubs grunted in disgust. "Ain't that just like a Mexican? Couldn't just say no and let it go at that. Got to nail on a couple insults in the process." He turned toward the door. "Pay the old coot what he's got comin' so far, but tell 'im to get back here 'fore sundown. We'll be leavin' for town then. I'll take care of our ponies."

Willoughby counted out the coins Fernandez had coming for watching the place at the rate of fifty cents a day, then added a dollar bonus on the sly. Brubs would throw a fit if he knew Willoughby had wasted a whole dollar on an old Mexican. A few minutes later Fernandez rode away on a half-asleep burro, tapping the animal with a stick. The burro showed no inclination to wake up.

Willoughby stirred the coals in the cast-iron stove to life, fed in a few wood chips, and added kindling to the growing blaze. Brubs came through the back door a few minutes later, grunting under the weight of two tin water buckets. "What's this?" Willoughby asked. "I had plenty of water for cooking dinner."

"Man's gonna take a bath, he's gotta have water."

"A bath?" Willoughby's eyebrows went up in surprise. "I think I just felt the earth quiver. Brubs, you had a bath only a month ago."

Brubs heaved the buckets onto the top of the stove. "Yeah. But Kat's awful persnickety. 'Specially for a whore. Gets plumb frumped up when a man smells like a man."

"I thought we had agreed that Kat could wait until we had done some serious planning," Willoughby said.

"She could, I reckon. I can't." Brubs stripped off his shirt, poked a finger through a hole in the elbow, and shook his head. "Damn. I paid four bits for that shirt not more'n six months ago and it's wearin' out already. Just don't make stuff like they used to." He glanced up at Dave. "Reckon you can patch it for me?"

Willoughby sighed heavily. "I can mend it, yes. But it wouldn't hurt you to learn how to use a needle and thread. I may not always be around to take care of you."

"You're mighty handy at that, partner. Better'n fair with a skillet and keep a clean house. You was put together some different, I'd plumb be tempted to ask your hand in marriage."

"I've had better offers."

Brubs strode to the wall, plucked a number two washtub from its hook, and let it clatter to the floor beside the stove. "You're the one always fussin' about needin' a bath and shave. Want to use this water when I'm done?"

"No," Willoughby said, grimacing. "I'll start over with fresh water. By the time you get through with it, a man would be able to plant a garden in that tub."

Brubs sniffed in mock indignation. "Damned if you ain't near as persnickety as some women I know, Aunt Mary." He rummaged in the bottom of a cabinet for a moment, then straightened, disgusted. "I had me a quart of two-dollar whiskey stashed back here. That old Mex musta done went and drunk it up, and here I am thirstin' somethin' fierce. Ought to fire that greaser. I never could abide no thief."

Willoughby checked the coffee water, found it boiling, and dumped in a handful of grounds. "He didn't steal it, Brubs. It's in the corner behind the broom."

"What's it doin' there?"

"I figured that was the last place you or Fernandez would look for it."

Brubs cast a peeved glance at him, then retrieved the battle. "Damned if you ain't gettin' more like a wife all the time. Hidin' a man's whiskey's a shootin' offense in Texas."

"I'll keep that in mind." Willoughby nodded toward the stove. "Your bathwater's hot."

LaQuesta wasn't much for looks, Brubs had to admit as he reined the little gray mustang called Mouse down what would have been the settlement's main street if LaQuesta had streets.

The town was a jumble of adobe shacks thrown up with no particular pattern in mind. A good half the buildings were in various stages of collapse. But it had everything a man needed, as far as Brubs was concerned. It was a good two days' ride from the nearest lawman. Hardly anyone in Texas even knew where it was. LaQuesta had a saloon. And a whore. Brubs couldn't think of anything else a man might need.

He sniffed the air and grinned at Willoughby, riding alongside on the big roan horse called Choctaw. "Nose music if I ever smelt it, partner," Brubs said.

"All I smell is dust and outhouses," Willoughby said, "but then I can't sniff out a saloon from twenty miles away like you can."

"Some folks got talent, some don't." Brubs reined Mouse to a stop before LaQuesta's only two-story building. Faded, handpainted lettering on the sun-bleached false front proclaimed the building to be *Symms' Dry Godds and Salon*. Brubs didn't care if Barley Symms could spell or not. The "Salon" part served whiskey — bad whiskey, but still whiskey — just like the saloons in San Antonio. As he dismounted and wrapped the bridle reins around the sagging hitch rail, Brubs wondered again if the "Dry Godds" part of the sign had anything to do with thirsty deities. He decided it didn't. He figured any being with enough power to be a god would have an ample supply of fine Kentucky bourbon at hand.

Brubs led Willoughby inside. The interior of

43

Symms's place was dark and dingy, lit only by a couple of guttering lamps at each end of the bar.

Kat Symms sat on a tall stool behind the bar, her chin cupped in her hands. It was an effective pose, Brubs decided at a glance. The woman could make an entrance sitting down.

The lantern light sent gold waves shimmering across her shoulder-length blond hair. It also deepened the shadow between Kat's ample breasts. A substantial amount of skin showed where the top buttons of her dress were undone.

"Howdy, Kat," Brubs said. "You're lookin' mighty fine. It's a plumb pleasure to see you again."

Kat Symms's smile put dimples in her full cheeks. "Hello, boys," she said, her voice on the husky side but musical, "it's good to see you again, too. It's been a while." Her gaze lingered for a moment on Willoughby. "I was afraid you two might be in some jail somewhere."

"I was. For a spell. Dave got me out." Brubs glanced around. "Where's that no-account husband of yours, girl?"

Kat glanced down at the floor behind the bar. "In his usual place. Passed out cold about a half hour ago."

"Barley stay drunk all the time? I never seen him sober."

"Neither have I," Kat said. "At least not for the last few years. What will you have, fellows?"

"Whiskey first." Brubs closed one eye in a lecherous wink. "Then a little trip upstairs."

Kat didn't blush at the lewd suggestion. "Dave?"

Willoughby's face colored. He still hadn't gotten accustomed to Brubs's blunt approach to women. Even those that were for sale. "A beer, please." He glanced around as Kat fetched a bottle and a drew a mug of beer from the keg behind the bar. There were no other customers. It wasn't an unusual condition for Symms's place. "Seems awfully quiet tonight, Kat. No drinkers?"

"Not unless you count Barley." She put the mug in front of Willoughby, leaned forward, and stared for a moment into his eyes. "And Barley hasn't counted for much of anything for the past few years." Willoughby saw the open invitation in Kat's gold-flecked blue eyes. He felt his neck redden.

Brubs poured a hefty slug of whiskey into a water glass, lifted it in a toast to Kat, then downed it in two swallows. His eyebrows shot up. "Damn, Kat. That's *good* whiskey, not ol' Barley's usual rotgut."

Kat smiled at Brubs. "I slipped in a special order for a case in the last shipment, just for my preferred customers," she said. "I only have two."

"Why, Kat, that's plumb neighborly of you," Brubs said. "Now, how's about you and me goin' upstairs and gettin' a tad more neighborly?"

Kat patted him on the arm. "In a bit, Brubs. It's Dave's turn to go first."

Willoughby felt his face turn even redder. He had never been able to accept such direct lan-

45

guage from a woman. And after several months, he was still trying to come to terms with the fact that Barley Symms used his wife as a whore. Barley had said *he* didn't "use her" anymore, and that he liked money better than he liked Kat. It still didn't seem proper to Willoughby. He downed half his beer to cover his embarrassment.

Kat strode from behind the bar and leaned against Willoughby. The scent of rose water and woman wafted to his nostrils. It started a stirring he hadn't felt for weeks. "Watch the bar for us, will you, Brubs?" Kat said.

Brubs wiped a hand across his mustache and chuckled. "That's like leavin' the coyote guardin' the henhouse, Kat. But don't you fret none. I'll keep count. Dave'll settle up later." He reached for the bottle, leaned over the bar, and glanced down. "Don't look like ol' Barley's gonna bother nobody for a spell. You kids have fun."

Kat slipped her hand beneath Willoughby's elbow and led him toward the stairs.

Brubs watched them go, then downed the last of Willoughby's beer and refilled his glass. "Here's to you, Barley," he said to the unconscious man facedown behind the bar. "Much obliged for the hospitality. Don't bother to get up."

Brubs had lowered the level of the bottle by half before Willoughby and Kat wandered back down the stairs. Kat had a mighty calm look about her, Brubs thought, relaxed as a kitten on a new feather pillow, cheeks flushed, eyes sparkling, damp tendrils of blond hair plastered to her neck. She had a firm hold on Willoughby's arm. Dave didn't look so bad, either, Brubs decided. Kat was more than just good at her work. Everybody should have a job they liked as much, he mused.

"You done with my woman, Dave?" Brubs asked.

Willoughby sighed. "Never been doner, as you might say." He leaned against the bar. "Barley still out?"

"Yeah." Brubs poured Kat a drink. "He wakes up in the next few minutes, tap him upside the noggin with that bung starter he keeps by the cash box. Be a damn shame to let the old skinflint spoil a right fun evenin'." He waited until Kat polished off her drink, then reached for her arm. "You ready, hon?"

Willoughby watched the two go upstairs, then strode behind the bar, surprised that his knees still held him upright. He had to step around Barley Symms. The bald saloon keeper and store owner lay on his side, spittle bubbling at the corner of his mouth as he snored. An empty whiskey bottle lay beside Symms's hand. Willoughby no longer felt any sympathy for the man. Nobody forced Symms to drink himself into oblivion every day. Willoughby had even gotten over the guilty feeling when he pilfered Symms's beer barrel these days. As Brubs pointed out, Symms charged three prices for everything when he was awake. This was just a way of balancing up the ledger sheet.

Willoughby drew a fresh mug from the keg, perched on Symms's stool behind the bar, and rested his elbows on the rough wooden planking.

A wry smile touched his lips as he wondered what his straight-laced family would think of the crooked limb on the family tree. Not every wealthy and politically powerful Cincinnati family could claim an offspring who was a horse thief, a barroom brawler, had a price on his head, got involved in gunfights, and consorted with common — in Kat's case, he corrected himself, make that uncommon — whores. It would drive them stark, raving mad, he decided. He liked that idea.

Willoughby glanced up, startled, as the front door banged open. "Keep them hands on the bar, feller," a growling baritone voice said. "I been lookin' for you damn hoss thieves."

THREE

Dave Willoughby turned slowly, making no effort to reach for the holstered Colt at his waist.

The man standing in the doorway was almost too big to fit through the opening. His dark, broad face seemed to rest on his shoulders, he had no visible sign of a neck. He held a Sharps Fifty rifle in a fist almost as big as a cured ham. A wide grin spread below an oft-broken nose smashed flat against his face.

"Howdy, Willoughby."

"Hello, Tige. It's good to see you again. I thought you were in Mexico."

Archibald Thibadeau Tilghman kicked the door shut and strode to the bar, light on his feet for a man of his bulk. Most of that bulk was solid muscle. Tilghman propped the Sharps against the bar and offered a hand. Willoughby shook it, hoping he'd get his own hand back with no broken bones. "Ran into a speck of trouble down there," Tilghman said casually. "That sawed-off little runt partner of yours around?"

"He's upstairs. Should be down in a few minutes. Buy you a drink?"

Tilghman nodded eagerly. "That'd be mighty neighborly of you. Been a long, dry ride."

Willoughby found a reasonably clean glass,

49

poured it half full from Brubs's special bottle, and waited as Tilghman tossed the liquor back in two swallows. Tilghman's heavy brows arched in surprise. "Damn, that's prime stuff," he said as he wiped a hand across his lips. "Last time I was in here, I got sheep dip."

"Our status has improved since then, Tige. We're favored customers now." Willoughby heard a snort, then a stirring from the lump on the floor behind him. Barley Symms seemed to be waking up. Willoughby considered giving the bar owner a tap with the bung starter as Brubs had suggested, but didn't. Hitting a man while he was down, drunk or otherwise, didn't seem fair. The issue became moot almost immediately. Symms's head thumped back against the floor. He started snoring again.

"Tige!"

The shout from the top of the stairs broadened the grin on Tilghman's face. Brubs's boots clattered on the stairs. Moments later Brubs's hand disappeared in Tilghman's big fist. Brubs slapped him on the shoulder with his free hand. Dust flew.

"You damned old bandit," Brubs said. "I thought we was shut of you a good spell back. What the hell you doin' in LaQuesta?"

Tilghman released Brubs's hand and shrugged. "Had to leave Mexico quicker'n I'd planned."

"Woman trouble again?"

"A little bit."

Brubs laughed aloud. "Tige, you ain't never

50

done nothin' little in your misbegot life." Grubs turned to Dave. "I ever tell you about the time Tige and me stole that Yankee general's horse right from under his nose?"

Willoughby nodded. "Several times. Along with numerous other adventures you two shared on behalf of the Confederacy." He lifted an eyebrow at Tilghman. "Is that lawman from Little Rock still after you, Tige?"

"Nah. He found me." He didn't expound on the comment. Willoughby didn't press for details. "How the blue-eyed hell you boys been?" Tilghman asked.

"Better'n a pot-licker hound with a gravy skillet," Brubs said. He reached for the bottle, poured two drinks, and hefted his glass in a toast. "Here's to General Bobby Lee," he said.

Willoughby lifted his beer mug and joined in the toast.

"Never knowed a Yankee to drink to Robert E. Lee," Tilghman said.

Willoughby licked the foam from his lips. "Nobody in the Union blue ever said Robert E. Lee wasn't a good soldier. He may have enhanced the profanity proficiency of the Army of the Potomac, but he gained a lot of respect in the Union ranks. Besides, that war's over. And good riddance."

"You got that right, Willoughby," Tilghman said. "Set up another round. I'll buy this one."

A half hour later, Brubs and Tilghman were already well into the third bottle, but hardly seemed to have tapped their inexhaustible supply of war stories. Willoughby stifled a yawn. The drone of voices and the warmth of the saloon interior added to the heaviness of his eyelids.

Kat came back downstairs, her "freshening up" complete, and nodded a greeting to Tige. "What brings you back to LaQuesta, Mr. Tilghman?" she asked.

Tilghman drained the last shot from his glass. "Had me three choices. I could marry that little Mex gal down to Cerritas and raise a passel of little half-breeds. Or I could maybe get skinned by a half dozen of her brothers and uncles. Or I could get out of Mexico for a spell. Didn't like either of them first two possibles. So I got out of Mexico. Thought I'd maybe drift on up north, maybe west."

"Well, if that ain't a kick in the bloomers," Brubs said. He clapped Tilghman on the shoulder again, raising more dust, then turned to Willoughby. "Partner, that patron saint of ours done come through again."

"What you talkin' about, patron saint?" Tilghman's words were beginning to slur a bit.

"Saint Augustine," Willoughby said. "The patron saint of horse thieves, duly adopted as such by the Texas Horsetrading Company."

"Tige, you couldn'ta walked in at no better time," Brubs said. "Dave and me's headin' north, too. Gettin' a hoss drive together. Gonna move 'em to Kansas come first grass. Good ponies bring top dollar up there."

"Horse drive?" Tilghman sounded a bit befuddled at the concept. "Never heard of such a thing."

Brubs emptied the last shot from the whiskey bottle and chuckled. "That's 'cause it ain't been done before, Tige. Ever'body in these parts is gettin' cow herds together for railhead, but nobody's doin' it with hosses. Ought to turn right smart a profit."

Tilghman swirled the liquor in his glass. " 'Specially when you're sellin' rustled hosses."

"Hell, Tige, them people up north ain't gonna be picky about where the hosses come from." He poured himself a refill. "Anyhow, ol' Dave's passin' fair at makin' out bills of sale, should anybody get over curious. Might as well come along with us, you goin' north anyhow. We need some good help. Pay you top hand wages, a dollar and a half a day and all the chuck you can eat."

"How many head we talkin' about?"

"Nigh onto three hundred," Brubs said, a touch of pride in his tone.

Tilghman hesitated for a moment, then shrugged. "Might as well. I ain't got nothin' else to do."

"Good. Now all we got to do is find us a couple more wranglers and maybe a cook. Kat, how's about goin' along with us?"

"I'd like to, but I can't," Kat said. "Someone has to be here to keep an eye on the place. We may not have many customers, but those who do come have to ride for a day or more to get supplies from us. It wouldn't do to have them make the trip for nothing if Barley's passed out. Which he is most of the time."

Brubs leaned over the bar and looked at the floor. "Speakin' of Barley, he's still snoozin'. You want some help rasslin' him into bed?"

Kat shook her head. "He's spent more time on the back bar floor than dust. He'll keep. But speaking of time, the night's getting a bit long in the tooth, boys. I have to lock up soon."

Disappointment flickered over Brubs's face for an instant, then he shrugged. "Reckon a girl's gotta get her beauty rest at that — not that you special need it, Kat. How much we owe you?"

Kat scribbled on a scrap of paper with the nub of a pencil. "Bar bill and other considerations comes to thirty-four dollars and thirty cents."

Brubs pursed his lips in a silent whistle. "That's a passel of money."

Kat smiled brightly. "It's been a busy night."

"Give us a bottle of that good stuff so's we can get to the house without catchin' our death from the night air." Brubs waved a hand toward Willoughby. "Dave'll settle up with you, him bein' the head cipherer and all."

"Brubs, I just remembered something."

"What might that be, Kat?"

"If you're needing to hire more people, there was a young man in here a few days ago. He bought three pounds of flour and paid for it with pennies, then asked if there were any odd jobs around he could do for pay. He's young, but he

54

seems like a good boy, and he obviously needs work. His name is Cal Hooper. He said he and his grandmother have settled on the old Pedersen place east of here. I can draw a map on how to get there, if you want to speak with him."

Brubs touched the brim of his hat with his fingertips. "Thanks, Kat. We'll have a little talk with 'im. Pay the lady, Brother Dave. We'll wait for you outside."

Willoughby drained the last of his beer and reached into his pocket.

"Dave, stay awhile?" Kat's voice was soft in his ear, little more than a whisper. Her cheeks were slightly flushed and her gold-flecked blue eyes seemed to twinkle in the lantern light. "My treat," she said, "literally."

Willoughby's face reddened. He glanced over at Brubs. "You two go ahead. I'll be along later."

Brubs sighed. "Damned if I know how he does it, Tige."

"Does what?"

"Never mind. You'll find out, you ride with this outfit a spell." He led Tilghman outside.

Kat barred the doors while Willoughby counted out forty dollars. She finished closing up, blew out all but one lantern, then pushed ten dollars back to Willoughby. "No charge to you for personal services," she said. A lecherous grin dimpled her cheeks. She dropped the remaining cash into a box, stowed it under the bar, and reached for his hand. "Bring the lantern,

Dave. I'd hate for you to trip and break a log. Especially on the way *up*."

Brubs reined his sorrel to a stop on a rocky ridge overlooking the Hooper homestead and glanced at Willoughby, riding alongside.

"Now that," he said, "puts a whole new meanin' to what a man might call a hardscrabble outfit."

Willoughby nodded as he studied the place below. What passed for a house was a half dugout carved from the side of a rocky hill. A door sagged on one hinge, and the roof was missing a chunk of sod in one corner. The yard was bare, but that came as no surprise. There wasn't a decent patch of grass for five miles around. The only visible water on the homestead was a shallow, reddish-brown ribbon twisting sluggishly in front of the dugout.

At the side of the house, the posts of a one-horse corral sagged against the weight of neglect and poverty. There was no barn. The only sign of life in the barren, dun-colored vista was a small herd of goats scrounging for something edible among the rocks and stunted shrubs on the hillside. Even the mesquite trees looked wilted and bedraggled. Prickly pear and bush cactus seemed to be the only reasonably healthy vegetation.

"It doesn't look exactly prosperous," Willoughby said. "No wonder the Hooper boy was looking for odd jobs."

"Has got one thing goin' for it," Brubs said.

"What?"

"It'd be safe from bandits and rustlers." Brubs snorted in disgust. "Ain't one damn thing down there worth stealin'." He clucked the sorrel into motion. "Let's go see if this kid's lookin' for work serious-like."

The two horsemen checked their mounts a few feet away from the front door. "Hello, the house!" Brubs called.

There was no reply.

"Maybe they done pulled out," Brubs said. "Sure looks like there ain't nobody home."

A frown creased Willoughby's brow. "Perhaps they're ill and in need of help. We'd better take a look." He started to dismount, one foot above the black's rump.

"Hold it right there, you young whelps!" The voice was a woman's. Willoughby froze, his boot still in the air. The twin bores of a double-barreled shotgun pointed straight at him from a crack in the sagging doorway.

"Damn me for a Baptist preacher," Brubs grumbled, "but it appears to me ever'body in this country's got a gun and is just a-steamin' to point it at us."

The door opened, screeching on a rusty hinge. The woman in the doorway was somewhere between 40 and 110, Brubs figured. It would be hard to tell which number was the closest. She was as wide as the door and about half as tall. Wild, gray hair framed a weathered, deeply lined face. Tobacco juice-stained wrinkles led from the corners of her frowning mouth to her chin. She wore bib overalls and a man's shirt, both slick from wear and bearing so many patches they looked like they were made of checkered cloth.

"You two rascals make a move and I'll touch off this here ten-bore." The woman turned her head and spat, tobacco juice dribbling down her square chin, but she never took her eyes off the horsemen.

"Mornin', ma'am," Brubs said. "Mighty fine day out, ain't it?"

"Shut your mouth, you sawed-off little runt. Damn fool whelps think you can jist ride around the country, rapin' poor defenseless old widder women —"

Brubs raised a hand. "Whoa up a minute, ma'am! That there's the last thing we had on our minds. We got nothin' but honorable intentions."

"In a pig's butt," she snorted. "There ain't no honorable men left. Woman can't get no respect no place these days. And we ain't got nothin' to steal, so you better git whilst I'm still in a Christian mood or I'll splatter you plumb over this valley. You ain't seen guts fly till you seen what this here goose gun'll do to a man."

"Ma'am," Willoughby said, "my friend is right. We mean no harm to you and yours. We may not even have the right place. Are you Mrs. Hooper?"

"What bizness of yours be that?"

"We came to speak with your grandson. We

seek to offer him employment."

The old woman's beady eyes narrowed as she glared at Willoughby. "You sure talk funny, mister."

"He's a Yankee, ma'am," Brubs said apologetically, "but there ain't no need to shoot him for that. He's gettin' over it some. Why, he's near as much a Texan as I am."

"That ain't exactly no character endorsement, you low-down jackass." She dismissed Brubs with a withering glance and turned her gaze on Willoughby. "What kinda job you got for my Cal?"

"Would you mind lowering the weapon, Mrs. Hooper? I think I'm getting a cramp in my leg."

"You sure you ain't got rape on your mind?"

Willoughby shook his head emphatically. "No, ma'am. I promise you that."

"Well, hell, then either git back in the saddle or git down. You look plumb silly, half on and half off that broomtail." She finally lowered the shotgun. "What's this about givin' my Cal a job?"

Willoughby finished dismounting with a sigh of relief. He removed his hat. "Mrs. Hooper, we rode out here to see if Cal might be interested in helping us with a trail drive. We'll be moving out soon, trailing a remuda of horses to Kansas —"

"Hosses? Kansas? That's the silliest damn idea I ever heard tell of. You pullin' my leg, son?"

Willoughby shook his head again. "No, ma'am, we're not. We're quite serious about the idea. My name is Dave Willoughby. This is my friend and co-owner of the Texas Horsetrading Company, Mr. Brubs McCallan."

"I'm Emeldeline Hooper. Most folks call me Granny. Cal ain't here jist now." She stared hard into Willoughby's face for a moment. Her expression softened slightly. "All right. Come on inside. But I'm keepin' the shotgun handy. I ain't trustin' you two jist yet. Woman can't be too careful, this part of the country. Bandits all over, stealin' and rapin' —"

"Oh, for the love of Pete!" Brubs said. "Can't you get it through your head we ain't gonna rape you?"

"Eve thank that. Look what it got her."

Willoughby sighed. "Look, Mrs. Hooper, all we want to do is talk to you and your grandson. We'll even pay you for your time."

"How much?"

"Two dollars," Brubs broke in. "Not a dime more."

"Cash? American silver?"

"Cash," Willoughby said. "American silver."

"Come on in. Mind you, behave yourselves, or —"

"I know, Granny," Brubs said, "you'll blow guts all over creation with that goose gun. We'll behave."

Granny Hooper backed through the doorway. Brubs and Willoughby followed. The inside of the half dugout was almost bare. A skillet sat on the crumbling hearth of a sooty fireplace. A rust-streaked water bucket rested on a rough pine shelf propped up by sticks of firewood. In the center of the small room, a crude table listed to one side. The floor was nothing more than hard-packed dirt. Yet, Willoughby noted, things were reasonably neat and clean considering the circumstances.

Granny Hooper waved the shotgun toward a couple of spindly chairs. "Sit down. Ain't got no coffee. Want some goat's milk?"

Brubs winced. "No, ma'am," he said, "milk's for baby critters, not growed men. And I sure can't abide nothin' that comes from a stinky old goat."

"That's all I got, 'cept cistern water, and a badger drownded in that last week."

Willoughby also declined the offer. He pulled out a chair, knocked a scorpion from the flat pine seat with his hat, waited until the insect scurried away from the table toward the fireplace, and sat down. He breathed a silent sigh of relief when the old woman finally propped the big goose gun against the wall.

Willoughby suddenly realized there were only two chairs at the table. He stood. "Mrs. Hooper, please take this chair. I don't mind standing."

Granny Hooper's wrinkled face crinkled even more with the ever-so-slight smile that lifted the tobacco-stained corners of her thin lips. "Keep your seat, young man. But it's a sure-enough pleasure to find a man with a little common decency toward a woman out here. Poor defenseless widder woman don't git no respect." She paused

61

for a moment to stomp Willoughby's scorpion into oblivion, picked the squashed creature up by a clawed foreleg, and chucked it into the fireplace. She spat an amber stream after it, then turned back to Willoughby. "Little feller said you was a Yankee. What outfit was you with?"

"First Ohio Volunteers, ma'am."

"My boy, rest his soul, was Union, too. He died at Gettysburg. Got lung fever." She lifted a gray eyebrow at Brubs. "Was you in the war?"

"Yes'm. Hood's Brigade. Confederacy."

"You boys cavalry?"

"No, ma'am," Brubs said. "I was infantry. Walked through the whole war. Dave was artillery. Officer, yet. Lieutenant."

Granny Hooper's brow furrowed. "Never held much truck with officers. My brother-in-law was one. A colonel. He was a horse's ass."

Brubs chuckled aloud. "I reckon you and me are gonna get along fine, Granny. Never held much truck with officers myself."

"Fergit the damn war," the old woman said. "It's done with. Damn foolishness, that's what it were. Wonder either side won. Now, tell me about this here job —" She cocked her head, listening. "Wait a minute. Cal's comin'."

"I don't hear nothin'," Brubs said after a brief silence.

"Son," Granny said, "I may not be no belle of the ball no more, but my eyes and ears is still good. I can still read the look in a hawk's eye at a hunnerd yards and hear a quail fart in a whirlwind

62

plumb across the ridge."

The door creaked open a moment later. A gangly youth stood in the doorway. Ears like jug handles stuck out from the sides of his head, which was topped by a mop of tousled hair the color of a carrot. He held an ancient .22 Remington, rolling block, single-shot rifle, the fore stock held to the barrel by several twists of rusty wire. The muzzle pointed toward Brubs.

The stocky Texan groaned aloud, a pained expression on his face. "Damned if this ain't the most suspiciousest country I ever been in," he grumbled. "Man can't even turn around without what somebody's pointin' a gun at his gizzard."

"These men bothering you, Granny?" The boy's eyes were wide, but the rifle muzzle was steady.

"Naw, Cal. Put the gun down. They come to talk about maybe hirin' you on." She cut a sideways glance at Brubs. "For cash money. The nice-lookin', polite, clean young man's Dave Willoughby. Little grubby runt's named Brubs McCallan. Boys, my grandson, Cal."

The boy lowered the rifle. "What kind of job?"

Cal didn't look to be more than thirteen, Brubs thought. Beneath the tangled red hair and a respectable accumulation of dirt, Cal's sunburned face sprouted more freckles than Brubs had ever seen on one kid. He was almost painfully skinny.

"Don't know if you're hoss enough to handle it, son," Brubs said. "How old are you?"

63

"Fifteen. Goin' on sixteen."

"You sure don't look it," Brubs said skeptically.

The boy stared at him for a moment, then shrugged. "I need a job bad, mister. But if you want an old coot instead of a good hand, that's up to you. I got two rabbits and an armadillo to skin outside." He turned for the door.

"Wait a minute, Cal," Brubs said. The boy turned. "I didn't say we wasn't gonna hire you. Can you ride?"

"Some."

"Handle horses much?"

"We never had more than one at a time."

"Well, that don't matter none." Brubs leaned back in his chair. "We'll supply you a string of saddle horses and gear some decent guns and ammunition, and all the chuck you can eat. Greenhorn wages is a dollar a day. Payday comes when we get our ponies delivered and sold in Kansas. We're talkin' two, maybe three months' work. Sound okay by you?"

The youth's brow furrowed. "That's a heap of money. But who'd watch after Granny?"

Willoughby cleared his throat. "I've been pondering that very thing, Mrs. Hooper. This place doesn't appear to be awfully prosperous."

Granny Hooper snorted in disgust. "Damned land agent sold us a rattler in a poke. Said it was knee-deep in grass and watered good. Should have knowed you don't get good land for two bits an acre. Only reason I bought it was I thought it might be somethin' for Cal someday. Hell, you called it, mister. This place won't grow nothin' but rattlers and scorpions or graze nothin' but goats."

Willoughby nodded. "Can you cook, Mrs. Hooper?"

"How you think I got this girlish figger and wasp waist? Hell yes, I can cook. If I got somethin' to cook."

Willoughby turned to Brubs, a question in his gaze.

"Granny, my partner's right," Brubs said. "We need us a cook. You game to take it on? We supply the chuck and cookin' stuff. Pay you a dollar a day. This place'll still be here when we get done."

Granny spat and shifted the chew to her other cheek. "Wouldn't miss it if it weren't. Dollar and a quarter a day. Cooks is worth more than cowboys or horse wranglers. And you throw in three months' supply of chewin' tobacco. Started my last twist this mornin'."

"One more thing, Mrs. Hooper," Willoughby said solemnly. "Before you or Cal agree, you should know that this trip could be dangerous."

"You think this place ain't, son? Rattlers under ever' rock, nineteen ways to starve. And this country's plumb slap-dab full of hoss thieves, robbers, and rapers."

Brubs nodded solemnly. "I reckon that's a pure enough fact, Granny." He pushed his chair back and stood. "You're hired, then. Both of you." He turned to Dave. "We got near a full crew now,

65

partner. One more hand and we'll be all set."

"I know somebody," Cal said cautiously. "Friend of mine. He's a little older and he doesn't talk much, but he's stout and a hard worker. If you want, I can ride over to his place — he's livin' over in Zavala County with an aunt and uncle he doesn't like much — and ask if he's interested."

"You do that, son," Brubs said. "If he wants to give it a shot, fetch him out to the Texas Horsetradin' Company north of LaQuesta and we'll look 'im over." He extended a hand. Cal hesitated for an instant, then took it.

"Good to have you with us, Cal," Brubs said. "I'll learn you the hoss business mighty quick, just like I did ol' Dave here." He ignored Willoughby's caustic glance. "We move 'em out in a week, ten days tops. New grass already showin'. Should be good grazin' all the way to Kansas."

Cal shook hands with Willoughby. "I'd better go clean the rabbits and that armadillo before they get too stiff on me," he said, then strode outside.

"You boys wanna stay for supper, we'll have us a bait of armadillo and jackrabbit stew," Granny said.

Brubs winced. "Thanks, Granny, but I et more'n enough diller and rabbit stew when Dave and me was just gettin' started, back when we was poor as church mice. Besides, we need to get on back. Like you say, the country's full of hoss thieves and bad men."

Willoughby reached for his hat, then paused.

"Mrs. Hooper, we'll bring a wagon around in a few days to move your belongings."

Granny Hooper paused long enough to spit and swipe a hand across her mouth. "Won't take a big wagon. Ain't got much. I gotta figger out what to do with my goats, though."

"We know a man in LaQuesta by the name of Francisco Fernandez," Willoughby said. "He's done some work for us from time to time. I'll ask if he might be willing to watch your goats in your absence. If so, we can trail them to LaQuesta for you."

Brubs raised a startled eyebrow. "Drive goats? Now, Dave Willoughby, I ain't gonna do no such a thing!" He snorted in revulsion. "That's the most humiliatin' idea I ever heard. A top hand like me herdin' goats? That'll be the day hell freezes over!"

FOUR

Willoughby tried in vain to suppress a grin. "I'll bet old Satan would give up a few thousand souls for an armful of firewood along about now," he said.

Brubs, riding alongside, shot a bleak glare at him. "You don't have to be so damn smug about it. Herdin' goats." He spat in disgust. "I never been so humiliated in all my borned days."

The bleating goats milled about uncertainly as the two harness mules leaned into the traces of the spring wagon bearing Granny Hooper's meager possessions. The wagon creaked and jolted into motion at the front door of the run-down half dugout.

Willoughby crossed his forearms over the saddle horn and chuckled softly. "Yes, sir, this adventure will go down in Texas history. Perhaps even a whole chapter devoted to Brubs McCallan's Great Big Bend Goat Drive. Why, it's the stuff of which legends are made. Cowboys will be telling the story around every camp fire in five states."

"Dave Willoughby, you ever mention a word of this, I'll whup your butt." The sorrel between Brubs's knees snorted and stamped his front feet, ears pointed toward the cluster of shaggy, scrawny goats. Brubs tugged on the reins. "Settle down, Squirrel. Them's just goats, not booger bears."

Willoughby glanced at the sorrel. The gelding's eyes were wide, the skin on his shoulders trembling. "Doesn't look like old Squirrel's ever seen such an animal before, Brubs," he said. "If I were you, I'd keep a short rein, a deep seat, and my toes turned out. The first time one of those goats tries to break out, Squirrel may buck you off or pull a runaway."

Brubs snorted. "Hell, I don't blame him none. Ol' Squirrel's likely more humiliated than I am. Gotta be pure embarrassment for a top cow horse, gettin' stuck behind a bunch of shaggies." His nose wrinkled. "Them's the stinkiest critters the Creator ever made."

"As Emperor Vespasian said, *'Pecunia non olet.'* "

"Talk American."

"It means, 'Money has no smell.' "

"What's goats got to do with money?"

Willoughby shrugged. "It appears to me that most of this country can support goats where it can't support cattle. The day might come when goats are the major viable livestock venture in this part of West Texas."

"Silliest damn idea I ever heard." Brubs sniffed. "Creator meant this to be cow and horse country. Won't never be nothin' else." He tugged on the reins and rammed a spur into the sorrel's ribs. "Squirrel, I told you to settle down." The horse flinched, danced sideways, and snorted again.

Willoughby sensed that his own black wasn't overly keen on the idea of goats. He could feel the horse's nervous uncertainty through the reins and against his knees. But at least the black wasn't on the verge of throwing a walleyed fit the way Brubs's sorrel was.

The wagon had pulled clear of the cabin, Granny Hooper on the hard wooden seat, one hand holding the reins, the long-barrel 10-gauge goose gun across her lap, and her tongue lashing the surly mules with oaths that would bring a blush to a teamster's cheeks.

"Look on the bright side, Brubs," Willoughby said. "You'll be an accomplished goatherd by the time we get to LaQuesta. You must admit it would be nice to have a trade to fall back on when we run out of felonies to commit."

The Texan pinned a cold, hard stare on Willoughby's face. "You got a flat-out mean streak in you, Dave. Rubbin' a man's nose in it like that. Now, I done warned you. Not a word about this to nobody, or I'll climb your tree."

Willoughby chuckled aloud. "Your secret is safe with me, friend." He nodded toward the bleating herd. "You're the trail boss on this drive, Brubs, but I think we should move them out now."

The Texan sighed and reined the sorrel toward the milling goats. Squirrel didn't want to go. The sorrel minced along, head held low to the ground, ears perked forward. Brubs waved a hand at the goats. "Move on, you —" His yell ended in a startled squawk as one of the goats broke from the herd and bounded straight toward the sorrel. Squirrel bolted two strides, then bogged his head with a squeal and fell apart. Brubs lost a stirrup on the first jump, his hat on the second, and his seat on the third. He fell on his side in the rocky soil, bounced, and rolled into the edge of a prickly pear patch.

Willoughby managed to coax the black into turning the goat back toward the herd. The gelding did his job, but Dave could tell the horse wasn't too comfortable doing it. He trotted the black up to Brubs, who had struggled to his feet and was trying to pull a prickly pear pad from his right buttock.

"Are you all right?" Willoughby tried to keep the amusement from his tone. He wasn't completely successful.

Brubs glared at him for a moment. "Am I all right? Hell, yes, I'm all right. Why shouldn't I be? I got a scobbed-up elbow, sand in my britches, a crick in my neck, and a damned prickly pear stuck in my butt. I ain't never been happier. Catch that idiot horse of mine. We got livestock to move."

By the time Willoughby retrieved the sorrel, Brubs had yanked the prickly pear pad from his rump. He spent a couple of minutes running through his impressive vocabulary of profanity, then toed the stirrup. The sorrel looked around at him. "Don't even think it, Squirrel," he grumbled. "I ain't in the mood right now."

Willoughby shook his head as Brubs settled, wincing, into the saddle. "That sorrel sure can buck," he said. "Looked like you flew ten feet into the air. I think you're losing your touch with the rough string, Brubs. Maybe you should consider riding gentler horses."

"Losin' my touch?" The Texan's lower lip protruded in a wounded pout. "I swear, I don't know what's got into you, Dave Willoughby. All of a sudden you just can't pass up a chance to insult a man."

"When it comes to flinging insults," his partner responded, "I've had an excellent teacher. A man learns a lot riding with you."

"Aw, hell." Brubs squared his shoulders and patted the sorrel's neck. "Old Squirrel's a good hoss. I'd a blowed up myself, I'd been him."

Willoughby glanced up at the sound of iron wagon wheel rims on the crunchy soil. Granny Hooper had turned the wagon back. She sat for a moment on the seat, her wide, weathered face creased by frown lines.

"I sure hope you two clodhoppers know more about horses than you know about goats," she said. "Like to have spilt the whole bunch already and we ain't even left home yet." She leaned over and spat. The amber glob splattered onto a green lizard's head. The lizard bounced several inches into the air, landed with feet churning, and dashed out of range. "You bucked down mighty hard, son. Bust somethin'?"

Brubs shook his head. "Don't reckon. Just got a few cactus stickers in me, that's all."

"I'll dig 'em out for you when we get to this ranch of your'n. Now, you boys see if you can bunch them goats up without crowdin' 'em none. They'll foller the wagon."

"They didn't before, Mrs. Hooper," Willoughby said.

"Didn't have no reason to," Granny said. She climbed from the wagon seat. "Toss me your rope, McCallan." She caught the rope on the fly and called one of the goats by name. The scraggly billy trotted up to her. Granny snubbed the rope around the goat's horns and tied him to the wagon tailgate. "They'll come along now," she said.

Brubs sighed. "I reckon I'll never get the goat smell off that good rope. Granny, how come you didn't do that in the first place? Woulda saved a mess of trouble."

Granny glanced around, found no living target, and spat a brownish glob against a rock. She raised an eyebrow at Brubs. "Tried to tell you earlier, you wouldn't pay no mind to no mere woman. You boys learn somethin' here today?"

"Yes, ma'am," Willoughby said. "We will certainly give careful consideration to your suggestions in the future."

" 'Bout time you whelps showed a little respect to a poor old widder." Granny sniffed in disdain and climbed back onto the wagon seat. "Next

73

time, maybe you'll listen to your elders some."

Brubs lifted himself in the saddle and rubbed his hand over his cactus-ravaged buttock. "Ain't gonna be no next time with goats. I done had all the truck with 'em I want."

Granny lifted the reins. "Let's go. You honyocks try not to scatter the herd. And don't you go chousin' them goats, neither, or I'll take a buggy whip to the both of you. *¿Sabe?*"

Willoughby nodded emphatically. "Yes, ma'am. We understand."

"Good." Granny tapped the reins against the off mule's rump. The wagon jolted into motion. The goat she had tied to the tailboard sat back against the rope, got dragged a few feet, then gave up the fight and trotted amiably along behind the wagon. The other goats followed.

"Don't just set there admirin' your shadows, dammit," Granny yelled at the two men. "We ain't gettin' a bit closer to Kansas and we ain't gettin' there fast, the way you two keep lolly-gaggin' around."

Willoughby glanced at Brubs. "Partner, do you think we might have made a mistake in hiring that woman?"

A slight grin tugged at Brubs's lips. "Hell, no," he said. "That there's the kind of granny I'd a wanted myself, I ever had one."

Willoughby sighed. "It figures. Let's go."

Brubs leaned across the table in the three-room adobe and yelped aloud as Granny Hooper

74

yanked a cactus spine from his butt with a pair of rusty pliers.

"Shut up your whinin', McCallan," Granny said. "Coulda been worse. You coulda landed on a porkypine. I tell you pure, it's hell's own frets, tryin' to pull porkypine quills outta a man. Or a dog. Sometimes I think they ain't no difference. Lay still."

"I ain't never been so — *Ouch!* — embarrassed in all my burned days," Brubs said. "Bent over — *Ow!* — like this. Plumb humiliatin', in front of a woman and all."

"Don't you fret that, son," Granny said. Brubs heard the "tink" as she spat a glob of tobacco juice into a tin can that served as a spittoon. "Ain't no part of a man I ain't seen, one time or another, and I still ain't much impressed at the sight." She yanked out another cactus spine and ignored his whimper. "Besides, you all look alike from here. I gotta say it wouldn't hurt you none to take yourself a bath once in a while."

"Bath! You cranky old — *Youch!*"

"You mind your tongue, you little runt. Show a tad of respect talkin' to me, or I might take a mind to get rough with these here pliers."

Brubs winced. "I thought you done had. Wouldn't a said nothin', but you don't know how bad it's been livin' with Dave Willoughby. Always wastin' water and cuttin' off good whiskers dealt to him by the Almighty and naggin' me about takin' a bath. It ain't like I was — *Yip!* — all that dirty or nothin'. I take a bath ever' couple months, most years." He glanced over his shoulder at Granny. "Ain't you done back there yet?"

"Hold still. I swear, you men is such a pain in the butt."

He grimaced as she plucked out another barb. "Speakin' of which, them prickly pear spines sting somethin' fierce."

Granny stepped back. "Reckon that'll hold you for now. Got most of 'em. It don't get infected, you'll be all right. Pull your britches up and go play with the rest of the boys. I gotta start supper."

Brubs buckled his pants, grabbed his hat from its peg by the door, and limped outside, favoring the raw buttock. He paused for a moment, wondering how Tige was coming along in Laredo. They needed more grub than Symms's place stocked, and Laredo was the closest supply point. Tige was the only one who could go, since Brubs and Willoughby had been banished. He was due back in a couple of days. If he didn't get robbed by bandits or waylaid by whiskey and women along the way. Then they could get moving toward Kansas.

Brubs idly wondered if spring came this quick in Kansas. The gentle breeze from the southwest smelled of greening grass and the lingering fresh scent of gentle showers. The sun had dropped halfway down the western sky, bathing the Texas Horsetrading Company headquarters in a soft, warm light. It would have been a downright peaceful thing to look at, he mused, except it was hard to get peaceful when guns were going off every couple of minutes.

Brubs thought about walking the two hundred yards upcreek to the spot Willoughby and Cal had picked for shooting practice. The thought didn't stick around long. A real genuine Texan never walked more than a few feet if there was a horse around. He saddled the little gray mustang called Mouse. The gray humped his back and snorted, but didn't pitch as Brubs trotted him toward the shooters.

Brubs checked Mouse a few yards short of the shooting range, waiting for Cal Hooper to finish firing the .38-40 Winchester taken from the Texas Horsetrading Company's considerable arsenal of guns, most of them appropriated from various bad men or bandits. Cal had no rifle except for the little .22 Remington. It would do for a camp meat gun, rabbits and quail and such, but Cal would need more firepower than that if they ran across Indians or outlaws on the way north. Brubs hoped the boy could shoot better than he showed now. The target was a syrup can fifty yards off, and it wasn't exactly punched full of holes yet.

Brubs kneed Mouse up to the trio after Cal lowered the rifle. "How's it goin', boys?"

Cal glanced up. "Not so good, Mr. McCallan. This rifle shoots low."

"Can't blame the shootin' iron without puttin' some blame on the shooter, Cal," Brubs said. "Maybe you ain't holdin' the sights right."

The youth picked up his Remington rolling block, chambered a .22 Short cartridge, and swung the rifle to his shoulder. The ping of lead against metal followed the flat splat of the rifle's almost silent report.

"Reckon you made your point, Cal," Brubs said. He pulled a coarse honing stone from his pocket. "File that .38-40 front sight down a tad. That'll make her shoot a touch higher." He glanced around. "Nick Chadburne show up yet?"

"Not yet," Willoughby said. "He said he'd be here by sundown today."

Brubs frowned. "Shouldn't take a man that long to pick up his stuff. Hope nothin' happened to him. I'd hate to be short a hand before we even start out."

"Don't worry about Nick, Mr. McCallan," Cal said, without looking up from his work. "If he said he'll be here by sundown, he'll be here."

Brubs nodded silently. He wasn't sure what to make of Nick Chadburne. The kid was sixteen but looked older, and when he did talk — which wasn't often — he sounded like he was sixteen going on thirty. Brubs still didn't know much about him except that he was an orphan. There was bad blood between Chadburne and his uncle, and Nick was more than ready to leave home. The kid hadn't gone into detail about the bad blood, and Brubs didn't push the point. It wasn't his business. He had learned to trust his instincts where people were concerned. Sometimes, he admitted, he got his fingers scorched. Most times, though, his gut feelings were right.

Chadburne wasn't a kid between the ears, or anywhere else. He stood about five ten, three inches taller than Brubs, and looked like he weighed about 180, ten pounds more than Willoughby. The boy was strong as an ox, with thick, sloping shoulders and heavy forearms. He was dark-skinned to the point of looking almost Indian. The first thing Brubs had noticed about him, though, was his eyes. They were green, and had a solemn look in them, like Chadburne was sorrowful inside. That didn't seem right in a man that young, Brubs thought. Life was too short to fret it away. He figured the youngster would get over it, once he'd learned how to have a little fun once in a while. Chadburne had the look of somebody who would make a fair hand on the trail. They had hired him on the spot.

Cal took one final, careful swipe at the front sight with the honing stone. "That should bring it pretty close," he said, handing the stone back to Brubs. The kid chambered a single cartridge, swung the rifle to his shoulder, and fired. The syrup can bounced and turned a flip, landing on its side. "That's better," Cal said.

"Fair shootin' there, son," Brubs said. "How are you with a handgun?"

Cal shrugged. "Passable. Only six-gun I got's an old .31 cap 'n' ball. Barrel's shot out. Haven't had the money to buy a new one."

"You can have the Colt we took from the man who owned that rifle," Willoughby said. "I

79

haven't fired the weapon, but it appears to be in good shape. We can cut down the cartridge belt to fit you, I think."

Brubs ground-hitched the mustang and loosened his Colt in his holster. "Meantime, son," he said to Cal, "I'll show you what handgun shootin's all about." He pulled his .45 Single Action Army from his holster, eared back the hammer, took careful aim at the syrup can, and fired. Dust kicked up a couple of feet right of the target. Brubs fired again; the slug again went right, and a bit high. He lowered the weapon and stared quizzically at it for a moment.

"Must have knocked the front sight off some when ol' Squirrel tossed me off," Brubs said.

Willoughby chuckled. "Don't let him kid you, Cal. Johnny Rebs never could shoot for sour apples."

"I recollect you Yankees wasn't much with a short gun. Or a long gun, neither," the Texan retorted. "They hadn't put you in artillery, you wouldn't have never hit nothin'."

Willoughby shrugged. "I never claimed to be a *pistolero*."

"You want to quit flappin' your lip and show us how it's done?"

Willoughby shook his head. "No sense in wasting ammunition. I know my limitations, unlike some folks around here."

"Tell you what, Dave." Brubs sounded slightly peeved. "Let's put a little bet up, just to make it interestin'. Say, a dollar apiece? Five shots?"

Willoughby sighed in resignation. "A challenge made is a gauntlet thrown. I hate to take your hard-earned whiskey money, Brubs, but if you insist —"

"Put that coin where your mouth is, Yankee." Brubs winked at Cal Hooper. "You watch, son, you'll see how easy it is to make money. You first, partner."

Willoughby pulled his .44-40 revolver, took his time, and fired five rounds. Two of the slugs kicked dirt against the can; a third pinged against the rim of the can.

Brubs snorted. "You Yanks couldn't hit an outhouse wall while sittin' on the two-holer plank. Wonder you ever won the war." He thumbed two fresh cartridges into his .45 and started to raise the weapon. "I'm gonna enjoy spendin' that dollar."

"Can I play?" Cal asked.

Brubs lowered the handgun. "Son, are you sure you want to do that? You're talkin' about a whole day's pay you'd lose."

"You can take it out of my wages when we sell the horses. If I lose."

"Your money, son." Brubs lifted the .45 and squeezed off five shots. One slug nicked the syrup can enough to rock it. The other four went wide right and high. Brubs glanced again at the smoking handgun. "No doubt about it. Them sights is off. Anyhow, we got us a tie."

"Can I use your revolver, Mr. McCallan?"

"Sure, son." Brubs ejected the spent hulls, re-

81

loaded, and handed the weapon to Cal. "Just try to keep 'em somewhere on that creek bank, boy. Don't want lead sailin' off and killin' a good hoss somewhere."

"Yes, sir. I'll be careful." Cal thumbed the hammer, raised the Colt, and fired almost in the same motion. The syrup can bounced and toppled. Cal cocked the hammer and fired again as soon as the powder smoke drifted clear. The impact of lead against metal sent the syrup can rolling. Cal lowered the weapon. "The sights are fine, Mr. McCallan," he said. "I think you may be yanking the trigger instead of squeezing. That can throw the bullet off course."

Brubs's jaw was hanging open. "I'll be damned, son," he said. "Where'd you ever learn to shoot a handgun like that?"

"Granny taught me."

"Granny?"

"Yes, sir. She can near shoot out a pine knot at thirty yards with Pa's old .36 Navy. It's nearly as accurate as these Peacemakers, but the .45's and .44-40's have a lot more stopping power. You want me to finish the round? I still have three shots left."

Dave Willoughby chuckled aloud. "That won't be necessary, Cal," he said. "You've already beaten us both with just two shots." He reached in his pocket, produced a dollar, and handed it to the boy. "Pay the man, Brubs."

The Texan found two four-bit pieces after an extensive search of every pocket. He handed them

82

to Cal and got his Colt back in return. He reloaded the two chambers and dropped the revolver into his holster. "I reckon you beat us fair and square on this one, son. But remember, syrup cans don't pack shootin' irons. It's a whole 'nuther game when somebody's slingin' lead back at you."

"Yes, sir, I expect it is," Cal said solemnly. "I sure hope I never have to find out what it's like."

Brubs abruptly turned away and mounted the mustang. "Playtime's over, boys. We got work to do." He kneed Mouse into a slow trot toward the barn.

Cal fingered the coins for a minute, then looked up at Dave. "Did I make him mad, Mr. Willoughby?"

The tall man grinned. "No, Cal, you didn't make him angry. It takes a lot to rile him. If you ever do, you'll know it." He nodded toward the cartridge cases at Cal's side. "Pick up your brass, son. We'll have to reload it. Unfortunately, .38-40 ammunition is hard to find out here."

Cal picked up the cases, blew the dirt from them, and dropped them into a shirt pocket. "Mr. Willoughby?"

"Yes?"

"How come you two are always picking at each other? I mean, insulting each other all the time? I thought you were the best of friends."

Willoughby smiled gently. "We are, Cal. The ragging is just a way of saying so without having to actually come out and say it out loud. If we ever stop joshing each other, then you can start worrying." He put a hand on the shoulder of the freckled, jug-eared youth. "Let's head back. It will be supper time soon and if Brubs gets to the feed trough before we do, there won't be anything left but crumbs and flies."

Brubs leaned against the wall of the adobe, listening to three sets of guts rumble as the scent of fresh-baked sourdough, chili beans, coffee, and frying venison wafted from the front door. Cal and Dave sat beside the door, taking up the stirrup leathers on a spare saddle to fit the boy's shorter legs.

Brubs glanced up as the door banged open. Granny Hooper clomped outside and put a bowl of water, a bar of lye soap, and a towel on a stump beside the door.

"What's that for, Granny?" Brubs said.

"Nobody bellies up to my table they don't wash up first," Granny said. She spat a glob of tobacco juice at a dung beetle, knocked the insect spinning, and glared at Brubs. "That goes special for you. You ain't puttin' them grubby hands on my biscuits."

Brubs groaned aloud. "Damn, Granny, if you ain't the persnicketyest old bat — I mean, woman —"

"Rider coming," Willoughby interrupted. He plucked his Winchester from beside the steps, squinted toward the approaching horseman, then relaxed. "Nick's back."

84

The three stood and waited as Nick Chadburne rode up, a blanket roll and gunnysack tied to an old McClellan saddle on the back of a mare that was little more than a walking bag of bones. Dried blood crusted the young man's right cheekbone. The knuckles of the hand that held the reins were torn and bloody, the hand swollen. Nick's shirt and pants were covered with dirt and bits of straw.

"What happened, son?" Brubs said.

Chadburne's green eyes didn't change expression. "Nothing I couldn't handle. My uncle didn't want me to leave. We settled it."

Granny Hooper strode to the mare's side and studied Chadburne for a moment, then snorted in disgust. "Damned if it don't look like I'm gonna spend more time patchin' up you whelps than I am a-cookin'. Get your butt down here, boy, and let's have a look." She glanced at Brubs. "Take Nick's horse to the barn. Don't forget to wash up before you come in my house."

"*Your* house?" Brubs sniffed indignantly. "I thought that was my house, and I was boss of this outfit."

"Don't argue with me, you whippersnapper. I ain't in the mood. Now, git!"

Brubs got.

FIVE

The horse's hoof caught Brubs square on the left buttock and flung him headfirst into the wall of the barn. The crack of skull against wood triggered a quick flash of white light before his eyes. He dropped the hoof rasp, sagged against the wall until his vision cleared, and rubbed his bruised butt before turning to glare at the coyote dun.

The dun stood passively, his head turned toward Brubs, ears pricked forward as if nothing had happened.

"Don't give me that smart-ass look, you sorry no-account slab of wolf bait," Brubs growled. He picked up the hoof rasp and noticed the blood seeping from his knuckles. Brubs weighed the rasp as if it were a weapon and glowered at the dun. "If it weren't agin' my religion to whup hosses, you miserable, mule-eared, cow-hocked idiot, it'd be a pure pleasure to peel your rotten hide."

The horse's eyes widened in what seemed to be an expression of innocence. Brubs would have sworn the damn dun was laughing at him.

"Ugly, you and me are gonna go at this till that last shoe gets hammered on if it takes from here to Christmas." He sidled up to the horse, keeping a wary eye on the lethal rear hoof. He shifted the rasp to his left hand, ran his right down the dun's leg to below the hock, and tapped the horse lightly on the fetlock with the rasp. The horse lifted the leg without resistance.

"That's better," he said. "I reckon you finally figgered out who's boss around here." The dun sighed and shifted. The movement threw a sizeable portion of the horse's weight onto Brubs.

"Stand on your own damn crooked feet, you son of a mangy she-hound," he grumbled over his shoulder. "Behave yourself and we'll get this done right —" Brubs yelped aloud as the dun twisted around and nipped a chunk of skin from Brubs's lower back. He jumped aside as the horse yanked his hoof free and kicked. It missed Brubs by inches.

"All right, dammit, that does it!" Brubs threw the hoof rasp down, limped to his saddle, and pulled the Henry from the boot. "You done went and made me mad now!" He racked a round into the rifle chamber. "It's maybe agin my religion to whup a hoss, but it sure as hell ain't agin my religion to shoot one." He raised the rifle.

"What's all the commotion?" Dave Willoughby said as he stepped into the barn.

"I'm gonna kill this sorry son of a bitch and put him outta my misery." Brubs's face was dark with anger. He cocked the Henry.

Willoughby reached out and pushed the rifle barrel down. "No need to do anything rash, Brubs. Malhumorado's a good horse."

Brubs glowered at him for a moment. "You got

mighty curious ideas about what's a good horse. Ol' Ugly here's done kicked me, bit me, scobbed up my hide and agitated me for the last time. Tryin' to shoe this idiot's a waste of time and iron, not to mention skin."

"Funny," Willoughby said calmly. "He never gave me any trouble. I'll finish up." He picked up the rasp, strode to the dun's side, and patted the horse on the rump. Then he reached for the hind foot.

"Watch out, Dave," Brubs warned. "That crazy bastard's got the sneakiest kick I ever seen."

"Oh, he won't kick." Malhumorado lifted the foot at Willoughby's touch and stood as calm as a Jersey milk cow while the tall man worked on the hoof. After a moment, Dave tossed the rasp aside, reached for a horseshoe and a few nails, and tacked the shoe in place.

The dun fluttered his nostrils as Willoughby rasped a shallow groove in the hoof beneath the protruding nail tips, but the horse never so much as twitched as Willoughby clipped the tips from the nails with hoof nippers, tapped them snugly into the shallow groove, and filed the exposed metal of the nails smooth. Willoughby dropped the hoof, patted the dun on the rump again, and stepped back.

"See? Nothing to it," he said.

The dun looked around at Brubs.

"That walkin' chunk of buzzard bait ain't never gonna get tired of tormentin' me," the Texan groused.

88

"By the way, I came to tell you that Tige's on his way in with the supplies," Willoughby said. "He'll arrive in a few minutes. I'll finish up here. How many more need to be shod?"

"Your black, that snip-nosed bay with the stockin' feet, and Choctaw. I done did the rest of the saddle ponies." Brubs massaged his bruised butt and gingerly probed the horse bite on his back. "Sure glad I don't have to blacksmith for a livin'. Man shouldn't ought to have to sweat over nothin' except a warm and willin' woman, and that ain't what I'd call work." He turned toward the barn door. "I'll send Cal up to work the forge for you."

Brubs limped from the barn, wondering if he had a spot of hide left somewhere that wasn't skinned, sore, bruised, full of thorns, or spotted with bug bites. He was still trying to find an un-damaged spot when Tige reined the two-mule hitch to a stop in front of the house.

"Howdy, Brubs," Tige said. "You look like you got worked over in a bar fight and then drug through the bushes."

"Been teachin' that damn coyote dun of Dave's some manners," Brubs said. "Get everything we needed?"

"Reckon so." Tige climbed from the wagon and grinned at him. "Even snuck in a few bottles of passable whiskey. Thought we might need us some prime snakebite medicine."

"Bless you, Brother Tilghman," Brubs said gratefully. "I knowed you'd remember all the necessaries." He clapped the big man on the shoulder, raising a cloud of dust.

The front door swung open and Granny Hooper stomped out, wiping her hands on a dish towel. She had a smudge of flour along one cheek. The other was distended by a wad of chewing tobacco only slightly smaller than a man's fist. She glowered for a moment at Tilghman.

"About damn time you got back, you lazy Arkie," Granny said. "Way you lunkheads is always dawdlin' around, we ain't never gonna get to Kansas."

Tilghman strode to Granny, embraced her in a big but gentle bear hug, and kissed her on the tobacco-bulged cheek. "I swear, Emeldeline Hooper, you get prettier all the time," Tige said. "Why, was you twenty years younger, I'd be snortin' in your flank like I was a young stud hoss."

Granny's cheeks flushed. "Let go me, you oversized prairie dog." She pushed him away, frowning, but the glint in her eyes gave lie to the scowl. "Show some respect for your elders, you young whelp. And if I was twenty years younger I'd a done had a damn sight better offer by this time of day, and it ain't much past noon yet." She strode past Tilghman to the wagon. "You fetch all the stuff I need?"

"Yes, ma'am. I reckon there's enough there to trail grub this bunch a fair spell."

Granny stretched on tiptoe to peer over the sides of the wagon. "You get me my tent?"

90

"Yes'm. It ain't brand-new, but it'll turn the wind and rain and give you a private place."

"Good. Poor defenseless widder woman's gotta have her privacy, travelin' with a bunch of skirt-crazy men like you young jackasses." She lowered herself to her heels. "Don't just stand there like a couple tree stumps, dammit! Get them mules unhitched and this here stuff unloaded so's I can tally it." She snorted in disgust. "Gotta be repacked, anyhow. You men don't know nothin' about loadin' a wagon. Or a helluva lot else for that matter." She turned and stomped back into the house.

"You done good, Tige," Brubs said. "Granny's plumb pleased with what you brung us. Can tell by the way she was sweet-talkin' you."

Tilghman grinned. "Yes, sir, I reckon I always been a ladies' man, at that." He flicked the harness buckles loose on the off mule, then glanced over the animal's rump at Brubs. "How soon we movin' out?"

"Soon's we get a few things done to this wagon to make life easier for Granny," Brubs said. "Gotta keep the cook happy. 'Specially that one. I figure a couple more days and we'll be ready to roll." He flipped the harness free of the hames and ducked a nip from the near side mule. "I tell you, Tige, I'm gettin' a tad anxious to get this outfit headed north."

"Me, too," Tilghman said solemnly. "Seen about half a dozen of that little Mex gal's brothers and cousins down in Laredo."

"They see you?"

"Don't reckon. Nobody stuck a knife in me."

Brubs McCallan stood at the end of the small dining room table, a swatch of butcher paper spread before him and the nub of a pencil in hand. He glanced around the table at the expectant faces. Even Granny Hooper seemed interested, maybe even excited. Although with Granny, it was hard to tell. She had a steady disposition, Brubs thought: cranky all the time.

"Well, boys and girls, here's how I got it figgered," Brubs said. He touched the pencil to the paper and made a small *x*. "This here's LaQuesta. What we'll do is trail these hosses to Lobo Springs, then straight north to the Pecos. We'll foller the Pecos up into New Mexico, then cut east once we pass the headwaters of the Red River. We head 'em northeast from there, cross the Canadian and Cimarron rivers, trail up through the Cimarron Strip to Skull Creek. Few days from there we catch the Dodge City Trail and mosey on into Dodge. Tad over six hundred miles, total."

Tige Tilghman's broad, flat-nosed face deepened in a scowl. "Brubs, that's a ways off the main trails north. There ain't more'n a handful of white men ever went up that way and fewer'n that who come back. Mighty empty country."

"That's one of the reasons we're goin' that way," Brubs said. "We're gonna blaze us a brand-new trail. They might even name it after us. I can see it on the maps now — the McCallan Trail."

Tilghman didn't seem impressed. "Water might be a problem once we top out on the Staked Plains," he said. "Not to mention there just might be a few bronco Comanches around that part of the country. Why not trail east from here to Fort Concho and catch the Western Trail from there?"

Brubs tapped the pencil point against the paper. "Got a reason for that, Tige. Some of these ponies we'll be trailin' come from up along the lower Concho and middle Brazos country. I'd just as soon they didn't get that near to home again. Some of 'em might take a notion to see their old pastures."

Tilghman cocked an eyebrow. "Didn't know you boys picked up horses that far north. Come to think on it, I did notice a couple Brazos brands on some of them animals."

Brubs winked at him. "That Brazos country's just crawlin' with horse thieves, Tige. Sure wouldn't want to lose any stock to 'em on the way north."

"Yeah," Tilghman said wryly. "I reckon you got a point. How about water? I hear it's a far piece between water holes on the Staked Plains."

"Talked to an old *mesteñero* — that's mustanger to you young fellers don't speak Mex good as me — up on the Cimarron once. He told me there was water on the Llano Estacado if a man just knowed how to look for it. Unless it ain't rained up there in a spell."

"Mr. McCallan?" Cal Hooper's eyes were wide. The expression made his ears seem to stick out farther. "What about the Indians Mr. Tilghman mentioned?"

Brubs shrugged. "Nothin' much to worry about there. Army done cleaned most of 'em out. Course, there could be a handful of bronco Comanch still hangin' around up there. All the Quahadis didn't quit. Might even be some Kioways or Kioway-Apaches, and them critters is a damn sight worse than even Comanches when it comes to mean."

"How many Indians," Dave Willoughby asked cautiously, "would you consider a handful?"

"Not more'n thirty, forty fightin' men, tops."

Willoughby sighed. "Brubs, you have perfected the art of bringing pure comfort to a man."

"Aw, don't fret none about redskins. Most likely we won't even see a feather." Brubs leaned over the table again, studied the sketch a final time, then grunted in satisfaction. "Reckon that's it. I'll ride point since I know the country some. Granny'll drive the chow wagon behind me. Dave, you and Tige'll have to double ridin' both swing and flank till these ponies get lined out and settled down good. Cal, you and Nick ride drag. Don't dawdle, but don't push 'em hard, neither. We'll sort of mosey along about grazin' speed, maybe ten, twelve miles a day. Time we hit Kansas, these ponies'll be slick and fat as a new baby on a full tit."

"McCallan," Granny Hooper snapped, "you mind your tongue in my house. By damn, I sure as hell won't put up with you jackasses cussin' around me."

"Yes'm," Brubs said. " 'Scuse me. I just got plumb carried away." He pushed away from the table. "Tige, you and Dave help Granny finish riggin' the wagon. Me and the two younkers got to top out some ridin' horses and get Nick fitted out with a decent saddle. Can't have nobody from Texas ridin' into Kansas on a old McClellan. Be an insult to the Lone Star flag."

Brubs led the two youths to the barn and nodded toward the small storeroom behind the feed trough. "There's a spare saddle in the tack room, Nick. Old center fire rig. It's got a high cantle and big swells, kind of a bronc saddle. You might need somethin' like that, on account of some of these jugheads look like they might pitch some."

Brubs waited until Chadburne fetched the old saddle, studying the dozen or so horses in the corral. "Nick, that old swayback mare of yours wouldn't make a dozen miles hard ridin'. We'll leave her here along with the other culls. Top out that snip-nosed sorrel over there to start with. We'll have you boys a fair string of saddle ponies put together before sundown."

Brubs turned to Cal and pointed toward a half-Morgan dozing at one side of the corral. "You use the big bay, son," he said. "Might watch 'im at first, though. When he ain't asleep, he got an ornery look in his eyes."

Cal nodded, the freckles standing out in sharp relief against his pale face. "Yes, sir."

Brubs leaned against the fence and watched as the two youths went to catch the horses. Cal was awkward with the rope. He blushed in embarrassment when he missed the first loop by ten feet.

"Don't fret it none, Cal," Brubs called. "If I could teach a Yankee college boy like Dave Willoughby how to rope, I can sure as hell learn you quick enough. Relax your wrist when you make the toss. Don't try throwin' the loop too hard unless the wind's blowin'. Which it normal is, where we're goin'."

Brubs grunted in satisfaction as the next loop settled over the bay's neck. Cal led the horse to the corral fence, slipped a bit in the bay's mouth, and held the catch rope out to Chadburne. The dark-skinned youth shook his head.

"Now this," Brubs muttered to himself, "is gonna get downright comical. Took me ten minutes runnin' before I caught that sorrel the first time."

Chadburne strode slowly toward the snorting sorrel, taking his time and talking softly. Brubs couldn't make out the words, but at least it proved the kid could talk. Brubs's jaw dropped when the walleyed sorrel let Chadburne walk up and slip a bridle over his head.

Cal was the first to saddle up. He toed the stirrup and swung aboard the bay. The horse immediately bogged his head and fell apart. Brubs

96

started to yell instructions, then realized there was no need. Cal sat firm in the saddle, feet forward, riding by balance rather than brute strength, as the bay bucked around the corral. The kid was a natural. Brubs couldn't remember having seen anyone ride that rank a bucking horse and make it look that easy.

The bay finally gave up. Cal reined the sweaty gelding around a few times, then trotted up to Brubs. "He'll do," the kid said. "Don't buck as hard as I thought he would."

Chadburne pulled the cinch tight on the sorrel. The horse's nostrils flared and his hide trembled. Nick led the horse in a tight circle a couple of times, patted the sorrel on the neck, and swung into the saddle.

The horse snorted and fidgeted, but didn't try to buck. A few minutes later Nick had him answering the rein. The sorrel was light on his feet and quick as a cat. Brubs shook his head in wonder. "Them sprats can flat handle horses," he muttered to himself. "At least I won't have to learn 'em that."

Brubs picked up his rope, caught a leggy brown wearing the Fishhook brand, and saddled up. The brown crow-hopped a few times, then settled down. Brubs leaned from the saddle and swung the gate open. "Let's take 'em out, boys," he said to the two youths. "Pull a few wet saddle blankets off 'em, they'll get shut of any idea of pitchin' ever' time we catch 'em. And don't you two get no ideas about racin' back to the barn. I ain't gonna have no barn-soured horses in this outfit."

The sun had dropped to near the top of the western mountain range before Brubs decided to call it quits for the day. He, Cal, and Chadburne had topped out a dozen horses. One of the horses, a palomino with a flaxen mane and tail, was a complete idiot. Brubs had fought the yellow horse every step of the way before pronouncing him a worthless jughead in the most colorful terms he knew. The rest of the animals they had ridden were decent horses. Nothing special like Choctaw or Squirrel, but they would do.

Brubs swung down and opened the gate. "Un-saddle, boys and give 'em all a bait of grain. Don't dawdle. Supper'll be ready pretty quick, and we don't want Granny on the prod at us for bein' late. Better wash up in the horse trough before comin' in. I swear, I never seen so persnickety a woman. You'd think a little horse slobbers and sweat was pure rattler poison, the way she carries on."

"Mr. McCallan," Cal said as he loosened the back cinch of the double-rigged Mexican saddle, "when do you think we'll be moving out?"

Brubs stripped the saddle from the palomino. "Day after tomorrow, most likely. You boys ready to see some new country?"

Cal Hooper's eyes brightened. "Yes, sir. This should be quite an adventure."

Brubs shook his head. "Son, what it's goin' to be mostly is long days and eatin' dust and bein' hot, dry, wet, hungry, thirsty, tuckered out, and bored on top of that. At least I'm hopin' that's all it'll be."

"Will we see any Indians?"

"That's one of the things I'm hopin' to be bored over. I'd just as soon not have no truck with Injuns on this trip." Brubs cocked an eyebrow at Chadburne. "How about you, Nick? You ready to leave?"

Chadburne shrugged. "I've got no reason to hang around here."

"Okay. You boys finish up here. I'm gonna see how the work on that wagon's comin'."

At least, Brubs thought as he strode toward the house, he had finally gotten a complete sentence out of Chadburne. There was something about Nick that seemed a little out of whack, something that didn't set just right in a man's biscuit pouch. Brubs shrugged the feeling away. If Nick developed into a good hand on the trail, his personal boogers were his own business.

Brubs found Tilghman under the wagon and Willoughby heaving a freshly greased rear wheel back onto the axle. Dave was getting to be a fair hand with cusswords, Brubs noticed.

Tilghman tightened the linchpin nut into place with a grunt, tossed the heavy wrench aside, and sucked at a freshly skinned knuckle.

"Mighty fine job you boys done on this here wagon," Brubs said.

Tilghman crawled from beneath the wagon as Willoughby tightened the hub nut. The big man straightened and massaged the small of his aching back. Willoughby's clothes were dusty and streaked with wheel grease. "Tige and I didn't notice you exactly busting your butt getting this thing ready, Brubs," he groused.

"One of the good things about bein' trail boss," Brubs said. "Man don't have to do near so much sweatin'. Course, it ain't easy bein' the brains of the outfit."

"If you're the brains of this outfit, you sawed-off little misbegot runt of a hoss thief," Tilghman said, squinting at Brubs and slapping the dust from his backside, "we ain't gonna make a dozen miles, let alone Kansas."

Brubs chuckled. "Glad you're feelin' perky, Tige. I was sort of frettin' that maybe you wasn't havin' a real good time."

Tilghman snorted. "I'll have me a good time when we get to Kansas. If we get to Kansas." He flexed the hand with the skinned knuckle. "Damn, I thought when I left Arkansas I was done with blacksmithin' hammers, anvils, and drawknives. Somethin' can't be done from horseback, it ain't supposed to be done at all, and I ain't been in the saddle since I rode back into LaQuesta."

"Just think about all them gold pieces you'll have in your pockets, Tige," Brubs said. He walked around the wagon. Tilghman had done a good job. The double harness tongue had been replaced with a four-mule hitch rig for more pulling power in sand and up hills. The harness leathers were mended, cleaned and oiled, the wagon wheels freshly greased and spokes tightened, new wooden brake blocks in place. Three hardwood bows arched over the wagon bed. A canvas sheet lay nearby, patched and ready to be spread over the bows to cover the load in the wagon.

Granny Hooper's chuck box at the back of the wagon was a touch on the crude side, Brubs mused, but functional. It had storage racks for small utensils, baking soda, spices, and other truck needed on the trail. A roll of canvas rested beside the chuck box, ready to be spread as a fly sheet to protect the cook and her fire from rain and heat. The small tent that would be Granny's sleeping quarters was mended and ready. The rest of the crew would sleep in the open or under the fly. All that was left now, Brubs saw, was the final loading of supplies.

"Well, gents," Brubs said as he finished his inspection, "I reckon we're about ready to roll. How's them ponies doin', Dave?"

Willoughby wiped the grease from his hands on a burlap sack. "Generally speaking, they're in good shape. Just the usual bites and scrapes from fights. I greased up the raw spots. If the blowflies don't get to them, they should hair over all right." He tossed the greasy rag onto a wheel rim. "That big paint with the Fishhook brand has a pretty bad limp. Either he got himself kicked or he's developing ringbone."

Brubs shrugged. "No big loss. That jughead ain't worth two dollars, anyhow. Keeps his head right up in your face, just like that palomino

Fishhook idiot. Couldn't neither of 'em see a cow unless she was flyin' overhead. We'll leave 'em with a few other culls." He spat in disgust. "Damn, you'd think somebody with Old Man Turbyfill's money would at least have hosses worth stealin'. Gettin' so a man can't hardly make a decent livin' in the hoss business."

SIX

Dave Willoughby slouched in the saddle, fighting the heaviness in his eyelids.

Saying good-bye to Kat Symms had turned into a longer night than he had expected. Kat took a lot of saying good-bye to. It hadn't been Willoughby's idea, but a gentleman didn't turn down a direct request from a lady.

He still remembered the sad look in those big blue eyes when he had finally dressed to leave. He hadn't been able to figure out why Kat looked so solemn. Women were a puzzlement. A soft and warm puzzlement, maybe, but still a puzzlement.

Willoughby had barely gotten back to headquarters in time to throw his personal belongings together and saddle up. That had been better than nine hours ago, and Brubs had called only a half hour halt for nooning — just long enough to grab a couple of biscuits and some cold bacon, a cup of coffee, and a change of horses. Then they were back in the saddle.

The early March sun seemed to have its seasons mixed up, Willoughby thought. It felt more like late June or early July. He could feel the warmth of the sun's rays on his shoulders and the trickle of sweat down the small of his back. The easy gait of the roan gelding also threatened to lull him into nodding off. He shook himself back to a semblance of alertness and concentrated on the horse herd.

The remuda moved along at a slow walk, strung out over more than a quarter mile. Horses seldom moved in a massed herd, like cattle. They drifted along in groups, as many as thirty in some bands or as few as two in others. Often, several yards separated the bands. Willoughby's black gelding and the coyote dun were, as usual, side by side when neither was under saddle. At least when the black was around for Malhumorado to buddy up to, the dun caused less trouble.

The horses were a mix of breeds and types. Most carried the distinctive mustang stamp — small, wiry, alert, and quick of foot. Others stood nearly sixteen hands — deep-chested, powerful mounts. In between were the mixed bloods and pure Mexican stock, most of them broken to saddle if not polished cow horses. Almost all the remuda was made up of geldings. Less than sixty of the animals were mares, and they were chosen for their promise as breeding stock. The mares would bring a good price in Dodge from ranchers looking for new blood for their brood mare bands. Four spare mules and a pair of aging, swaybacked burros rounded out the cavvy. The burros weren't worth much as work animals, but they were better watchdogs than any hound and could find water in the middle of nowhere. And when the Texas Horsetrading Company drive reached the Llano Estacado, those mangy jackasses just might be worth more than the rest of the outfit combined, Willoughby conceded.

The loosely herded animals moved along at a respectable pace. Graze was still scant despite a wetter than normal winter. Only a few isolated clumps of bunchgrass and low shrubs showed tinges of green. The horses were content to pause for a few seconds to crop the tender shoots and leaves. It wasn't hard to keep them moving.

Willoughby knew that true spring was at hand. The mesquite trees were showing buds. Mesquites, not the calendar, determined the end of winter in the Big Bend. They didn't put out new leaves until all danger of frost had passed.

Early season wildflowers daubed small patches of red, white, and yellow across the dun-tinted land. Willoughby knew that with the next warm rain, the desert would be a sea of color, entire valleys blanketed with every hue known to man. The blooming would be brief but spectacular. At such times, the desert seemed to lower its guard against the encroachment of man, to soften its usual brooding air of menace. During those short periods, Willoughby thought, the desert was one of the most beautiful places on earth, with magnificent vistas spread from horizon to horizon.

He forced his musings aside with a conscious effort and tried to concentrate on the work at hand. He lifted himself in the stirrups to scan the countryside.

Brubs and his sorrel, Squirrel, had the point, ambling along a hundred yards or so in front of the remuda. The heavily laden chuck wagon and its four-mule hitch followed Brubs, Granny Hooper at the reins. Two nanny goats were tied to the tailboard, one with a kid at her side and the other's belly swollen with new life. Brubs hadn't been happy about having goats along on a trail drive. Granny hadn't wasted many words bringing him to salvation. Goats gave milk. Cooks needed milk. Therefore, goats. End of argument.

The wagon lurched from time to time as a wheel jounced over a rock or rut. Willoughby was too far away to hear, but he expected the air would be tinged more than a bit blue around the wagon. Granny Hooper had a better command of mule skinner vocabulary than most teamsters. She had a way of getting a mule's attention.

Brubs reined Squirrel alongside the wagon, spoke to Granny for a moment, then kneed the sorrel into an easy lope up the valley.

Willoughby drifted back to the flank position, confident that he could relax and leave the actual herding chores to the roan between his knees. Choctaw knew more about moving livestock than any three men. Willoughby had spent most of the day riding swing until the remuda settled down. The horses had been restless and frisky at first, eager to get back on open range after being confined for so long. After a couple of hours the lead horses had accepted the idea of heading in the right direction.

Tige Tilghman's tall, rawboned buckskin trotted along on the other side of the remuda.

Tilghman slapped his coiled rope against his leather leggings, easing a couple of wandering horses back into the remuda before they strayed too far.

Cal Hooper and Nick Chadburne rode drag, keeping the stragglers moving. Willoughby heard their occasional soft calls as they pushed a laggard horse or two into motion. The kids were green, but they were already learning. Moving horses wasn't a time for whooping and hollering and going rope crazy. It was a time for slow and easy and hope for the best.

All in all, he decided, it was a peaceful scene that spread before him. Almost a whole day gone, and not a single serious calamity yet. That was unusual for a Brubs McCallan project.

Willoughby scanned the horizon all around. There was no other sign of human life. An eagle sailed the wind currents high above the shallow valley they followed, and a covey of blue quail scurried away, legs moving so fast as to be almost invisible.

He lowered himself back into the saddle. In a few days the procession would move beyond the rocky, broken desert country through the narrow pass between the Delaware and Apache mountain ranges. That would bring a welcome change. Beyond the mountains the grass would be better and water more abundant. Once they reached the Pecos, another fifty miles or so beyond the pass, they would have a reliable, if less than tasty, water supply. In the lower reaches of the Pecos, the water was salty and laden with minerals, but not enough to give a man the green apple trots and clear enough that the horses would thrive on it. Higher upriver in New Mexico, the Pecos water was more palatable, fed by spring rains and melted snow from the mountains.

Willoughby shifted his weight in the saddle and rubbed a hand over eyes that felt gritty. A bit over twelve miles down, he thought, and only 580 some odd to go. Kansas seemed as far off as the moon at the moment. He suddenly realized what had left that empty feeling in his belly. It wasn't lack of sleep. It was the first time in years he had felt homesick. He had glanced back once, just before the Texas Horsetrading Company headquarters faded below the first ridge. Leaving home seemed harder this time. He knew why. It would be months before he saw the place again. The thought hurt, somehow.

The sun had dropped low in the western sky before Brubs trotted Squirrel back to Willoughby's position.

"Lobo Springs got plenty of water and enough graze to keep the ponies happy," Brubs said. "We'll overnight there. Seen anything worth worryin' about?"

Willoughby shook his head. "Not a thing."

"Good," Brubs said. He pulled his hat off and ran a hand through his mop of unkempt, sandy hair that always looked to be in need of a trim even fresh from the barbershop. "Could be a speck of trouble waitin' to happen, though. Fresh

108

painter sign up by Lobo."

Willoughby frowned. Call them painters, panthers, mountain lions, catamounts, cougars, or whatever, the scream of the big cats — a sound like a tortured woman's screech of agony — could spook a herd of nervous horses quicker than the thunder of a six-pounder cannon. Sometimes just the scent of the big cats would trigger a stampede. "Any sign of a fresh kill?"

"Didn't see none," Brubs said. "No buzzards circlin', either. I'd say that cat ain't et in a spell. Painter ain't likely to tackle no grown horse, but them ponies don't know that. I reckon we better double up nighthawkin'." He clapped his hat back on his head. "Somethin' else, too. Seen the tracks of that red roan stud and his *manada*. That mustang stud's the best mare thief I ever seen, not countin' Comanches. Tracks was left about an hour after sunup, best I could tell."

Willoughby's shoulders sagged. "You are just full of sunshine and good cheer today, Brubs McCallan. Panthers, mustang stallions, and us with a remuda of half wild horses that aren't broke to trail yet. Just what we need for the first camp out. I suppose next you will be telling me there are a thousand Indians up ahead?"

A hint of a grin twitched Brubs's mustache. "No need to get fretty over that, partner. Only feathers around here's got wild turkeys growed to 'em. We ain't likely to see no Injuns for at least a whole 'nuther month."

"You are a pure comfort to a man, Brubs," Willoughby said despondently. "A pure comfort."

"Like to keep my partners happy," Brubs said. "You move up and take the point. I'll send Cal up to give Granny a hand pitchin' camp at Upper Lobo Spring. We'll hold the ponies in that open meadow south of Middle Lobo."

Cal Hooper had the mules unhitched and the cooking fly staked into place at the side of the wagon when Brubs, Chadburne, and Willoughby rode up. Tilghman stayed behind to watch over the horses at Middle Lobo.

Granny squatted behind a nanny goat, squeezing milk into a foaming tin bucket. She looked up at the horsemen, her face a storm cloud ready to spout lightning. "You whelps keep them horses thirty feet from my fire," she yelled, "or I'll peel your ears like an onion!"

Brubs's sorrel danced sideways on nervous hooves, eyes wide and nostrils flared, ears pointed toward the goat. "Ain't gonna be no trouble keepin' ol' Squirrel back," Brubs said as he tried to quiet the boogered horse. "No way he's gonna get close to that damn goat. I swear, I ain't never seen such a coward of a horse in my life."

Willoughby swung down, rope in hand, and set a picket line between sturdy cottonwood trees at the edge of the spring-fed stream. It took Brubs a good ten minutes to coax Squirrel up to the picket line. The sorrel finally settled down, but he wasn't happy. Every twitch the goat made brought Squirrel's ears to a point.

Granny finished with the goat, lifted the pail

over the tailboard of the wagon, and turned to the three men. "Don't just stand there with your mouths open catchin' flies, dammit," she snapped. "McCallan, you get that tent of mine set up. Dave, lend me a hand with the cookin' stuff. Nick, you gather some firewood. Hop to it, boys, if you want any supper tonight."

Willoughby raised an eyebrow at Brubs. "I thought you said you were the boss of this outfit."

"Not if I got to cross that old woman, I ain't," Brubs said solemnly. "Let's get crackin'. I'd sure hate to see her slip out of that good mood she's in."

The sun was about to touch the western rim of the desert mountains when Brubs made his last swipe at the grease in his tin plate with a sourdough biscuit and popped the bread in his mouth. Crumbs clung to his mustache as he swallowed, patted his stomach, sighed, and leaned back against the rear wagon wheel.

"Granny," Brubs said, "you are one mighty fine cook. I ain't et such good camp grub since ol' Hairbelly Johnson's buffalo camp up on the Cimarron."

Willoughby watched in curious amusement as Granny's milk goat stretched her neck and sniffed at the back brim of Brubs's hat.

"Ol' Hairbelly," the Texan continued, warming to the story, "was a right colorful character. Done his cookin' nekkid most of the time when it weren't too cold." The goat strained against the rope. Brubs's hat was almost within reach now.

"Used to knead that sourdough by rollin' it up and down on that big bare gut of his." The goat's lips twitched. "That's how he got his name, Hairbelly —" Brubs squawked in surprise and outrage as the nanny snatched the hat from his head and bounded beneath the wagon. He barked a curse and scrambled after the goat. "Gimme my hat, you ugly, stinkin' son of a — *Ow!*" The crack of skull against wood was loud.

"Don't you hurt my goat, you mangy runt!" Granny yelled. "I'll skin your hide, you abuse that animal!"

Brubs crawled from under the wagon a moment later, an outraged scowl on his flushed face. The goat peeked out, contentedly chewing on a mouthful of felt torn from the hat brim. Brubs glared at the goat. "You smelly, flea-bit chunk of worthless," he growled, "I got half a mind to roast you over a mesquitefire and roll you up in a tortilla."

Willoughby chuckled and glanced at Granny. He could tell the old woman was having a hard time keeping a straight face.

"That's the nastiest, most disgustin' thing I ever heard of," Granny said.

"Damn sure is," Brubs grumped. "That was my best hat."

"I meant Hairbelly Johnson," Granny said. "You gonna finish the story?"

Brubs clamped his goat-ravaged hat on his head. "Ain't in the mood now." He glowered at the goat for a long moment, then glanced at his partner. "You don't have to look so damn tickled about it, Dave Willoughby."

"Sorry. Couldn't help myself."

Brubs stalked to the far side of the camp away from the wagon and gestured to Cal and Chadburne. "Gather round, boys. Another lesson in the McCallan Horse Wranglin' School's about to start."

Cal leaned forward eagerly, his lifted eyebrows flaring the jug ears even more. Chadburne merely sat and waited. There was no expression in his eyes.

"Now," Brubs said, "a lot of these ponies is still about half wild, so we'll ride double nighthawk tonight. Dave, you got the best night eyes, and it'll be darker'n pitch till we get a little bit of moon along toward midnight. You and Nick take first watch."

Willoughby nodded, but groaned inside. The call of the bedroll would have to wait.

"Cal and me'll stand second," Brubs continued. "I reckon Tige can handle third by hisself."

"Mr. McCallan, do we sing to 'em? Like cowboys around a herd?"

Willoughby shook his head emphatically. "No, Cal. The way Brubs sings would be enough to *start* a stampede, not head one off. The first time I heard him, I spooked and ran a couple hundred yards myself before I figured out what the caterwauling was all about."

Brubs glared at him. "You ain't exactly no songbird yourself, partner. More like a crow with its tail feathers in a fox's mouth. Go spell Tige so's he can come eat some supper."

Willoughby heaved himself to his feet and deposited his eating utensils in the washtub Brubs called the "wreck pan" beside the fire. He toed the stirrup and swung aboard Choctaw.

"Boys, I ain't sayin' it'll happen," Brubs said, his words clearly audible to Willoughby, "but I got to tell you it could. There's a catamount been hangin' around here. That critter squalls tonight, we could have us a stampede. I reckon neither of you whelps ever been in a hoss stampede before, so I'll tell you what to do, does it happen . . ."

Brubs's voice faded as Willoughby trotted Choctaw from camp. The tall man suddenly stiffened in the saddle. He realized that he himself had never been in a real horse stampede — not three hundred animals worth. And neither had Brubs, as far as Willoughby knew.

"Well, Choctaw," he muttered to the roan, "as the Book of Saint Matthew says, 'If the blind lead the blind, both shall fall into the ditch.' "

The roan snorted and bobbed his head as if in agreement.

It seemed to Willoughby that his head had barely touched the bedroll before both eyes snapped open, his heart in his throat, the lingering scream still echoing in his brain. A split second later he felt the earth tremble beneath his blankets; the squeals of horses and the rumble of hooves jarred him fully awake.

"Stampede!" Tilghman yelled.

Willoughby threw back his blankets and grabbed the picket rope that tethered the coyote dun near his bedroll. He had slept in his boots and with the dun saddled and bridled. He yanked the cinch tight.

Tilghman and Chadburne were already in the saddle, driving spurs to their mounts, shadowy lumps racing through pale moonlight, as Willoughby mounted. The thunder of hooves was louder now; he realized with a start that the stampeding horses were headed straight for their camp. He yanked his slicker from its tie behind the cantle and reined the dun about, putting himself between the camp and the charging remuda.

Willoughby felt the dun's muscles quiver as the first wave of horses swept toward him at a dead run, less than a hundred yards away. He glanced over his shoulder; Granny Hooper, in an oversized nightshirt, stood beneath the canvas fly, a white rag in hand.

Willoughby felt the sudden push of terror against his bladder as the lead runaways bore down toward him. If they didn't turn and the dun went down, there wouldn't be enough left of Dave Willoughby to bother about burying. He whooped and waved the slicker. It was like a boulder trying to stop a river. The horses shied from the commotion, raced past a few feet away, then closed ranks again as soon as they thundered by.

Then Willoughby was in the middle of the run, the bulk of the remuda tightly bunched and bearing down on him. He felt Malhumorado stagger and almost go down as a horse's shoulder hit the dun a glancing blow. Willoughby's heart skipped a beat as Malhumorado struggled to regain his balance. Then the dun got his feet under him, spun, and raced along with the stampeding remuda.

A few yards away Willoughby saw the sea of horses part again, dodging the white cloth in Granny's hand. Then one of the horses' feet hit a stake rope holding the fly. The horse went down. The fly billowed and collapsed, trapping Granny underneath the coarse canvas. Willoughby choked back a cry; within seconds the fly would be shredded under scores of churning hooves. He spurred the dun toward the downed canvas, dropped his slicker, and pulled his Colt. He fired twice into the air. The charging horses ducked aside at the powder flashes from the muzzle and the flat bark of the Colt's report. One horse, caught in the crush of other animals, was unable to change course. The horse tried to leap over the fly, caught its hooves in a tangled stake rope, fell, and rolled onto the sagged canvas. The others shied from the gunshots, veering to Willoughby's left, narrowly missing the chuck wagon. Just before the dust cloud they raised blotted out the weak light from the sliver of moon, Willoughby saw Cal Hooper on the far side of the remuda, leaning over the neck of his horse and spurring for all he was worth, trying to catch up with the leaders.

Willoughby slapped the spurs to the coyote dun and plunged into the mass of horses, trying to work his way through to help Cal. He had no choice but to trust the surefooted dun not to step on a round rock or stumble over a bush. The dun bobbed and weaved, checked up short, leapt sideways as he worked his way through the remuda — and suddenly broke into the clear on the far side.

Willoughby's chest ached; he realized he had been holding his breath during the run. He gasped for air and spurred the dun toward the front of the stampede. Through the faint moonlight he saw Cal pull ahead of the leaders, attempting to slow them down and turn the run back onto itself. Willoughby ignored the mesquite limbs that raked his legs and tore at his clothes. A few more yards and he would be in position to help Cal. Then his blood went cold as Cal's bay stumbled, went down, and a mass of dark bodies swept over the spot. Willoughby cried out in dismay and frustration, knowing there was nothing he could do for the boy. He leaned over Malhumorado's neck, spurring even more speed from the fleet dun. It seemed to Willoughby that hours had passed before he managed to pull alongside the now-winded leaders. He heard the yells and whoops of the other hands, louder now as the stampede began to lose its momentum. The leaders slowed, then tried to bolt again as the crush of horses from the bulk of the remuda pushed against them from behind. Willoughby felt the dun's heart hammer against the inside of his knees and heard the horse's heaving gasps for air.

Brubs's wiry little gray mustang pulled up behind Willoughby. The lead horses began to turn. Tilghman and Chadburne were vague shapes in the dust on the far side of the remuda, turning the run back against itself. The stampede slowed and finally stopped in the first gray light of dawn. The winded horses milled, snorting and blowing, their hides streaked with sweat and lather. Willoughby wasn't sure, but he thought the run had covered at least four miles.

"Where's Cal?" Brubs yelled from a few yards away.

Willoughby had to swallow against the tightness in his throat. "Horse fell with him! Mile or so back!"

Brubs barked a sharp, bitter curse. "Let's get back there and see if there's anything left of him. Tige, Nick, watch these idiot horses," he called. "The run's out of 'em now!"

At Tilghman's acknowledging wave, Brubs and Willoughby urged their exhausted horses into a stumbling trot back down the valley. Neither spoke. Brubs's jaw was set, streaks of white showing through the dust trickling down his face in the growing light of sunrise. Willoughby felt the leaden chunk of fear grow in his gut as they neared the spot where Cal's horse had gone down.

The bay was on his side, motionless, his head twisted grotesquely back along his neck. A small bundle lay between the horse's feet.

Brubs bounded from the mustang's back, Willoughby close behind, and knelt beside the crumpled form. He put a hand on Cal's neck and glanced up at Willoughby. "He's still alive, partner."

Willoughby sighed in relief. Cal's eyes fluttered open. The boy's left cheekbone was scraped, his skin sallow and cool to the touch. His right leg was pinned beneath the bay's belly.

"Cal, son," Brubs said softly, "can you hear me? Are you hurt bad?"

Cal's face scrunched up in pain. "What . . . what happened?"

"Horse fell with you, boy. Where are you hurtin'?"

"All . . . over. My horse?"

"Dead, Cal," Willoughby said. "Broke his neck in the fall."

Brubs glanced at Willoughby. "I reckon Cal's got the makin's of a top hand," he said. "First thing he asks about's his horse. Don't fret about the bay, son. We got plenty of horses. Now, let's let ol' Doc Willoughby here take a look at you and see what's busted."

Willoughby finished a quick examination and sighed in genuine relief. Cal had numerous cuts and scrapes, a black eye, a bloodied nose, possibly a broken rib, and a strained knee. But there did not seem to be any serious head or internal injuries.

"It appears you will be all right, Cal," Willoughby said. "You'll be sore for several days, and you'll be hoping not to sneeze or cough until that rib knits up. If you can ride behind me, we'll take you back to camp."

"Granny?"

Willoughby shook his head. "I don't know, son. Try not to worry about it for now."

There was no sign of life when the horsemen rode back into camp, Cal and Willoughby riding double on the coyote dun. The chuck wagon was intact, but the cooking utensils and the stones used as a fire base were scattered. The collapsed fly was crumpled and wadded.

"Granny?" Brubs's call seemed loud in the stillness of uncertainty and fear.

A lump under the fly wiggled. "Don't just stand there yelpin', you damn fool!" The voice was muffled by the canvas. "Get me out from under this thing!"

Brubs swung from his horse and started pulling the canvas away. Granny Hooper lay on her belly, her nightshirt riding high up on her back, and a scowl of impressive proportions on her face. "You hurt, Granny?" Brubs asked as he helped her to her feet.

"Hell, no, I ain't hurt," she snapped as she tugged the nightshirt down, "and you better not say one smart-ass word, you whelp, on account of I never been so mad in my whole —" The rage abruptly faded from her voice. "Cal — what's the matter with Cal?"

"His horse fell with him during the stampede, Granny," Willoughby said. "I don't think he is se-

120

riously injured. We were afraid he might have been trampled, but it appears none of the horses stepped on him. He — all of us — were quite lucky tonight."

"Yeah," Brubs said. "Coulda been worse. At least those broomtails stampeded in the right direction." He turned to help ease Cal from behind Willoughby's saddle. The coyote dun took a half-hearted nip at Brubs's backside, bringing a yelp of outrage from the stocky Texan.

"Wish to hell it'd been that damn dun busted his neck 'stead of Cal's bay," Brubs muttered. "At least then there'd a been one good thing come out of this." He eased Cal to the ground. "Granny, reckon you can patch this young'un up? Dave thinks Cal's maybe got a cracked rib."

Granny Hooper gathered the boy to her breast. "I'll take care of him if I can find my hide-patchin' kit." She glanced around the camp. "Damn fool horses done wrecked my camp. You boys ain't gettin' no breakfast this mornin'."

Brubs reached for the mustang's reins. "Don't reckon that'll matter much, Granny. Dave and me's got a smart bit of work ahead, anyhow." He glanced around. "Them damn goats get run over and stomped?"

A frightened bleat sounded from beneath the wagon. Brubs swore. "Figured them no-account shaggies'd come through." His voice softened. "Cal, you done good out there."

Brubs swung into the saddle. Granny had already found her hide-patching kit and was clucking over the boy. "Didn't get a good count, Dave," Brubs said, "but I reckon we spilled about fifty, sixty head in that run. See can you find your hat, partner. We got some hoss huntin' to do."

Willoughby realized for the first time that he was without his hat. There hadn't been time to put it on when the stampede started. He found it fifty yards from his bedroll, covered in about a pound of dirt, stomped out of shape, and the crown torn in two places. The slicker he had dropped was beyond salvation, ripped to shreds. Willoughby slapped the hat against his leggings and wiggled a finger through one of the rips.

"Sure glad my head wasn't in it when that happened," he said. "It's still a shame, though. That was a nearly new hat."

"Hell, partner," Brubs said, "she's just now lookin' broke in good. Looks like a real Texas hoss wrangler hat now. Mount up. We got to go find us some ponies."

Willoughby could barely stay in the saddle. He couldn't remember ever feeling quite so exhausted. His eyelids seemed to weigh twenty pounds each, his shoulders sagged, and he couldn't even muster the effort to wave a hand at the deerflies buzzing around his eyes and ears.

Even the rawhide-tough coyote dun was near exhaustion. The horse stumbled from time to time, and carried his head low to the ground. The sun was halfway down the western sky as Willoughby and Brubs trailed the last group of horses toward the main remuda. The gather had covered a good twenty square miles, but at least they had managed to find all but a handful of the horses that had broken away during the stampede.

Brubs rode at Willoughby's side, whistling "The Bonny Blue Flag" — off-key, as usual — as if nothing had happened and he was just out for a pleasure ride. Except for the heavy coat of dust and sweat, a few new skinned knuckles, rope burns, and thorn punctures, the stocky Texan still looked fresh and rested. Willoughby began to wonder if the man ever got tired.

"Well, partner," Brubs said, "I reckon we had us a pretty fair day. Got all but twenty head back, countin' the six mares that scrawny hoss thief of a roan mustang stud stole."

"Right now," Willoughby said, "he's welcome to them. I'd just about trade my share of the rest for a bath, a shave, a change of clothes, and at least a ten-hour nap."

"Has been kind of a long day, at that," Brubs said with a brief nod. He glanced at the coyote dun. "First time I ever seen that damn horse tuckered out." He leaned over and patted his lathered gray mustang on the neck. "Old Mouse is feelin' the miles, too. You know, we'd a been on fresh horses, we mighta got them mares back, too."

Willoughby lifted a worried eyebrow at him. "You aren't thinking of going after them later, are you?"

Brubs shook his head. "I reckon that's part of

the game. We don't lose more horses than that 'tween here and Dodge, we'll be some lucky."

"If we get there," Willoughby said. "It hasn't been an especially auspicious start."

Brubs reined Mouse aside, shooed a gelding back into the cavvy, and grinned at Willoughby. "When we get to Dodge, partner, you'll be jinglin' plenty of gold and silver in your pockets. Now, you gotta admit that'll be more fun than bein' broke."

Willoughby sighed. "I suppose you're right. 'Indocilis pauperiem pati.' "

"Talk American."

"Horace wrote that. It roughly translates as, 'It is hard to train to accept being poor.' "

Brubs nodded solemnly. "No doubt about it. This Horace feller knowed him some cowpunchers and hoss wranglers. Reckon he ever made it to Dodge?"

"The question," Willoughby said with a sigh, "is whether *we* will ever make it to Dodge."

Brubs shifted his weight in the saddle and spat. "Sure we will, partner. We got us a patron saint and a guardian angel. And they was watchin' over us last night."

"How do you figure that?"

"We're still alive, ain't we?" Brubs clucked Mouse into a shambling trot. "Come on, amigo," he said, "let's kick these ponies in the butt a little. I'll feel a right smart better when we get to the Pecos."

SEVEN

Brubs McCallan stretched out with his bedroll for a pillow, listened to his gut digest his second helping of beans, antelope steak, and biscuits, and savored the idea of a whole afternoon without so much as a lick of work ahead.

The east bank of the Pecos was their best camp yet. For once it was peaceful and quiet. Not even Granny Hooper had cussed or fussed much, and then not near as loud as she normally did, since they had reached the river on the tenth day out of LaQuesta.

After the stampede at Lobo Springs, the horses had only run once, and that didn't last long. Brubs figured the horses bolted just for the hell of it that time. Horses had a way of aggravating a man sometimes out of pure orneriness. Sort of like women, come to think on it. Brubs thought on women a lot.

Dave Willoughby and Cal Hooper were helping clean up the noon meal wreckage, Willoughby washing, Cal drying, and Granny stowing the utensils. Granny was downright picky about where things went. Brubs noticed that the second night out, when he'd casually plunked down a water bucket into the wagon bed. Granny had lit into him something fierce. He hadn't had a tongue-whipping like that since he'd left the farm over by Nacogdoches.

Cal was healing fast from the fall at Lobo. The youngster winced from time to time when the cracked rib ouched him, but he didn't whine and didn't use it as an excuse to dodge work. Cal was back in the saddle already, even taking his turn at nighthawking. Brubs liked Cal, with his jug ears and wide-open eyes. The boy's expression always reminded Brubs of a big question mark, like he was seeing everything around him for the first time and soaking it all in.

Nick Chadburne was a sight harder to figure. The boy hadn't said a dozen words since LaQuesta. And he still had that look in his eyes like his drawers were too tight. Not exactly surly, but not the friendliest man Brubs had ever ridden with. Next to Chadburne, Willoughby was a downright chatterbox, and Dave sometimes didn't say more than five words a day. Brubs forced himself to quit fretting about what was going on in Chadburne's head. Whatever was eating on him, the boy had to fix himself.

They had been lucky finding those two youngsters. Both were making good hands. They made mistakes like any greenhorn, but never made the same one twice. Which, Brubs had to admit, was a touch better than his own record.

Something else about Chadburne was a bit spooky. It was like he could look at a horse and tell what the horse was going to do before the horse knew it. He was always in the right place at the right time. He didn't mistreat his mounts, but Drubs noticed that even the rankest horse tried his damnedest not to rile the kid.

Granny stowed the last skillet, draped her apron over a wagon wheel, and disappeared into her tent. She came out a minute later, a bundle in one hand and the big ten-bore goose gun in the other, and paused to glare at Brubs.

"I'm goin' down to the river, wash some clothes, and get me a bath," Granny said. She wrinkled her nose. "Sure wouldn't hurt you none to get next to some soap and water yourself."

Brubs sniffed indignantly. "Granny, havin' you and Dave Willoughby around's like havin' two full-time wives underfoot. I ain't never been around such a soap-crazy pair in my life. By tomorrow mornin', the Pecos won't be fittin' to drink from here to the Rio Grande. Be plumb full of soapsuds."

Granny's perpetual frown deepened. "I ain't *askin'* you to take a bath, McCallan. I'm *tellin'* you to, or you ain't gettin' supper tonight. They was two buzzards circlin' over you yesterday. Looked to me like they was plumb puzzled, tryin' to figger how come somethin' that smelt like it'd been dead a week was still movin'."

Brubs sighed and heaved himself to his feet. "All right, all right. I know when I'm whupped. I'll go with you."

Granny's face flushed. "You ain't doin' no such thing. I ain't havin' no young woman-crazy fool leerin' at me whilst I'm bathin'." She shifted her sizeable chew of tobacco to the other cheek and spat. "Damn if it ain't plumb disgustin', the way a poor defenseless woman can't get no respect around here. You go when I get back. And it wouldn't hurt none to take that damn Arkansas hillbilly with you. Gettin' downwind from Tige Tilghman'll make a body's eyes water." She spun on a heel and waddled toward the plum thicket that lined the riverbank on the edge of camp.

Brubs chuckled softly as he watched Granny Hooper try to thread her broad beam along the narrow game trail through the thicket, cursing every thorn along the way. He was still grinning when he strode to the camp fire and re-filled his coffee cup. The coffeepot was one utensil that never got washed, partly because it was always in use in camp and partly because Granny wouldn't stand for it. Willoughby found that out the hard way. He'd washed the pot and Granny pitched a fit. She ranted that washing the pot spoiled the character of the coffee. Brubs couldn't argue. The cantankerous old bat made mighty fine coffee.

Brubs felt something tug at the bottom of his chaps, swatted the goat that had been chewing on them away, then squatted by the fire and watched as Cal and Willoughby finished their chores. The two spread a canvas ground sheet and started dis-assembling Cal's rifle for cleaning. The boy could smooth handle the .38-40, Brubs acknowledged. He had dropped the supper antelope with one shot from near two hundred yards.

Chadburne lounged against the wagon tailboard, mending a frayed pair of hobbles as he waited to relieve Tilghman on remuda watch. It was an easy job these days. The ponies were trail-broke now, content not to drift much as long as they had plenty of grass and water.

A mockingbird sang from a grove of cottonwoods at the river's edge. A cottontail bobbed past the edge of the thicket and disappeared as a hunting hawk's shrill cry sounded overhead. The horses picketed nearby grazed on new spring grass, the ripping sounds and occasional low snort or snuffle audible over the soft gurgle of water flowing in the Pecos.

Brubs sipped at his coffee and soaked in the sights, sounds, and smells of the camp for a few moments, then rose and ambled over to face Chadburne. Wouldn't hurt to make one more try at talking to the boy, he thought.

"Nick, I been studyin' on somethin'," Brubs said. "This here's a good horse camp. Plenty of new grass and good water. I'm thinkin' we might lay over here two, maybe three days. Fatten them ponies up some before we move on. What's your thinkin'?"

Chadburne suddenly stiffened and stared past Brubs's shoulder. "I think," he said softly, "we've got trouble."

Brubs turned and muttered a curse. He was getting damn tired of looking down the barrel of a gun.

Tige Tilghman sat glumly aboard his buckskin, hands crossed over the saddle horn, his belt holster and rifle scabbard empty. At Tilghman's side, a man wearing a gray derby hat and riding a muscular dun horse held a Winchester almost in Tige's ear. Two other men flanked the rider in the derby, one stocky and swarthy as an Indian, the other tall and fair-skinned with blond hair. Their rifles were pointed at Brubs.

"Sorry, Brubs," Tilghman said, disgusted. "Must be losin' my touch. These three boys snuck up on me like I was a real greenhorn."

"No reason to fret that, Tige." Brubs's tone was tight. So was his gut. "These boys wrote the book on snuckin'." He nodded to the man on the dun. "I'd say howdy and how you doin', Jamison, but this don't look like no social call."

"Don't try reaching for any weapons, boys," Texas Ranger Sergeant Tobin Jamison said. "Behave yourselves and nobody will get shot."

Brubs took a half step away from the wagon and glared at the sergeant for a moment. "Jamison, I'll sure be mighty glad when you grow out of that habit of pointin' guns at me. You better have a damn good reason for ridin' in here like this."

"I do, McCallan." Jamison's tone was as cold as the expression in the pale blue, almost colorless eyes. Brubs had seen eyes like that before. Killer's eyes. "I've come to arrest one of your men. I intend to do that without bloodshed if possible."

"That a fact, Jamison? Who you after?"

Jamison nodded toward Chadburne. "That one."

"What you want him for?"

"Suspicion of murder."

Brubs glanced at Chadburne. The youth's somber face showed no emotion. "You kill anybody, Nick?"

Chadburne shook his head. "No, sir."

Brubs turned his attention back to the Texas Ranger. "You heard him, Jamison. He didn't kill nobody. Take that gun outta my friend's ear and let's talk this out peaceable."

Brubs chanced a quick glance around. Cal Hooper stood with his hand on the butt of his revolver, his face stark white behind the freckles, eyes wide. Willoughby was an arm's length from Cal, a worried look on his face. Brubs figured it was prime worrying time. He shook his head at Cal, a silent warning not to try drawing the handgun, and turned his gaze back on Jamison.

"I don't trust you when it comes to talking, McCallan," the sergeant said. "I'd put the whole bunch of you in irons if I had papers on you. As of now, Chadburne's the only one I want." He waggled the Winchester muzzle. "I'll brook no interference from you or your men. Unbuckle the gun belts and step away from the rifles. I don't want any shouting if it can be avoided."

Brubs glared at the sergeant for a long moment, then shook his head. "Can't do that, Jamison. I gotta stick by my hands." He paused for a moment, the growing tension in the camp broken

131

only by the soft snuffle of a horse and the creak of saddle leather.

"I have to take Chadburne back. I have a warrant issued by the Zavala County sheriff. I'll kill you if you force me to." Brubs knew Jamison didn't bluff. If he made a try for the Colt at his hip, he would catch a pound of lead before the six-gun even started to clear leather.

"Jamison, I ain't sayin' you owe me," Brubs said, "but Dave and me pulled a few Comanches off your neck a spell back, you recall." He shifted his gaze to the swarthy man. "Casey, you ain't forgot how Dave chanced gettin' hisself killed pullin' you out of a pickle down to Hangtree Pass in the scrap with Gilberto Delgado's bunch of bandits. He hadn't rode out after you, you'd be dead now."

Casey Sinclair shook his head. "I haven't forgotten," he said calmly, "but I'm still a Texas Ranger. We have a job to do."

Brubs shifted his gaze to the tall blond man. "You gonna throw down on us, too, Lee? That'd be a mighty unsociable thing to do, and you ain't got a mean streak in you like Jamison here."

Lee Denton shrugged. "I will if I have to. Like Casey said, it's our job. We don't necessarily have to like it all the time."

Cold sweat beaded Brubs's forehead. "I ain't in no rush to kill no Rangers, Jamison, but I can't let you have Chadburne."

"I don't believe you can stop me, McCallan."

"By God, *I* can!"

Jamison's head snapped around at the bellow from the edge of the thicket. Granny Hooper stood in the narrow trail, the goose gun in her hands. Both barrels were lined on Jamison's chest. The Ranger lifted an eyebrow, but he didn't look overly spooked, Brubs noticed.

"And who might you be, madam?" Jamison asked.

"I might be the madam who cuts loose on you with a ten-bore, you whippersnapper. I reckon that's up to you." Granny's voice was as sharp and hard as Jamison's was cold and deadly.

The Ranger stared silently at the old woman for a moment. "Madam, you are very near to being in deep trouble. You are threatening an officer of the law with a firearm and obstructing justice. Those are serious charges."

Granny loosed a spurt of tobacco juice without lifting her cheek from the stock of the goose gun. "Son, I ain't in no trouble. You are. As far as them serious charges goes, I got 'em right here in this smoothbore. Double-nought buck charges. You gonna try and shoot a poor ol' defenseless widder woman, that's your pick. Now either put them guns up or use 'em, son. Makes me no never mind whichaway."

For a brief, panicked moment, Brubs thought Jamison was actually going to try. Then the sergeant lowered his Winchester and glanced at his companions. "Put the weapons away, men. I can't bring myself to shoot a woman."

Brubs breathed a deep sigh of relief as the

Rangers sheathed their weapons.

" 'Bout damn time we had somebody around here showed a little respect for the fair sex," Granny grumbled. She waggled the barrels of the shotgun. "You boys climb down slow and easy, and like McCallan said, we'll talk it over."

Brubs nodded to Jamison. "Texas Ranger Sergeant Tobin Jamison, meet Granny Hooper. She ain't one to mess with."

"I got that impression, McCallan."

"Granny, the stocky one there's Casey Sinclair. Tall one's Lee Denton."

"Seems like I recollect you makin' mention of these boys," Granny said. She didn't lower the shotgun.

Brubs shrugged. "They was the ones we rode with a spell back. Fought a few Injuns and Mex bandits together."

"They got a damn funny way of showin' grateful."

"Jamison's one of the suspiciousest fellers I ever seen," Brubs said. "Comes with the badge, I reckon. Well, Jamison, you gonna sit there like a lizard on a tree stump, or we gonna talk this little problem out?"

"It doesn't appear that I have much choice at the moment," Jamison said. He dismounted. The others followed suit.

"Granny," Tilghman said, "I'd hug your neck right now, you wasn't packin' that smoothbore."

"Shut your mouth, Tige. This ain't no time for sweet-talkin'." Granny glowered over the shotgun barrels at Jamison. "Don't you Ranger boys do nothin' stupid now. I get plumb out of sorts when somebody disturbs my bath. Git over there by the wagon — and you leave them damn flea-bit nags right where they's at. I got a rule. No hosses within thirty feet of my cook fire."

The Rangers did as they were told. Granny finally lowered the hammers of the shotgun, but kept it in hand.

"Now, Jamison," Brubs said, "what's this killin' thing all about?"

The Ranger reached into a shirt pocket, produced a paper, and handed it to Chadburne. "It's spelled out in the warrant."

Chadburne glanced at the paper, at the sergeant, and shook his head. "I can't read," he said.

Willoughby strode to Chadburne's side and reached for the paper. He studied it for a moment, his jaw clenched. "Nick, you're charged with the murder of your uncle, Elton Forrest. It says here he was beaten to death."

Chadburne's expression didn't change, except for a slight narrowing of the eyes. "Can't say I'm sorry to hear he's dead, but I didn't kill him. I fought him, right enough. The old bastard was due a good whipping. I busted his jaw and knocked out a couple of teeth, but he was sure enough alive when I rode out."

"That isn't the way we heard it from your aunt, Chadburne," Jamison said. "And the Zavala

135

sheriff said he found Forrest's body lying beside the kitchen table, his head bashed into a pulp. There was a singletree covered with blood just outside the back door."

Chadburne shook his head. "We fought out in the barn, Sergeant. Not in the house. I reckon you ought to talk to Harriet again. If anybody had a reason to knock Elton Forrest's brains out, she did."

"Why would she do that?"

Chadburne squared his shoulders and stared into the Ranger's eyes. "Because he was a mean son of a bitch, that's why. He beat her damn near to death several times."

"I can vouch for that, Sergeant," Cal Hooper said. "I saw Forrest hit her smack in the face with his fist once. Just because she was five minutes late getting supper on the table. Several other times I saw Mrs. Forrest all bruised up and kind of hunched over like she hurt something awful inside."

"So," Jamison said to Chadburne, "you finally couldn't stand to see her being beaten any longer, and you killed him. I've heard worse reasons before."

Chadburne raised his chin defiantly. "I thought about killing him, Sergeant. I wanted to. I should have. But I didn't."

"I suppose that explains why you didn't express any remorse at hearing he was dead," Jamison said. "Why didn't your aunt just leave him?"

"You didn't know Elton Forrest. He would

have found her and killed her. Now he can't follow her."

Jamison ran a thumb along his stubbled jaw, his brow wrinkled in thought for a moment. "What do you think happened after you fought with your uncle and rode away?"

"I left him in the corner of the barn, about halfway knocked out," Chadburne said. "It wouldn't have been too hard for Harriet to help him to the house, set him down at the kitchen table, then crack his skull with a singletree before he got his wits back."

Jamison stared hard at Chadburne. "Assuming that I believe your story so far — and I'm not saying that I do or I don't — why would she try to blame you for it?"

Chadburne shrugged. "She had to blame somebody. She didn't like me much. I was riding out, leaving the country. Maybe she thought no one would ever find me. And even if they did, it wouldn't have bothered her to hear that I'd been hanged for killing him."

Granny Hooper stepped alongside Chadburne. "What these boys says is true, Sergeant."

"I suppose you have firsthand knowledge of that, Mrs. Hooper?"

"Damn shootin' I do. I know these boys." She shifted her chew to the other cheek and spat. "Maybe they ain't angels, but I never caught neither of 'em in a lie. Nick's right. Elton Forrest was sorrier'n buzzard droppin's. Thought about killin' the old bastard myself, way he treated Harriet, and her not well and all."

Jamison frowned. "What do you mean, not well?"

Granny sighed. "Harriet and me was the only females in most of two counties, not countin' town women. She didn't live more'n fifteen miles from my place, so I visited a few times." Granny shifted the shotgun to her left hand and scratched her rear with her right. "Harriet got funny in the head durin' the past year. Like a hoss eatin' loco-weed. She'd be happy and grinnin' one minute, bawlin' her eyes out the next, then she'd jump up and go runnin' around all walleyed and talkin' stuff that didn't make no sense."

Willoughby cleared his throat. "I've read about cases like that, Sergeant," he said. "A person can take just so much abuse, and then they snap."

"Heard about it, hell," Tilghman said with a snort. "Brubs, you remember that woman out by old Fort Davis on the Brazos?"

"Sure do. Went out one night while her old man was passed out drunk, got her a double-bit ax, and hacked his head clean off. Jury said she didn't commit no crime. More like a public service. They cut her loose and took up a collection to buy her a new ax on account of she nicked the first one up pretty bad on his neck bone."

Jamison held up a hand. "All right, all right. This case obviously merits further investigation. But I still have to take you back, Chadburne. Your name's on an official warrant. I'll make sure you are well treated until a grand jury rules on your case."

Brubs grunted in disgust. "Dammit, Jamison, we're right back where we started. I told you I wasn't gonna let you have him. I need every hand I've got to get these ponies to Kansas."

"Wait a minute," Willoughby said. "There may be a way to resolve this." He tapped the warrant against the heel of his hand. "Sergeant, according to *Langstrom versus the State of Texas*, it is possible for an unindicted suspect to be remanded to the custody of a second responsible party in lieu of arrest, pending a grand jury investigation."

Jamison frowned at him. "What's your point?"

"It's simple," Willoughby said casually. "You remand Nick Chadburne into my custody. You have my pledge that I will offer my share of the horses as a guaranty bond. Nick goes with us. You complete your investigation into the death of Elton Forrest. If Nick is not cleared as a suspect by your investigation, you wire the Dodge City marshal's office and Nick will surrender to the authorities there."

"Now, that there's a right fine idea," Brubs said eagerly. "Why, Jamison, you can just hand this boy over to me to watch out for."

The Ranger cut a piercing glance at Brubs. "McCallan, I wouldn't put a setting hen in your custody. I strongly suspect you would steal the eggs, eat the hen, and try to charge the state for watching the empty nest."

Brubs shook his head sadly. "Jamison, you are the most suspiciousest man I ever met. And after

I rangered with you, at that."

"An episode which I am still attempting to forget," Jamison said. "By the way, do you remember those Bar F brand horses we recovered from Delgado's gang?"

"Sure do. Mighty fine mounts, that Bar F stock."

Jamison lifted a suspicious eyebrow at Brubs. "Curious thing happened to those horses. They were stolen only a night or two after we returned them to the Bar F. I don't suppose you might know something about that?"

Brubs looked astonished at the news. "That a fact? I tell you, Jamison, this here country's just crawlin' with hoss thieves. Why, it's got so a man can't even let loose of the reins without somebody steals his mount. I swear, I just can't abide no dishonest horse thief."

"Neither can I, McCallan. I suggest you keep that in mind." Jamison turned to Willoughby. "Okay, you've got a deal. I'll wire the marshal's office in Dodge with the results of the investigation. I warn you, though — if Chadburne remains a suspect and you fail to surrender him as agreed, you will take his place in jail and I will sort out the charges later. Understood?"

Willoughby nodded. "Nick and I will uphold our end of the bargain, Sergeant."

"One more word of caution," Jamison said. "If Chadburne is indicted, I'll obtain warrants on you and McCallan for aiding and abetting a fugitive, threatening duly appointed officers of the

140

law, obstructing justice, and anything else I can think of. Fair enough?"

"Agreed," Willoughby said. The tension slowly began to drain from the gathering around the wagon. Even young Chadburne looked relieved, Brubs noted. It was the first outward expression the kid had shown since he'd joined the outfit.

"Say, Jamison," Brubs said, "you boys got an invite to stay for chuck tonight."

"I don't think so, McCallan." Jamison's tone took on a suspicious edge. "I might get to wondering more about where these horses of yours came from. It might be best for all concerned if I didn't dwell too much on that at the moment. Besides, I have other things to do on this scout." He turned toward his ground-hitched dun, Lee Denton following.

Casey Sinclair lingered a moment. "Dave," he said, "if you're planning to trail these horses north along the Pecos, you'd better keep a sharp eye out once you get into New Mexico. The Seven Rivers Gang owns the lower Pecos. That bunch would kill you for a twist of tobacco, let alone three hundred horses."

Willoughby offered a hand. "Thanks for the warning, Casey. We'll be careful."

"There's something else you should know. Those 'other things' Sergeant Jamison mentioned was a reference to Comanches. A band of young Quahadi bucks jumped the Fort Sill reservation a week or so ago."

Cal Hooper's eyes went wide as saucers.

"How many?" Brubs asked, frowning.

Sinclair's swarthy face turned darker. "Twenty or thirty of them."

Brubs sighed in relief. "Damn. There for a minute I thought you was talkin' about a *bunch* of Injuns."

Sinclair frowned at Brubs then turned back to Willoughby. "They're wearing war paint. Led by a bronco who's looking to make himself a wealthy man. To a Comanche buck, that means horses and perhaps scalps. We think they're headed for their old hangouts in the Palo Duro and Tale Canyon country of the Staked Plains. We've also gotten word that there may be a lot more Indians getting ready to bolt the reservation and follow them. If you go into that area, watch your horses — and your hair."

"We will, Casey," Willoughby said. "Watch your own."

Sinclair mounted and spurred his horse after the other two Rangers. Brubs watched him ride away, then grinned and clapped Willoughby on the shoulder. "By damn, partner," he said, "you are plumb full of surprises. Didn't know you was a lawyer. What happened to that Langstrom feller you mentioned, anyway?"

"I'm not a lawyer," Willoughby admitted, "and as far as I know, there is no Langstrom. I made the whole thing up."

Brubs's face lit up. "You mean you done went and *lied* to a lawman? Son, you're gonna make a first-rate Texan after all."

Willoughby shrugged. "It's been my experience that if you sound like you know what you're talking about, even if you don't, people will believe the story. It worked. For now." He frowned at Brubs. "Speaking of sounding like you know what you're talking about, what do we do now?"

"Come again?"

"From what Casey said, we have a dangerous outlaw gang to the north and Indians to the northeast. Where do we go from here?"

Brubs ran a hand over his stubbled jaw. "I had my druthers, I druther not tangle with them Seven Rivers boys. That there's a tough outfit. They can't find nobody else to shoot, they shoot each other."

"More words of comfort from our fearless leader," Willoughby said wryly. " 'Quidquid agas, prudenter agas, et respice finem.' "

"Talk American."

" 'Whatever you do, do cautiously, and look to the end.' "

Brubs sniffed in disdain. "Never knowed a cautious man to get rich, boys. But that don't mean we're gonna go up again them Seven Rivers boys. We'll head east. Out onto the Llano Estacado."

"What about the Indians?" Cal asked.

"Cal, them Injuns ain't nothin' to fret over if there ain't but a little bunch of 'em."

"Brubs," Willoughby said, "one Comanche is a bunch."

"Don't fret, partner. You're just spookin' Cal." Brubs smiled. The grin seemed a bit forced to

Willoughby. "I don't expect we'll have no Injun trouble at all. I figger we can make the Canadian in two weeks, Skull Creek in three."

"You mentioned this Skull Creek before," Willoughby said frowning. That name has an ominous sound."

Brubs shrugged. "Just a little stream up in the Cimarron. Good water and graze. Got its name from an Army scout twenty, twenty-five years back. Found the banks lined with human skulls." He scratched his armpit. "Nobody ever figgered out what happened or how them skulls got there or who wore 'em whilst they still was tied to neck bones. Some folks says they's ghosts around there. Don't know about no ghosts, but I do know they's a mess of outlaws up there. Don't nobody packin' a badge go into that Cimarron Strip country."

Willoughby sighed. "Once again, Brubs McCallan, your words are a true comfort."

"Partner," Brubs said, "you ain't gonna booger at a little ghost story, are you?"

"I get boogered," Willoughby grumbled, "whenever you say there is nothing to worry about. That particular phrase of yours always seems to summon the thundering hooves of famine, pestilence, and death."

"Don't go givin' yourself the vapors over Skull Creek," Brubs said. "We got a long ways to go before we get there, anyhow. Speakin' of which, I reckon we better pull out first light tomorrow. Sure hate to leave the ol' Pecos, but that Seven

144

Rivers bunch might take a hankerin' to wander down thisaway. You truly want to fret on somethin', Dave, you might study on what we got lookin' at us the next hundred miles or so."

"What's that?"

Brubs sighed. "That country we got to cross now. It's just one long, big dry."

EIGHT

Brubs had always thought jackasses were the ugliest critters the Creator had ever put on earth, but he still felt like hugging that potbellied old burro's neck.

They had been in big trouble before the burro had smelled the string of playa lakes on the Llano Estacado. They had been in the middle of nowhere when the burro had thrown up his head, brayed, and set off on a dead run. Brubs and Granny Hooper had barely been able to get out of the way before the water-starved remuda stampeded and almost ran them down in a run for water.

The last ten days were little more than a bad memory now, ten days without one water hole that wasn't alkaline or little more than thin mud. Ten days of slogging along bone-tired, grimy and parched to the point where tongues were beginning to swell, across shinnery covered sandhills and then wide open stretches of treeless prairie as flat as a billiard table in a San Antonio saloon. The sky even looked washed-out, the sun brassy.

Still, Brubs figured they'd come through the long dry in pretty good shape. They had lost only a dozen horses on the way. And a goat.

Brubs had to admit that he was starting to look

at Granny's goats as something other than potential suppers. The damn things seemed to be able to go for weeks without water, and they laid on fat from weeds and bushes no self-respecting horse would put a lip on.

The second nanny had dropped a pair of kids just as the first mama goat dried up. One of the baby goats was a big, strapping fellow with long legs. The other was a runt. The bigger kid never would take his mama's teat and died the next day, in spite of Granny's staying up all night trying to keep him alive. Granny seemed downright sorrowful when the critter died.

The runty little goat went straight for the teat as soon as he could stand. Granny promptly named him Brubs Junior, which Brubs McCallan took as something of an insult. The moniker soon got shortened to Junior because Brubs McCallan kept answering when Granny called the goat.

Junior's mama produced enough milk for her offspring and a cup each day for the humans. Brubs was beginning to develop a taste for goat's milk. That set his teeth on edge. No cowboy with an inch of backbone would ever admit to such a perversion. Not even if it was spiked with good whiskey.

The playa lake campsite was like a St. Louis hotel after the miserable, dry camps on the long drive from the Pecos, Brubs mused. The playas were little more than oversized buffalo wallows that still held water from the last rain, whenever that had been. The playa water wasn't exactly spring-fresh, but it wasn't gyppy or brackish either. Brubs had been so dry he had even taken a bath without Granny Hooper nagging him to death first.

The horses had filled out in the two days and nights they had been here, their once-gaunt flanks now swollen with decent water and rich spring grass. Two more days, Brubs figured, and they would be fattened out enough to move on.

The largest of the playas lay in a shallow valley, its wind-rippled water dancing under the sunlight. The lake was at least two hundred yards across and three hundred yards long, its banks lined with reeds and full of bullfrogs that grumped in the night. New grass stood tall, bright and green around the playa. Scores of doves wheeled in the sky, coming in for their morning drink.

Brubs finished his coffee, pushed Junior aside before the baby goat got serious about nibbling on his shirtsleeve, and mounted and trotted Squirrel toward the remuda at the east end of the lake. The day was warming fast as the sun climbed higher above the flat horizon.

Tige Tilghman was rolling a cigarette, his right knee hooked around the saddle horn, when Brubs rode up alongside.

"All quiet, Tige?"

"Ain't sure," Tilghman's tone was somber. "Could be we got company." He paused to lick the edge of the paper and twist the ends of the quirly. "That jackass's been actin' funny ever since I come on watch. Just before daylight he kept lookin' up, sniffin' the wind like he smelt somethin'."

Brubs frowned. "Coyote, maybe?"

"Doubt it. Never seen a jackass fret over coyotes, 'less they was runnin' in a pack." Tilghman scratched a match on his saddle horn and fired his smoke. "Ain't just the jackass, neither. That big roan of Dave's been actin' nervous, too." He shook the match to extinguish the flame, pinched the burned end between thumb and forefinger, and tossed it aside.

"Don't much like the sound of that," Brubs said, frowning. "That jackass might be just gettin' twitchy in his old age, but I never knowed old Choctaw to booger without there was somethin' to booger at. You see anything?"

"Maybe, maybe not." Tilghman dragged at the cigarette and let smoke trickle from his nostrils. "Thought I seen somethin' move out yonder an hour or so before sunup. Couldn't tell for sure."

Brubs's right hand instinctively dropped to the stock of the old .44 Henry in his saddle boot. "Could be we got us an Injun problem," he said. "That roan can smell feathers further'n a buzzard smells dead." He studied the rolling, grassy countryside and saw nothing. "Reckon I'll scout around a bit, see can I cut some sign."

Tilghman unhooked his right leg and slipped his boot into the stirrup. "I'll give you a hand. You want me to tell the rest of the crew?"

Brubs shook his head, trying to ignore the cold lump in his gut. "No need to fret anybody just yet. Don't want to holler 'wolf' without we see a pelt." He slid the Henry from its scabbard, cracked the action to make sure a cartridge was chambered, cradled the rifle in the crook of an elbow, and surveyed the remuda. The horses were strung out along the south and west banks of the playa, some nuzzling the water, others grazing. There was no sign of alarm among the horses. Brubs hoped it stayed that way. The playa wasn't an ideal spot to defend. It was open country with no cover.

All of a sudden he wasn't quite as comfortable with the playa camp as he had been.

Brubs's edgy feeling got worse a quarter hour later as Tilghman squatted beside a Spanish dagger clump and studied the tracks in the soft soil. Tige glanced up at Brubs and frowned. "No doubt about it. Unshod horse, moccasin tracks. We had us an Injun here last night."

"Damn, Tige," Brubs said through clenched teeth, "just for once I wish you'd be wrong about somethin'." He leaned from the saddle, studied the prints for a moment, then sighed. "Never knowed a Comanch to travel by his lonesome. Reckon we best foller a ways and see what else turns up." He waited until Tilghman pulled the big Sharps Fifty from the saddle boot and mounted, then he kneed Squirrel into motion.

They rode in silence for the better part of two hours, Tilghman keeping his head down to follow the trail and Brubs scanning the empty countryside, the Henry resting across the pommel of his saddle.

Then Tilghman pulled his horse to a stop. "Looks to have picked up a couple of his partners here. All of 'em ridin' northeast. Scouts, most likely, or we'd a struck the main bunch's tracks by now."

Brubs scowled. "Headin' for the Palo Duro country, sure enough. Same way we're goin'."

"Maybe we oughta swing north by west," Tilghman said. "I'd as soon not tangle with them red varmints, I don't have to. Leavin' my hair hangin' on an Injun's war shield sure would sorrow a bunch of women I ain't met yet. Prob'ly put a saloon or two out of business, too."

Brubs sucked at his cheeks and finally worked up enough saliva to spit. "I ain't whoopin' for joy over the idea myself, Tige. I got to tell you, they ain't all that many critters I'm boogered of, but Comanches is right atop that list." His brow bunched in thought. "Can't go northwest. There ain't no water up that way until we hit the Canadian River. That's near a hundred fifty miles. Them ponies'd never make it that far."

Tilghman pulled his tobacco sack and started rolling a smoke. "Reckon it wouldn't make no difference to them redskins. They'd likely come after us anyhow, now they know we're here. This many horses sure would buy some young bucks a lodge full of pretty young squaws." He paused to light the cigarette. "So what's your druthers, partner?"

"My druthers," Brubs said, "is to be holed up in Mexico with a cold beer and a warm señorita, not ridin' toward no Injuns." He sighed heavily. "Hell, Tige. We ain't got no choice. Can't go around 'em. Can't go back. Headwaters of Palo Duro Creek's the only water for many a mile. Maybe we sneak past 'em."

"And if we can't?"

"I reckon we'll just have to go through 'em. Like General Bobby Lee said, when you got doubts, charge."

Tilghman squinted through the cigarette smoke at Brubs. "I'd feel a damn sight better about that plan had the South won the war."

Brubs came awake slowly, drowsing in his blankets in the pale gray of false dawn, relaxed and content. Their luck had held.

There hadn't been a single Indian sign on the long drive up the string of playa lakes to Whitehouse Draw and then on to Palo Duro Creek. Not a track or feather. The Staked Plains looked the same in every direction. Empty.

Brubs liked it that way.

Even the weather seemed to be working in their favor. A fast-moving storm system had brought rain along the creek watershed. The grama and buffalo grass were near knee-high, green and rich. A few bellyfuls of Staked Plains grass put the fat on a horse in a hurry. Palo Duro Creek flowed stirrup-deep with runoff water and the flow from springs scattered along the high, rocky banks of the stream.

The crew was still edgy, but the thick tension of the last four days had eased a bit. Even Granny Hooper had finally calmed down. Brubs grinned to himself, remembering Granny's suit when he'd first mentioned Indians. She still kept her ten- bore goose gun in easy reach and muttered under her breath about "them damn heathen redskins and their rapin' and pillagin' unchristian ways."

Dave Willoughby hadn't helped Granny's mood all that much when he pointed out that raping and pillaging were not pastimes limited strictly to non-Christian peoples. And that more people had died in the name of the Holy Mother Church — by whatever term it was called — than at the hands of the pagan hordes.

"Them red bastards'll learn a thing or two about takin' advantage of poor defenseless white women if they gets in range of this scattergun," Granny ranted. "And you mind your tongue, Dave Willoughby, or I just might be tempted to dust your disbelievin' backside with a little buckshot."

Cal Hooper's eyes were still wide as saucers at the idea of Indians, but the boy didn't booger at every shadow. Neither did Nick Chadburne. Brubs couldn't say the same for himself. Twice in the first day he had almost yanked the trigger on jackrabbits before he realized the long-eared critters weren't wearing war paint.

"Brubs —"

153

The Texan glanced at Willoughby, who sat bolt upright in his blankets.

"What's ailin' your partner?"

Willoughby silently pointed past Brubs toward the picket line less than twenty feet away, where the night horses were kept. Brubs turned his head and stared in disbelief. The picket line was empty — except for a pair of worn-out moccasins draped over the center of the rope.

Brubs yelped a curse, scrambled from his blankets, and racked a round into the chamber of the Henry. "Dammit to hell! Them thievin' sons of bitches!"

The commotion brought the rest of the camp to life in a hurry. Granny Hooper, nightshirt tail flapping behind, bustled from her tent, shotgun cocked and ready. Cal scrambled from beneath the wagon, clutching a rifle, his face ash-white in the weak light.

"What the hell happened, McCallan?"

Brubs cast a quick, icy glance at Granny. "What the hell does it look like?" His voice quavered in rage. "Them damn Comanches snuck in here and swiped ever' night hoss we had on picket. Right out from under our noses."

Cal's gaze flicked around, eyes wide, as if he expected an Indian to pounce from behind the nearest bush. "When? Why the picketed horses instead of the loose ones?"

Brubs spat in disgust. "They done thumbed their noses at us, that's what. Big Comanche medicine, stealin' an enemy's horses damn near outta his back pocket without so much as wakin' him up. Cal, run fetch Tige and Nick. We gotta have us a little war parley."

Cal sprinted toward the remuda grazing two hundred yards upstream, Brubs mouthing a cussword for every stride the boy took.

Willoughby stood at the picket line, staring at the moccasins draped over the rope. "Why did they leave these?"

"Message," Brubs grumbled. "Comanche way of sayin' he wore out a pair of moccasins to steal our horses and now it's our time to do the walkin'. Rubbin' a man's nose in it, that's what."

Willoughby was still puzzled. "Why didn't the horses make any noise? Surely we would have heard something."

"Injuns got a way of keepin' critters quiet," Brubs said. "I tell you, when it comes to stealin' horses, there ain't no human bein' better at it than a Comanche."

"My God," Granny said breathlessly, "they coulda killed us all and — and raped me!"

"Simmer down, Granny," Brubs said. "The boys is comin'."

Tige Tilghman reined his big buckskin to a sliding stop a yard away, Cal and Chadburne close behind, riding double on Chadburne's sorrel.

"Tige, you see anything last night? Hear anything?"

Tilghman took in the scene at a glance and shook his head. "Not a sound. Didn't see so much

155

as a coyote." He dismounted, studied the ground around the picket line with care, and fingered the worn moccasins. "Young bucks," he said.

"How do you know that?" Willoughby asked.

"Experienced warriors woulda killed the whole bunch of us and took all the horses, not just the ones in camp," Tilghman said calmly. "This wasn't no war party out for scalps. It's more prestige to a young warrior to steal horses this way than to kill white folks."

"They coulda raped me —"

"Shut up, Granny," Brubs said. "We got somethin' more important to fret over. Them thievin' redskins stole Squirrel. And Dave's black. Dammit, them's good horses. We're gonna get 'em back."

Willoughby lifted a hand. "Now, wait a minute. Let's think this through. We're out four horses —"

"And two of my mules," Granny interrupted.

"Best horses we got," Brubs grumped.

"Dammit, Brubs, four horses —"

"And two of my mules."

"Aren't worth getting killed over," Willoughby said, exasperated. "We still have plenty of horses. And mules. Let it go, and maybe we will have seen the last of the Indians."

Brubs shot a cold glance at him. "We ain't gonna let it go, Dave. Them damn redskins done made me hog-mean mad." He turned to Tilghman. "Tige, bring us some mounts. Mouse for me, old Ugly for Dave. Both of 'em got lots of bottom and could be we might have to do us some hard ridin' afore this is done with."

"Brubs, wait a minute!" Willoughby felt the cold knot of dread build in his gut. "Let's talk this over —"

"Maybe you could use some help," Tilghman said, ignoring Willoughby. "Be glad to tag along."

Brubs shook his head. "No. I want you guardin' the outfit while we're gone. You and Nick's top-hand rifle shots. Them Injuns decide to come scalp huntin' after all, or maybe take in after us, I want you two here. Cal, we'll need a horse holder, maybe a backup gun."

Cal swallowed hard, then nodded. "Whatever you say, Mr. McCallan."

"Wait just a damn minute, McCallan," Granny snapped. "You can't be takin' Cal after no Comanches. He don't know nothin' 'bout fightin' Injuns."

"She's got a point, Brubs," Willoughby said hopefully. "And for that matter, we aren't exactly qualified to teach Indian warfare tactics at West Point ourselves. One skirmish does not make us experts. Tell me you aren't serious about this insane idea."

"I ain't never been seriouser," Brubs said. A muscle in his jaw twitched. "More to it than just them ponies. By God, we'll show them Comanch a thing or two about hoss stealin'."

Willoughby moaned in exasperation. "Brubs, this is not a pissing contest over who is the better horse thief. The dubious honor of the Texas Horsetrading Company is not worth getting shot, knifed, lanced, arrowed, scalped, skinned alive, and baked over a slow fire."

"Reckon you know Comanch better'n I thought, partner," Brubs said, "but you left out gettin' dragged through cactus patches, cut up in little pieces by squaws, or gettin' tied between four horses and tore to bits."

"You are a true comfort to a man, Brubs McCallan," Willoughby said. "I apologize profusely and with great humility for my omissions of a few minor tortures employed by the Comanches. Which does not change the fact that I have no intention of accompanying you into a den of hostiles over four horses."

"And two of my mules," Granny said.

Brubs lifted both eyebrows at Willoughby. "You scared, partner?"

"Hell, yes, I'm scared! Any rational man would be."

Brubs turned to Cal. "How about you, son? You spooked, too?"

Cal swallowed hard, his freckles prominent against ash-white skin. "Yes, sir. I reckon I am."

"Good. Wouldn't want no men ridin' with me wasn't boogered somewhat of Comanches. Tige, fetch that leggy blue roan for Cal. Ol' Blue's near as fast as Dave's coyote dun, should it come down to a hoss race." Brubs swept the worn moccasins from the picket line and tucked them under his belt.

"What do you want those for?" Willoughby asked him.

"We're gonna take 'em back to the owner," Brubs said. "Get your stuff together, boys. We got some hard ridin' and serious trackin' ahead."

Willoughby waved a hand. "Deal me out. I'm not going. And this time, I'm making it stick."

Brubs McCallan lay beneath a wind-twisted cedar tree at the lip of Tule Canyon, studied the Comanche camp below, and grunted in satisfaction.

"Just like I figgered," Brubs said. "This here's a little bunch. Not more'n twenty Comanch in the whole camp."

At Brubs's side, Dave Willoughby winced. "Only twenty Comanches. No more bothersome than a pesky housefly."

"Glad you're thinkin' thataway now, partner. I was beginnin' to wonder if you was still on the prod at me."

"If I'm on the prod at anybody, it's myself," Willoughby said. "I don't know why I let you talk me into situations like this. If there was any doubt in my mind before, I now know for certain that insanity is, in fact, contagious. And that I have been exposed to the malady for months while riding at the stirrup of a bona fide carrier of the pestilence." He sighed in resignation. "So now that we've found them, what do we do with them?"

Brubs studied the shadows cast by the lowering sun. "Be dark soon. There'll be some moon after midnight, enough we can work by but not enough for good shootin' light, should it come to that. After them redskins down there get asleep good, we sneak in and steal our horses back."

"Just like that?"

"Just like that. It ain't no hill two top-notch hoss thieves can't climb. Won't be nothin' to it."

"It seems," Willoughby said, "that I've heard that line before. Usually before I get shot at, run over by horses, thrown in jail, or beaten up in a barroom brawl. Or worse."

Brubs nodded. "Yep, we have had us some fun, at that. But we can hash over them good times later. Right now, I reckon we best sneak back off this canyon rim before some buck happens to look up thisaway."

The two men crabbed back from the lip of the canyon and strode to where Cal Hooper held the horses in a brush-choked dry wash a few yards back.

"Did you see the Indians?" Cal's eyes were wide, the freckles prominent on his pale face. His ears seemed to stand out even more with the hat jammed far down on his head. Brubs wondered why those ears didn't flap like a buzzard's wings when the wind kicked up.

"Sure did, son. There ain't but a few of 'em," Brubs said. "Good trail leadin' down into the canyon and plenty of cover along that creek runs through camp. We can get in easy enough."

"What about sentries? Won't they have someone standing guard?"

Brubs shook his head. "Not this bunch. They're feelin' nice and cozy and mighty smug right now. Didn't even try to hide their tracks on the way. They won't figure anybody's comin' after 'em. Besides, Comanches ain't real big on standin' watch. Don't like to miss their naps. We might as well make ourselves to home, have a bite of supper, and wait for 'em to bed down."

Supper was not exactly steak and lobster — just a few strips of cold bacon jammed between Granny's sourdough biscuits and washed down by canteen water. The thin fare didn't matter to Willoughby. His gut was clamped so tight, there wasn't room for a biscuit anyway. He noticed that Cal Hooper didn't eat much, either. There was something about the prospect of imminent death and dismemberment that dulled a reasonable man's appetite.

Nothing went to waste, though. Brubs ate his own, half of Cal's, and all of Dave's.

Willoughby could barely make out the forms of his two companions as darkness fell. The terrain soon turned an inky black, broken only by faint starlight. Cal sat with a blanket draped over his shoulders against the chill of the early spring night air, his rifle in his lap. Brubs lay on his back, hat tilted down over his face, his snores a light buzz against the quiet night.

Willoughby started as a coyote yelped nearby. The knot in his gut clamped tighter, then eased as the predator's wail cracked on the final note. The sour finish meant that the yelper was really a coyote and not a Comanche. Indians made their coyote calls crisp and clean. Willoughby realized he was picking up quite a bit of Comanche lore of late. He could only hope that was all he picked up from the Indians before this little escapade was over.

The night seemed interminable, yet it sped by. Willoughby had felt the sensation before, the agonizing wait before a battle when fear and dread twisted a man's sense of time and space. It was almost as bad as the battle itself. Almost.

He started again as the coyote dun snuffled, a soft, rolling snort that sounded like a cannon shot in Willoughby's ears. He squinted at the dun until he was satisfied that Malhumorado was just blowing dust from his nostrils and not smelling danger.

Willoughby ran over the plan in his mind for perhaps the twentieth time. The layout of the Indian camp remained sharp in his mind. The four stolen horses were picketed on a riata line near a jumble of fallen trees and a wild plum thicket bordering the small stream that wandered through camp. They wouldn't be able to recover the mules. The Indians had already butchered one, and the second was with the main Indian herd fifty yards up the canyon. Granny wasn't going to he overly happy about losing the mules, Willoughby knew.

The Comanches hadn't bothered to raise lodges, content to sleep on blankets and robes near the central fire. There were no women or children. That, Brubs said with his usual talent for reassurance, meant that these Indians — young braves from the Quahadi band, most likely — were on a raiding party and not just hunting. Several of the braves had horses staked beside their blankets. Brubs said they were favorite war ponies. Brubs had seemed especially impressed with one of the Indian mounts, a stocky, mustang-type bay-and-white paint with strips of red cloth braided into its flowing mane and tail, and a yellow handprint in the middle of a bay splotch on its shoulder.

The paint horse, Brubs said, was the kind of war pony a young man who was working on soon becoming a senior warrior or even chief would fancy. "Bet a year's profits that buck's the leader of this outfit," Brubs said. "Yellow's big medicine color to a Comanch lookin' to make somethin' of hisself on a raid. Supposed to turn bullets and the like." The paint horse was obviously a treasure to its Indian owner. The lead rope of the horse's halter was tied to the warrior's right wrist.

The trail into and out of the canyon was narrow, steep and strewn with small stones and shale slides, barely wide enough to accommodate horses moving single file. The trail switched back twice on the way from rim to canyon floor, hugging the sheer wall of the west face. It was shadowed for part of the way by clumps of cedar trees and jumbled sandstone rocks. The rest of the way was open, exposed to view from the camp below, which did not help the knot in Willoughby's belly much.

"Mr. Willoughby?" Cal's voice was a shaky whisper.

"Yes?"

"Maybe you and Mr. McCallan shouldn't have brought me along. I haven't been so scared in my life. What if I do something wrong? What if it turns out I'm a coward?"

"Don't worry about that, Cal," Willoughby said, hoping to reassure the boy. "You'll do fine. It's all right to be scared. The measure of a brave man isn't his lack of fear. A brave man is one who can be bone-deep scared and still do his job."

Cal was silent for a moment, mulling over Dave's words. "Mr. McCallan said you won the Medal of Honor in the war. Were you scared then? When you won it?"

"You might say that, Cal. I wet my pants." Willoughby sighed. "I did that on more than one occasion during the war. And a few times thereafter."

"What was it like? I mean the war, not peeing in your pants."

Willoughby thought for a moment, trying to find the right words to express the terror of battle, the crushing boredom of idleness and waiting, the exhaustion of marching twenty miles a day through sucking mud and choking dust, the constant fear of cholera and smallpox and lung fever and infected flesh. The worry that the command-

164

ers who led knew little about military tactics — or worse yet, that they underestimated the enemy. Or even worse, that they didn't care, that it was the so-called glory of war that blinded them to realities of mangled bodies and the smell of blood and ripped-out guts. Glory didn't stand up to a canister of shot or a musket ball. There were no adequate words.

"It was bad, Cal," he finally said. "I hope you never have to go through something like that. A man named Virgil who lived a long time ago perhaps described it best. He wrote, '*Quaeque ipse miserrima vidi et quorum pars magna fui.*' In English it says, 'And the most miserable things which I myself saw and of which I was a major part.' "

Brubs's soft buzzing snores ended in a sharp snort. He yawned, shook himself, stretched, removed his hat, and stared at the sky. "Well, gents," he said, "looks as to how it's time to go work."

Willoughby realized with a start that the moon had peeked over the eastern horizon. The sliver of white cast a weak light that soon would trickle into the canyon below. The knot in his gut tightened.

Brubs stood, pulled his Colt from the holster and checked the loads. Willoughby did the same, then reached for his Winchester.

"Leave the rifle," Brubs said. "If any shootin' happens, it'll be short gun work. We do this right, won't be no lead flyin'." He crouched, pulled off his spurs and draped them around the saddle horn. "Gonna be a long walk down, and I purely do hate to walk. Get yourself shut of anything that clatters, jingles, or shakes, partner."

"Does that include teeth and fingers?"

Brubs chuckled softly. "Now I know you ain't comin' down with a case of the vapors, Dave. Howsomever, I knowed this gal once over in Jefferson — right pretty little thing she was, too, till she took her teeth out and put 'em on the washstand —"

"Brubs," Willoughby interrupted, "as fascinating as your amorous adventures may be, I don't believe this is the time and place for any long stories. If you are determined to get us spitted on a Comanche lance, let's get it over with."

Brubs clapped him softly on the shoulder. "Relax, amigo. Ain't nobody goin' to get hurt. At least not if you Yankee artillery officers can sneak half as good as us Rebel privates." He turned to Cal. "You know what to do, son. Have the horses ready, cinched up tight. Now, don't go gettin' jumpy, 'cause this may take Dave and me a spell. If you hear shootin' from down in camp, shinny up to the rim for a look-see. If we have to run for it, cover us with that rifle. If all you see is Injuns comin', forget us, plop your butt in the saddle, spur that blue roan for all he's got, and don't look back."

Cal nodded. "Yes, sir."

"Good man. One more thing. When we come back up that trail, we'd sure be mighty grateful if

166

you didn't put a slug in us. Could spoil the whole evenin'."

"Yes, sir. I'll make sure of my targets."

Brubs glanced at Willoughby. "You ready to go steal our ponies back?"

"No," Willoughby said honestly, "but I can't let you go down there alone."

"Spoke like a real genuine Texan," Brubs said. "Man's got to stick by his partners through thick and thin."

Willoughby sighed. "That's only part of it, Brubs. You're the only one who knows how to get to Kansas."

NINE

Brubs and Willoughby crouched behind a fallen tree trunk and studied the sleeping camp in the weak light of the quarter moon. So far, so good, Brubs thought; no sentries, no barking dogs. The stolen horses were only three or four strides away.

"You cut the picket line, partner," Brubs whispered. "I'm goin' after that paint war pony."

"Brubs, you can't be serious," Willoughby whispered back urgently. "We're pushing our luck as it is."

"I ain't never been seriouser. Them Comanch stole six animals from us. And that paint'll be some reward for the mule them damn redskins et."

"Brubs —"

"This ain't no time to argue. Get movin' before one of them bucks wakes up to pee. And be mighty quiet about it, you want us to keep our hair." Before Willoughby could reply, Brubs snaked over the tree trunk and squirmed toward the camp, belly down like a salamander, his belt knife in hand.

Brubs worked his way toward the paint, digging knees and elbows in the sand to inch his way along. He paused once, heart pounding, as a Comanche buck less than three feet away muttered aloud and shifted in his blankets. Brubs held his breath until the Indian stopped squirming and started snoring softly, then resumed his careful stalk.

He kept his movements slow and deliberate; the sound of a twig cracking beneath elbow or knee would wake the Indian camp in a hurry. His heartbeat quickened as he crawled past the remnants of the Comanche fire. The paint was only a couple of yards away now.

Brubs cautiously rose to his feet. He knew the paint would throw a walleyed fit if something that looked like a big terrapin crawled up on it in the dead of night. But the horse knew what a man standing erect looked like. Brubs just hoped the paint wasn't too picky about how much Indian smell a man carried. The horse's ears perked toward Brubs, the whites of its eyes showing. The paint seemed to be more curious than spooked. Brubs was the one who was spooked. One mistake now and he would all at once be butt-deep in mad Indians. He forced his concentration back onto his work. The honor of the ancient tradition of horse theft was at stake. Along with his hair.

Brubs eased closer to the animal's right, the side where most Plains Indians approached their mounts, until he could reach out and touch the bay-and-white hide. He eased a hand slowly beneath the horse's nostrils and let the paint have a good, long sniff of his scent. He ran the hand under the horse's jaw and down the neck, whispering softly into the paint's ear. The war horse snuffled softly and shuffled a front foot, but did not sound an alarm. Brubs blew a gentle breath into the paint's nostrils. He wasn't sure what that did for an Indian pony, but the old-timers had told him it worked, that it helped keep an animal calm. Brubs didn't care how it worked. He only cared that it *did* work.

He doubled a bit of slack in the picket rope, eased the blade of his knife into the loop, and sawed gently against the riata. The keen knife edge sliced through the tough horsehair with a raspy whisper. Brubs's heart skipped a beat as the Indian in the blankets stirred and sighed. It seemed that an hour passed in the few seconds before the Comanche grunted, rolled over on his side, and his breathing steadied into the measured rhythm of sleep. Brubs sheathed his knife, pulled the worn moccasins from beneath his belt, and tied them to the end of the riata secured to the sleeping warrior's wrist. Only then did he chance a glance toward the picket line.

The line was empty. Brubs heard the faint, distant clink of horseshoe on stone as Willoughby led the retrieved horses away from camp.

The easy part was done now, he thought. The hard part was getting back out of camp and up that canyon wall before the Comanches discovered what had happened. He slipped his revolver from its holster but did not cock the weapon. The distinctive metallic clicks of a Colt hammer drawn to full cock would be as loud as a blacksmith's hammer on an anvil in the stillness of the camp.

Brubs led the paint away, silently retracing his steps toward the creek and the dense cover along the banks. He fought back an almost overwhelming impulse to hurry. He was too close to getting out alive to rush anything now.

He glanced over his shoulder every third step, muscles tensed, ready to spring onto the stocky paint's back at the first yelp of alarm from the camp.

It didn't come.

Brubs finally allowed himself a deep, audible sigh of relief when he led the paint into the cover alongside the creek. The tension began to drain from his shoulders. Still, he didn't holster the Colt until he was two hundred yards away from camp.

Willoughby waited at the edge of a cottonwood grove in a bend of the creek, already mounted bareback on the black, the lead ropes of the other three horses in his hand.

Brubs checked a sudden urge to whoop in triumph. That could wait a few more miles. He grinned at Willoughby. "Told you we could do it, partner," he said softly. "I'd sure like to see that buck's face when he wakes up and finds them moccasins on the end of his rope instead of his horse."

"If it's all the same to you," Willoughby said, the tension thick in his tone, "I'd just as soon be a long way from here when that happens."

Brubs took Squirrel's lead rope from Willoughby and scrambled onto the sorrel's back. "If you're waitin' on me, partner, you're wastin' time. Let's get the hell out of here." He kneed Squirrel toward the twisting trail up the canyon wall, the paint war horse following on a slack line lead. Willoughby brought up the rear, leading the other two horses.

Neither man spoke as the small caravan threaded its way up the second switchback and neared the top of the canyon rim. Brubs winced as a horse's hoof dislodged a stone; the small rock seemed to make as much racket as a Union Pacific train wreck as it bounced and skidded down the canyon wall. A dozen heartbeats later, Brubs let himself breathe again. They were less than twenty yards from the canyon rim.

"By God, Squirrel," he muttered to the sorrel between his knees, "I think we've got her made —" The half whisper ended in a squawk as lead pinged off a rock twenty feet away. A second later the report of the rifle shot and outraged yelps sounded from the Comanche camp below. The blast of the gunshot spooked Squirrel and the paint; the Indian horse lunged back against the lead rope, almost yanking Brubs from the sorrel's back. Another rifle ball whirred overhead as Brubs fought the panicked horses. The paint finally gave in to the lead rope. Brubs thumped heels against Squirrel's ribs. The sorrel lunged up the trail, dirt and pebbles kicking and sliding beneath driving hooves.

Brubs glanced over his shoulder. Willoughby had his hands full with the other mounts as they lunged against each other, fighting the leads and scrabbling for space on the narrow, rocky trail. A horse's shoulder slammed into Willoughby's black. The black's back foot slipped over the edge of the trail; the horse tottered for a moment, seeming to dangle over the precipice before his flailing hooves found solid ground. The black scrambled up the trail, Willoughby clinging desperately to the horse's mane. A speck of red-yellow fire winked in the canyon floor. The ball fell short, struck a stone, and ricocheted over Brubs's head with a nasty whir. Two more flashes sparked from the Indian camp. The shots again went wild, the range beyond accurate reach of the warriors' rifles below. Brubs found little comfort in that. It didn't matter if a rifle slug hit by aim or accident. The hole it made was the same.

In the faint moonlight below, four horsemen quirted mounts toward the rimrock trail, closing fast. Behind the mounted men, other black shapes hurried toward the Indian horse herd up the canyon.

Brubs flinched as another slug slapped the canyon wall uncomfortably close to his shoulder. At least one of the Comanches not only had a long-range weapon, but was also more than a passing fair shot. Brubs settled in to riding hard, trying to keep his bareback seat on the lunging sorrel.

He glanced back once more and spat a curse.

The four Comanche horsemen were almost at the base of the trail now. They would be within accurate shooting range in moments. The lip of the canyon seemed a mile away.

Fire streaked out from a clump of cedars on the canyon rim, the distinctive whip crack report of Cal Hooper's .38-40 falling atop the flash. One of the pursuing Comanches jerked upright and reined his horse aside. Cal's rifle cracked again, and an Indian's horse went down, spilling the rider. Then Brubs's horse lunged up the final yard of the steep trail, Willoughby close behind.

Brubs reined Squirrel to a sliding stop beside the saddled horses and yanked his rifle from the scabbard. He whipped a half hitch in the paint's lead rope over his saddle horn and sprinted back to the edge of the canyon.

The remaining mounted Indians had reached the base of the canyon wall, quirting mounts up the first few feet of the trail. Cal's Winchester cracked twice more. Brubs threw the Henry against his shoulder and emptied the magazine as fast as he could work the action and yank the trigger. He didn't expect to hit anything, not shooting at night and blinded by the muzzle flashes of his own rifle. But the unexpected spray of lead served its purpose. The Indians wheeled their horses and raced back toward camp.

Brubs blinked rapidly, trying to get his night vision back, as Willoughby knelt beside him, Winchester in hand. Willoughby squeezed off two quick shots toward the fleeing Comanches. The echoes of rifle fire rolled up and down the canyon, seeming to come from all directions. Brubs's eyes finally adjusted enough so that he could see the Indians milling about in obvious confusion in the camp below. He glanced at Willoughby.

"Cut her a little closer'n I hoped there," Brubs said. "You okay, partner?"

Willoughby lowered his rifle and glowered at him. "Hell yes, I'm all right. Considering that I've spent the night slipping into a Comanche camp, dodging bullets, and almost getting thrown down a hundred-foot cliff, I'm fine. Never better."

"Glad to hear it. I was worried a speck back there. Thought we mighta been in a little trouble." Brubs glanced around. "Cal? Where you at, boy?"

"Over here, Mr. McCallan." The youth stopped into view from a cedar clump. Brass tinked against steel as the youth fumbled cartridges into the loading port of the rifle.

"Son," Brubs said, "that was some damn fine night shootin'."

"I never" — Cal's voice cracked slightly — "never shot at a man before."

"You done mighty good for the first time, Cal. I was a tad busy, but it looked to me like you nailed one of 'em square and put another'n afoot. Mighta saved ol' Dave here from losin' his hair sooner'n he plans."

"If I ride with you much longer, Brubs McCallan, my hair will turn snow-white and fall out of its own accord," Willoughby groused. "In case you haven't noticed, this isn't over yet. When those Comanches regroup, they'll come at us again."

"Quit frettin', partner," Brubs said. "You're thinkin' like a Yankee officer. Gotta think like an Injun out here. Comanches don't like fightin' in the dark. They believe a man gets killed at night, his soul spends eternity in the dark. They won't come after us until sunup. Then they'll most likely bring the whole bunch. I reckon we mighta made 'em some mad here tonight."

"A comforting thought, to be sure," Willoughby said. "It isn't that long until daybreak. I assume you have some grand strategic military maneuver in mind?"

"Sure do, partner," Brubs said. "We run like hell." He strode to the saddled mustang, reloaded the Henry, and mounted. Willoughby climbed into the saddle on the coyote dun. Cal was already aboard the blue roan.

"Well, boys," Brubs said as he reined Mouse about, "I reckon we done showed them redskins a thing or two about horse stealin'." He leaned over and patted Mouse's shoulder. "Now that we got our ponies back, let's see can we put some miles between us and them Comanches. We can get back to Palo Duro Creek in plenty time. Ain't but forty, fifty miles from here. We'll be ready when they come."

Dave Willoughby leaned against the wagon bed and rubbed a grimy knuckle across eyes that felt as if they had half the sand in Texas in them. He hadn't slept in twenty-six hours. The stubble on his neck and chin itched and his mouth was parched, not from lack of water but from fear and dread. Every unexpected noise or imagined movement on the outskirts of the Palo Duro Creek camp sent a start through his tense muscles.

Willoughby glanced around the camp, wondering if the defense they had set up would hold against a Comanche war party that outnumbered them three-to-one.

The terrain favored the defenders. The Palo Duro Creek breaks fanned into a stirrup shape here on the south bank, steep bluffs twenty to thirty feet high protecting the rear from a mounted charge. The bow shape in the bluffs behind the wagon formed a natural holding pasture for the remuda, narrowing to little more than thirty yards across before flaring out into the creek bottom. At least the Indians wouldn't be able to stampede the horses without a fight. The Comanches, if they came, would have to attack from the north, across an open stretch two hundred yards wide.

Willoughby and Brubs had thrown a shallow mound of sandy soil up as a bulwark and shooting stand in front of the wagon, where they would have a clear field of fire. Granny Hooper was in the wagon bed, crouched behind sacks of supplies and cooking utensils, the long-barreled goose gun at her side. Tige Tilghman and Cal Hooper, the best rifle shots of the crew, were stationed at the left and right wings where the bluffs narrowed. Nick Chadburne, mounted on a fast, leggy brown, prowled back and forth across the narrow opening. It was Chadburne's job to try to keep the remuda bottled up in the meadow when the shooting started.

All the defenders had at least forty rounds of ammunition close at hand and swift horses saddled in case they had to make a run for it.

Willoughby could see only one flaw in the defenses. They couldn't hold out against a siege. Brubs insisted that wasn't anything to worry about. Comanches didn't understand siege warfare, Brubs said. "They can't get your scalp quick and easy, they don't want it," he said. Willoughby didn't find that observation particularly reassuring.

The sun was halfway up the morning sky, a bright, brassy disk against a pale blue, cloudless backdrop. The wind had begun to pick up, blowing from the southwest, rippling the grama and buffalo grass and rustling the cedars along the rocky bluffs.

At Willoughby's side, Brubs was whistling "The Bonny Blue Flag," off-key, as if he hadn't a care in the whole world. Willoughby could never tell if Brubs was whistling his way through the graveyard, whistling because he truly wasn't worried, or whistling just to aggravate one Dave Willoughby.

He turned to Brubs. "Maybe they aren't coming," he said hopefully.

Brubs abruptly quit whistling. He nodded toward the north rim of the creek. "They're done here."

Willoughby's head snapped around. His heart caught in his throat. A line of Indians sat astride war ponies and stared in silence at the camp. The wind ruffled eagle feathers and scalp locks braided into the manes and tails of the Comanche mounts.

"Well, partner," Brubs said, "looks like we best rosin up the bow. This here dance is about to start."

A warrior in the center of the Indian line, a lean man wearing a buffalo headdress with horns still attached, held something above his head and waved it back and forth.

"Maybe I shouldn't a took them moccasins back," Brubs said. "Reckon it sort of ruffled their feathers." He tapped on the wood of the wagon bed. "Get set, Granny. We're fixin' to have us some company."

"Let the damn heathen, pillagin', rapin' savages come," Granny Hooper growled. Brubs ducked a brown stream of tobacco spit that sailed from the wagon. "Me and this goose gun ain't afeared of no unchristian red son of a she-dog."

A whoop sounded from the far side of the creek. The cry jolted Willoughby into action. He dove into the shooting pit behind the sand berm and racked a round into his Winchester. A puff of smoke blossomed from the Indian line; a split second later Willoughby heard the thunk of lead into sand. Brubs scrambled into the shallow trench and cocked the Henry. The sand seemed to tremble under Willoughby as the Indians charged, whooping and yelling. He raised the Winchester.

"Don't go wastin' lead," Brubs said. "Wait till they get close enough we can deal 'em some serious hurt. We don't bloody this bunch a tad, we just might be in a heap of trouble."

"I'm certainly relieved to hear we aren't already," Willoughby said caustically. He winced as a rifle ball pinged off the iron rim of a wagon wheel.

"Save that Injun in the buffalo horns for me," Brubs said as he raised the .44 rimfire. "That's the buck I stole the paint pony off of."

Willoughby had to grit his teeth to keep from yanking the trigger. The Indian skirmish line swept forward; water flew as the charging horses lunged through the knee-deep water of the main creek channel. Slugs buzzed overhead or drove into the sand as the Indians fired wildly from the backs of charging mounts.

"Them fellers can't shoot much better'n you Yanks," Brubs said. "I reckon they're close enough now. Cut the wolf loose."

Willoughby heard the heavy whop of lead against flesh a split second before the thunderous blast of Tilghman's Sharps reached his ears, and an Indian at one end of the skirmish line tumbled over the rump of his horse. The Indians were

180

scarcely fifty yards away when Willoughby pulled the sights fine and squeezed the trigger. The .44-40 thumped against his shoulder. The warrior in his sights jerked upright, then slumped over the neck of his pony.

Brubs's Henry cracked. Willoughby heard the Texan's sharp oath as his shot missed. Another warrior went down under a slug from Cal Hooper's .38-40. Willoughby slapped a quick shot, missed, and frantically levered another round into the Winchester. The Indians were almost upon them now . . .

The deafening whomp of Granny Hooper's goose gun shook the sand under Willoughby. The buckshot charge blew one warrior from his horse and put a second Indian pony down. The Comanche attack slowed, faltered momentarily, then regrouped under the shouts of the warrior in the buffalo headdress.

Willoughby's heart skidded. They would be overrun in a matter of seconds. He tried to slap a quick shot at a Comanche bearing down on him less than thirty feet away and heard the sickening click as his rifle misfired. He yanked frantically at the lever and muttered a curse. The faulty cartridge had jammed the action. He clawed for the Colt at his waist.

The charging Indian suddenly lurched in the saddle, rifle spinning from his hand. Willoughby finally yanked his revolver clear — and watched in disbelief as the Comanche charge faltered and broke. Only then did Willoughby hear the clatter

181

of hooves from behind. He spun on his belly, handgun raised.

Nick Chadburne spurred past on the leggy brown, a revolver in his fist, charging the retreating Indians.

"No, Nick!" Brubs yelled. "Rein in!"

Chadburne paid no heed. "That fool kid's gonna get hisself kilt for sure," Brubs said. He levered three quick rounds through the Henry. Willoughby fired twice in futility, knowing the chase had moved beyond effective reach of the Colt. Chadburne's brown neared the bank of the creek. The horse seemed to stop in mid-stride as a volley of rifle shots rattled from the far bank. The horse went down. Chadburne kicked free of the stirrups, and hit hard on his shoulder, the impact jarring the handgun from his grasp.

A Comanche warrior kneed his horse into the creek and splashed toward the downed man, lance in hand, ignoring the buzz of lead thrown by the frantic defenders in the camp. Chadburne came to his feet and stood, legs slightly spread, knees flexed. The warrior aimed his lance at Chadburne's chest.

Brubs barked a curse of helplessness. Willoughby's heart skidded as the Comanche closed the final twenty feet. Chadburne stood his ground as if braced for the shock of the lance tip. At the last second he leapt in front of the horse to the off side and rammed a doubled fist into the warrior's left hip. The Indian skidded his mount to a stop and sat for a moment facing Chadburne, his back to

Willoughby. Brubs squinted over the sights of the Henry, then abruptly lowered the muzzle. "What the hell?"

The warrior lowered the tip of his lance to the ground and inclined his head to Chadburne. He kneed his pony to the right, circling Chadburne at a respectful distance, and kicked his mount into a lope toward the gathering of Indians across the creek.

"What the hell?" Brubs said again, bewildered.

Willoughby sensed the motion from the corner of his vision and snapped his head around. Cal Hooper spurred his horse toward Chadburne. Smoke blossomed from muzzles of rifles on the far ridge. Cal's hat spun from his head. Dust sprayed at the horse's feet.

"Cover him, dammit!" Brubs yelled. He shouldered the Henry and triggered four quick, unaimed shots toward the ridge. The .44 rimfire slugs fell well short. An Indian horse went down as Tilghman's Sharps roared.

Willoughby dropped his handgun, swept up his rifle and frantically pried the jammed misfire free. He levered and fired wildly toward the Indians as fast as he could work the action. Through the growing fog of powder smoke and dust he saw Cal lean from the saddle, hook his arm beneath Nick's, and swing Chadburne up behind him.

The Indians on the far ridge stopped shooting.

The sudden silence seemed unreal, broken only by the sound of hooves, as Cal spurred back toward camp, Chadburne bouncing on the saddle skirts behind him. Brubs and Willoughby sprinted out to meet them as Cal pulled the winded horse to a stop. Willoughby glanced toward the ridge. The Indian skirmish line had formed again. It was shorter than before.

"What in the name of blue-eyed hell are you two tryin' to pull?" Brubs snapped. "You could have both got killed out there sure as sin."

Chadburne's dark face was streaked with sweat and dirt, but still without expression. Willoughby wondered if the kid ever showed emotion.

"Looked to me like you folks were in trouble here," Chadburne said, his voice steady. "I thought maybe the Indians wouldn't be expecting a one-man charge."

"Well," Brubs said grudgingly, "I reckon you was right. Boogered 'em off, sure enough, just when we was gettin' set to lose our hair." He cocked an eyebrow at Cal. "That was some fair ridin' there, son, even if it weren't too smart."

Cal dismounted, his fingers trembling on the reins. "I couldn't leave Nick out there afoot. I couldn't think of anything else to do but go get him."

Brubs eyed the two youngsters for a moment. "Maybe I ain't too pleased you boys didn't foller orders, but I sure can't say you ain't got bigger *cojones* than a pair of young Mexican studs." He shook his head. "Ought to tan your hides, takin' such a chance." But it was admiration, not anger, that tinged his words, Willoughby noted.

The wagon timbers creaked as Granny Hooper

climbed down. She crashed into Brubs, almost knocking him down, and gathered Cal to her more than ample bosom. She held the boy tight for a moment, glaring over his shoulder at Brubs. "If there's any butt-chewin' to be done, Brubs McCallan, it'll be my teeth and your butt," she snapped. "Them red savages woulda run us down sure, hadn't been for Nick and Cal here, and you damn well know it!" She pulled Cal tighter. "Are you hurt, son?"

"No, ma'am," the boy said, his head buried in several layers of flesh, his voice muffled, "but I can't hardly breathe."

Granny reluctantly eased her grip on the boy.

Willoughby glanced up at the sound of hoofbeats. Tige Tilghman reined in, the butt plate of the Sharps resting on his right thigh. "What in thunder's goin' on here?" he asked.

Brubs shrugged. "Just havin' us a little family reunion, I reckon."

Tilghman snorted. "Hate to bust up a happy bunch like this," he said, "but I reckon we still got us an Injun problem."

Willoughby's gaze swept the battlefield. Five Indians and four horses were down, either dead or wounded. Buzzards were already circling overhead, as if they knew the sound of gunfire meant dinnertime. On the far ridge, the surviving Comanches had gathered in a cluster, apparently arguing, arms waving and hands gesturing. Willoughby figured they were probably trying to decide whether to roast the whites over a slow fire, skin them alive, or just shoot them, scalp them, and go on about their business.

The Indian wearing the buffalo horns and the warrior who had almost lanced Chadburne reined their mounts away from the group on the ridge, trotted to the far edge of the creek, and stopped. Willoughby raised his rifle.

"Don't shoot, Dave," Tilghman said. "They're makin' parley sign. Want to talk. Them buffler horns means that one's boss hog of this bunch. Other might be the number two man. Could be a good idea to jaw with them Injuns a spell, Brubs."

The stocky Texan glared at the Comanches for several heartbeats, his jaw set. "Can't," he said, "I don't speak Comanch."

"I talk good Mex," Tilghman said. "Most these Plains Injuns talk Mexican. Learnt it from the Comancheros back in the old days. You want to parley, I'll do the yammerin'."

"Suppose we don't? Hell, Tige, we could take 'em down easy from this range."

"They know that. Don't reckon it'd be a good idea, though. Shoot at 'em, my guess is we'd mighty soon be butt-deep in Comanches again."

"Aw, hell." Brubs shrugged. "Might's well hear what he's got to say. Wave 'im in."

Granny Hooper loosed another wad of tobacco spit. "Get them damn savages in range of this smoothbore, I'll fix their bacon." She cocked the heavy hammers of the goose gun. "They ain't gonna rape no more poor defenseless white women."

Brubs reached out and pushed the barrels of the shotgun down. "Settle down, Granny. I don't reckon they got your bloomers on their minds right now. If they try to do somethin' but talk, then you can shoot 'em."

The Comanches didn't hesitate when Tilghman waved. The two reined in a few feet from the whites. Neither of the Indians showed any outward expression. The man in the buffalo headdress jabbered something in rapid-fire Spanish.

Tilghman nodded and turned to Brubs. "Says his name's Turtle Wind of the Quahadi band. He says Ugly One — that's you, Brubs — is a great horse thief. You took his best pony and left his worn-out moccasins. Big medicine."

"Just payin' back a social call," Brubs said casually.

"He also says Dark Skin — that's you, Chadburne — is a brave man, a fine warrior. You counted coup on a mounted and armed enemy."

"Counted coup?" Chadburne sounded confused.

"Struck a living enemy with your bare hand," Tilghman said. "To a Comanch on his way up and schooled in the old ways, that's a damn sight bigger medicine than killing an enemy with a weapon. That's how come the other Injun lowered his lance tip. Comanche salute." Tilghman and the head man jabbered a few more sentences, hands fluttering in sign language when a phrase wasn't understood.

"He says Boy With Eagle Wing Ears — that's you, Cal — is a fine horseman and a brave warrior. And that Walks Wide Woman — that'd be you, Granny — is *mucho hombre*. Not one to tangle with."

"Why, that smart-ass savage!" Granny fumed. "I'm half a mind to teach him some respect. . . ." Her voice trailed away in an outraged sputter of tobacco spittle.

"Be best if you didn't, Granny," Tilghman said calmly. " 'Specially since he just paid you a mighty high compliment. For a Comanche."

Brubs snorted impatiently. "Tell ol' Turtle Farts to get to the point. I ain't in the mood to stand around here tradin' pleasantries all day."

"Rein in, Brubs. We're comin' to that. Comanches like to ride around the herd a spell before doin' serious type talkin'." Tilghman turned back to the Comanche. The yammering and gesturing lasted longer this time.

Finally, Tilghman turned away. "He wants to make a treaty. Says if we let him collect his dead and wounded, give him back his paint war pony and five other good horses, a sack of sugar and a pound of lead, he'll call off the fight."

"What?" Brubs sputtered. "Six horses! That's the most high-handed thing I ever heard! Highway robbery, that's what it is. Dammit, we worked hard for them animals."

"That uppity redskin wants a present, by God, I'll give 'im one," Granny grumbled. "A double load of buckshot right in his red butt."

Tilghman ignored Granny. "It's a pretty cheap price, Brubs. Lets him save face with his warriors. Lets us keep from gettin' somewhat dead and losin' the rest of our hosses to boot. Might want to think on it some. 'Specially since he also mentioned there was three, four more bands, maybe a couple hundred warriors all told, headin' south toward these parts. Turn 'im down, he'd likely send runners out to gather some of them friends of his. That might amount to more Injuns than we can handle."

Brubs frowned. "Reckon he's lyin' about them other Injuns?"

Tilghman spat. "Maybe. Maybe not. Never trusted no Comanch in my life. But I ain't willin' to bet neither way."

"All right," Brubs said with a sigh. "Tell him this. We'll give him his Injuns and paint pony, four other horses and a pound of sugar, but no more. Tell him Ugly One must save face with his tribe, too. Turtle Farts will give us two good mules, two Comanche blankets, and a couple drags off a medicine pipe to close the deal. Then he's honor bound to let us alone."

Tilghman nodded and relayed the message to the Comanche. The Indian listened silently, then nodded.

"We got us a deal, Brubs. We'll make the trade down at the creek when the sun's straight overhead." Tilghman and the Comanche jabbered again for a few moments, the Indian staring at Granny Hooper all the while.

189

"What's that red bastard sayin' about me?" Fire flashed in Granny's narrowed eyes.

Tilghman shrugged. "Nothin' important."

"Damn you, you oversized saddle bum," Granny snapped, "I reckon they're tryin' to work in some trade for me, sealin' the deal with a good rape. Now, you tell me what that savage said or I'll whop you upside the ear with this smoothbore!"

"Promise you won't shoot 'im." Tilghman waited for Granny's reluctant nod of agreement. "He says he feels sorry for the men of this crew. Says wakin' up beside Walks Wide Woman would make a man run screamin' from his lodge to sing his death song."

"Why, that smart-ass son of a —" Granny tried to raise the shotgun. Brubs held the barrels down.

"Easy, Granny," Brubs said. He had a hard time holding back a grin. "At least you can quit frettin' about gettin' raped." He didn't let go of the shotgun barrels until the Indians had ridden well out of range.

Tilghman sighed in relief as the Indians disappeared over the bank of the creek, leading the paint war pony and four of the sorriest horses from the Texas Horsetrading Company remuda. He pulled a tobacco sack from his pocket. "Reckon that's that. If he wasn't lyin', we won't have us no more trouble. At least out of *this* bunch of Injuns." Tilghman rolled his smoke, twisted the ends of the quirly, and reached for a match. He lifted an eyebrow at Brubs. "Friend, you don't look so good. Got a bellyache?"

Brubs winced. "Gut's a little queasy. Got an awful taste in my mouth. What the hell do them Injuns smoke, anyhow?"

Tilghman fired his cigarette and grinned through the haze. "Touch of tobacco, crumbled cedar bark, few strands of badger hair, and a pinch or two of rat droppin's for flavor. Ain't bad, once you get used to it."

Brubs moaned aloud. "Thanks a hell of a lot, Tige. You got a way of bringin' comfort to a sufferin' man." He swung aboard the sorrel. "Let's get movin', folks," he said. "We got a lot of miles to make up and it's a far piece from here to the Canadian."

TEN

Brubs McCallan sidled up to the chuck wagon, tin plate in hand, reached for the molasses jar, and caught a sharp rap across the knuckles from the heavy spoon in Granny Hooper's fist.

"You whelp," Granny groused, "you know damn well you don't get but one syrup helpin'."

Brubs flexed his stinging knuckles and lifted a woeful eyebrow. "But, Granny, I can't get the biscuits and syrup to come out even. I got near a whole biscuit left and not a solitary syrup sop to go on it."

"Don't matter. You know the rules." Granny spat a glob of dark brown tobacco juice that landed at his feet. "One spoonful, no more. This here jar's got to last us till we get someplace we can buy more grub."

Brubs stared for a moment at the splotch of tobacco spit near his boot toe. It looked a lot like molasses. The sight pulled his sweet tooth in a hurry. He tucked the remaining sourdough bread into a shirt pocket and dropped his plate in the wreck pan. "How we fixed on other stuff?"

"Runnin' short on flour, sugar, salt, and damn near all else. Can't cook nothin' if I ain't got nothin' to cook. Ain't got but two tobacco twists left, neither, and I get downright out of sorts when I ain't got no chewin'."

Brubs brushed the biscuit crumbs from his hands and noticed that the knuckles were red where the spoon had whacked them. "Used to be a Mex sheepherder tradin' post over on the other side of the Canadian." He stooped to pry Junior loose from his leather leggings. The chaps were starting to look mighty ragged from baby goat chewings. "I'll scout over thataway and see if it's still there. It is, we can lay in some necessaries. Sure would hate to have you run out of tobacco and go gettin' cranky on us." Junior had hold of Brubs's shirttail. He pushed the goat aside. "I got to check out that river ford anyhow."

Granny sloshed a pail of hot water into the wreck pan. "Then get your butt outta my way, McCallan. I got work to do. And quit tormentin' poor little Junior."

Brubs glared at the baby goat. The kid stared back from behind the spokes of a wagon wheel, chewing contentedly on the bite of cloth from Brubs's shirttail. "One of these days I'm gonna have me some goat barbecue," he muttered as he strode toward the picket line where Mouse waited.

Willoughby shifted his weight in the saddle and fiddled with the bridle reins, trying to shake the feeling of uneasiness that had dogged him all morning.

He wasn't sure why the cold lump had formed in his belly. Or why he felt the need to glance around every few seconds. The early afternoon sun was warm, almost hot. Maybe, he told himself, it was the deathly stillness of the spring air. There was no wind. Not a blade of grass rippled except where disturbed by the passage of men and horses. The air seemed strange in the nostrils, a clear sharpness that held no detectable odor but still seemed to carry a faint wisp of something that left a brassy taste on the tongue and set the nerves jangling.

The animals sensed something, too.

The horses walked or trotted along with ears alert, nostrils flared as if testing the air for danger. They did not graze, even though the new spring grass was past anklehigh, green and tender. There were none of the usual squabbles among them, no nips or kicks. Normally the animals spread out singly or in pairs, keeping a bit of space between themselves and other horses. Now they crowded together as if searching for some sort of security or protection in sheer numbers. Willoughby had been around horses long enough to know that the animals could often sense danger well before any threat became apparent to men. Even the roan gelding between his knees was twitchy; Willoughby could feel the tension in Choctaw's solid muscles at each mincing step. The roan's ears flicked back and forth; he carried his head higher than normal and snorted softly from time to time. That wasn't like Choctaw.

Even Granny's goats seemed to have the yips. The two nannies stayed so close to the wagon that

194

they had their heads under the tailgate, bleating almost constantly. Brubs Junior walked at his mother's flank, pressed against her as if seeking reassurance.

Willoughby twisted in the saddle to study the back trail. A slight cloud of dust raised by the passage of nearly three hundred horses lay close to the prairie. Even the dust looked spooky, he thought. It was more of a fog bank than a cloud.

The tip of the peak over Willoughby's right shoulder stood shrouded in a blue haze. They were less than a full day's ride past the prominent landmark. The canyon Brubs called Buzzard Roost should be straight ahead, and beyond it, the Canadian River ford. Brubs had checked the ford, pronounced it passable, and now rode a wide-ranging scout to the south. He should have been back two hours ago.

Willoughby's gaze slowly moved over the rolling, grassy prairie dotted with stirrup-high cactus, Spanish dagger plants, and prickly pear clumps. There was no sign of life, not even a buzzard or eagle or antelope.

Willoughby tried to convince himself he was just "boogerin' at shadows," as Brubs would say. He lost the argument. The whole crew seemed to be wrapped in the same blanket of expectant tension. Granny Hooper didn't even bother to curse the mules. Tige Tilghman rode with his Sharps drawn and resting across the crook of an arm, his gaze flicking back and forth over the countryside.

On impulse, Willoughby eased Choctaw back through the remuda and rode to Tilghman's side.

"You feel it, too?" Tilghman said by way of greeting.

Willoughby nodded. "I don't know why, but I must admit I'm more than a little nervous right now. So are the horses. It's like they'd stampede if somebody so much as sneezed."

Tilghman shifted the Sharps and reached for his tobacco sack. "They're boogery, sure enough."

Suddenly Brubs rode up and reined in alongside the two men, the neck and shoulders of the tough little gray mustang dark with sweat. He looked worried, too. "Looks like we got us a real fret buildin', boys," he said.

The hairs on Willoughby's forearms rose up. "What?"

"Smelt air like this a couple times before," Brubs said. "Storm's comin'. Bad one. Heavy rain, lightnin'. Maybe some hail. We got to get these ponies to them river breaks before it hits. If it catches us in open country with no cover, we could lose half the cavvy."

Willoughby quickly scanned the horizon. There wasn't a cloud in sight, only a brassy disk of sun in a pale blue, washed-out sky. "I don't see any sign —"

"This ain't no time to argue, Dave," Brubs interrupted. "Buzzard Roost Canyon ain't more'n five, six miles straight up this little draw." The Texan studied the washed-out sky for several heartbeats. "Got to get the wagon down in that canyon, too. The boys and me'll help Granny once we get them ponies steppin' smart. Tige, trot over and tell her to get set to do some bouncy ridin' and mule whuppin', then take the east swing. Dave'll take point."

Willoughby started. "Me? Why me? I don't have the foggiest idea where this canyon is."

"Just head up that draw, partner, and get ready to ride like hell. We'll trot 'em part of the way and let 'em run the last two, three miles. That'll yank enough sweat off 'em they won't stampede when the storm breaks. When they hit the bottom of the canyon, let 'em find whatever cover they can and hunt up a hidey-hole for us." Brubs reined the mustang about and spurred Mouse into a long lope toward the drag where Cal Hooper and Nick Chadburne rode.

Willoughby touched spurs to the fidgety roan. He heard the whoops and yelps from the other riders and the growing rumble of hooves behind him as the remuda picked up the pace. He kneed Choctaw into a swift trot, the trail-wise brown at the lead of the cavvy following fifty yards behind.

They had covered a couple of miles at a fast trot before Willoughby felt a sudden chill in the air. He glanced to the west. A towering thunderhead seemed to have bloomed above the horizon, blotting out the sun. Huge sections of the massive cloud twisted and boiled. The cloud flickered with near-constant lightning flashes. A gust of cool air touched Willoughby's cheek. The cloud seemed to hang above the ground, the sky beneath it a ghostly green.

The rumble behind Willoughby grew to a roar as the drag riders pushed the horse herd into a hard run. He glanced over his shoulder at Tilghman. The big man already had his horse in a long lope, the Sharps back in its sheath. Willoughby spurred Choctaw into a run and leaned over the roan's muscular neck for the race to the river breaks.

The last two miles of the run were a blur. Willoughby rode hard through cactus flats and over increasingly rough terrain dotted with fist-sized stones and prairie dog holes. The wide, shallow draw grew more narrow and rocky, angling steadily down toward the river beyond.

Willoughby's heart hammered against his ribs as the tiring Choctaw stumbled, almost went down, then regained his feet after what seemed to be an eternity. Willoughby barely had time to recover from that quick blast of raw terror before the roan was lunging and sliding down a steep slope littered with large rocks and treacherous swatches of loose shale. He gave Choctaw his head, trusting the horse to keep his feet under him. The winded roan finally reached the bottom of the trail, jumped a shallow creek, and raced into the floor of a rapidly widening canyon. Willoughby glanced over his shoulder. A solid mass of horses poured down the slope; a bay near the lead went down, spilling two more horses crowded against his rump.

Dave settled in for the final sprint to the tree-lined river basin below. Choctaw's heart hammered against Willoughby's knees as the big roan labored for air. The rumble behind him seemed to intensify. He finally realized the rumble was not from the remuda, but a constant cannonade of thunder from the darkening sky. Scattered drops of windblown rain spatted against his hat. Willoughby glanced over his shoulder. Tilghman was a few yards behind, riding swing. Nick Chadburne spurred his horse toward the flank. The three finally managed to slow the leaders. Willoughby's heart still hammered as the run finally ended.

Fat, heavy raindrops hammered against him as he straightened in the saddle to stare back up the canyon. Granny Hooper sawed against the reins of the mule hitch, her foot jammed firmly against the wagon brake. Smoke boiled from the wood brake blocks screeching against iron rims. Cal Hooper and Brubs had lariats secured to the tailgate irons, their horses' haunches almost dragging the ground as they strained to help keep the wagon from careening out of control down the slope. Willoughby held his breath as a wagon wheel jounced over a rock; the jolt almost bounced Granny from the seat. The wagon slewed precariously and would have overturned but for the drag of ropes dallied to the two horsemen's saddle horns.

The chuck wagon finally reached the relatively

open flat, then bounced and skidded toward Willoughby as Granny released the brakes and slapped the mules' rumps with the reins, cursing at every stride, the goats darting first one way and then the other in confusion and terror. Brubs and Cal undallied the drag ropes and let the lariats trail behind the wagon.

Brubs reined Mouse to a stop before Willoughby. He had to shout to be heard above the constant rumble and sharp cracks of thunder.

"Overhang there!" He jabbed a thumb toward a rock formation bulging from the upper rim of the northwest wall of the canyon. "Get the saddle horses under it! Mules, too, soon's we can get 'em unhitched!"

Willoughby started as a pure white light suddenly slashed through the increasing rain; a bolt of lightning shattered a cedar tree atop the canyon, followed instantly by a sharp crack that set his ears ringing. He spurred Choctaw toward the overhang.

Minutes later the crew huddled against the side of the canyon, protected from the direct onslaught of the storm but soaked to the skin by rain carried on swirling wind gusts. Granny's goats crowded against her; she held the young kid in her arms. A solid sheet of rain lashed the canyon. Willoughby could barely make out the dim outlines of the wagon only ten yards away. Lightning bolts ripped overhead and sent jagged streaks of white fire against the canyon rim and into the flats below. Thunder cracked and boomed almost constantly. Willoughby flinched as something pinged off the top of the overhang. A quarter-sized hailstone splatted near his feet, bounced, and rolled down the slope.

"Brace up, folks!" Brubs yelled above the tumult. "She's fixin' to get serious!"

"I thought it was already!" Willoughby shouted back.

"Be over quick! These storms don't usual last —" Brubs's words were lost under the crash of thunder, crack of lightning, and growing clatter of hailstones.

Willoughby huddled against the canyon wall and watched in awe as the hail hit with a vengeance. He could hear the ice clumps pop against the wood of the wagon bed and ping off the iron wheel rims. He watched in amazement as a hailstone the size of an orange thumped into the mud a few feet away, leaving a fist-sized crater as it bounced. It was, he thought, like watching a New England snowstorm, except that the flakes were huge and jagged, like grapeshot and shell fragments. Man wasn't the only being with artillery, Willoughby realized. Nature had some impressive ammunition of her own.

Granny Hooper suddenly cried out in dismay. The young goat had squirmed from her arms and, panicked, dashed toward the wagon. The kid made four bounding jumps before a big hailstone slammed into his neck. The goat crumpled without a sound. Within seconds he was a small, gray lump pounded into the mud. His mother bleated frantically. Granny dropped her head into her hands.

The storm passed as abruptly as it had hit. The barrage of ice slowed to an occasional chunk and the rain lost its intensity. Thunder still boomed and lightning bolts danced, but now the target was the east rim of the canyon and the flats beyond.

Willoughby's eyes widened as the river valley floor slowly came back into view. Huge trees smoldered from lightning strikes. Thigh-sized limbs torn from tree trunks littered the valley beneath cottonwood and elm groves. Hailstones blanketed the battered soil and banked up on the east side of deadfalls and rocks. Through a break in the storm-hammered trees, Willoughby saw the wide ribbon of reddish Canadian River water swell and spread from the main channel. The scene reminded him of the aftermath of the Battle of the Wilderness, but this time the destruction was not the fault of man.

Granny Hooper slogged through the mud and hailstones toward the wagon. She paused for a moment beside the broken body of the young goat, then shook her head sadly and strode to the wagon.

Willoughby finally regained his voice. "My God," he said, awestruck, "I have never seen a storm like that."

Brubs shrugged. "Just a little pissant of a cloud by Texas Panhandle standards. Seen one throw hailstones so big it killed full-growed buffalo bulls. Just dropped straight down like they'd been hit with a Sharps slug. At least there weren't no twisters with this 'un." He pushed himself away from the canyon wall. "Let's go see what we got left." Brubs stopped beside the dead goat and stared at the body for a moment. "Junior was a pain in the butt, sure enough," he muttered, "but I reckon I'm gonna miss havin' the little bastard underfoot."

The inspection took the rest of the day. The wood of the wagon was dented and splintered in places. The canvas sheet that covered the wagon bed was in shreds. Their supplies had taken a beating, most ruined by rain or hail. Granny went through her entire vocabulary of English and Spanish cusswords and even borrowed a couple of Comanche epithets from Tilghman as she surveyed the ruins in the wagon.

"Tige, you and Nick take a look-see downriver," Brubs said. "Dave, take Cal with you and ride upstream. See how many ponies we lost and how far they strayed. Push 'em back this way. We'll overnight here. I'm gonna see how much of a tear that ol' Canadian's gone on."

Willoughby's stomach lurched as he rode past one grove of cottonwoods. The carcasses of three horses lay beneath one lightning-struck tree whose splintered top still sparked and smoked. They found two more dead horses, one beaten to death by hailstorms when it was caught in the open, another hit by lightning. The lightning bolt had hit the horse between the ears. The scorched entry wound was barely the size of a half dollar, but the bolt had melted the iron shoes on the animal's hooves.

Willoughby started at the echoes of two pistol shots from upriver. Someone had put a horse, perhaps two, out of its crippled misery. He was relieved that the chore had fallen to someone else. Having to shoot a good horse was the most gut-wrenching thing a man had to face. He became aware of a distant rumble, glanced at the sky to see if another storm was building, and then realized he was hearing the rush of floodwaters in the river nearby. It wasn't a reassuring thought.

Night had fallen before the crew regrouped, the horses rounded up and a tally taken. Most of the horses that had survived the storm sported knots on withers, backs, and hips from the impact of hailstones. Willoughby suspected they'd be riding sore-backed mounts for several days to come.

Dave helped Granny cover Brubs Junior's battered remains in a shallow, muddy grave. The blasting nanny sniffed at the low mound and looked at Granny as if asking, "Why?" Granny stroked the nanny's neck in sympathy and reassurance — and, Willoughby suspected, a feeling of mutual loss. He strode to where Brubs was finishing up a preliminary tally.

"Well, it weren't so bad," Brubs said. "We lost eight ponies dead or crippled, ten more missin'. We'll find 'em come daylight if they ain't strayed too far." He turned to Cal Hooper. "Watch the horses awhile, son. One of us'll spell you directly so's you can eat. If we got anything to eat." He sighed. "Sort of hate to go face Granny. I'm feared she might be just somewhat cranky now."

She was.

Brubs tried his best to reassure her as Granny ranted that she didn't have enough stuff left now to feed a field mouse let alone the hollow-legged chow hounds in this crew. "I can maybe fix somethin', but it ain't gonna be no uptown hotel fare like you whelps is used to," she fumed.

Brubs patted her gently on the shoulder. "Don't fret it none, Granny," he said. "It weren't like it was somebody's fault. We'll just ration out what we got left till we hit that sheepherder tradin' post across the river. Tell you what — let's all have us a good, stiff shot of whiskey. That'll set the world right again."

"Don't know where you're gonna get it," Granny grumped. "Damn hailstones busted ever' last bottle they was."

Brubs grimaced and moaned aloud. "Now that," he said woefully, "is the saddest thing I heard since the hogs et little Jimmy Smithers back in Nacogdoches. Made them hogs sick, too. I tell you, it makes a growed man want to just break down and bawl." He sighed in resignation. "All right, children, let's see what we can do with this here wagon and get us some supper and a bit of rest. Tomorrow's shapin' up to be a tad on the busy side."

Willoughby jerked erect in the saddle and stared

in disbelief at Brubs McCallan.

"You want me to *what?*"

"Now, don't go gettin' the vapors on me, Dave. Crossin' a little ol' creek like that ain't gonna be no problem."

Willoughby turned to stare at the rain-swollen river. The Canadian was nearly a hundred yards wide. Driftwood logs, broken stumps, and whole trees rode the waves of reddish brown water tumbling downstream. "A little ol' creek? What in the blue-eyed hell would you call a flood?"

Brubs shrugged. "Somebody's gotta go across first, and you got the best river horse. Ol' Choctaw's maybe a little tired from that set-to yesterday, but he's the best we got."

"So we'll trade horses. *You* cross that raging sea. I am not Moses. I cannot part the waters." He thought he saw a smile touch Tige Tilghman's lips. Willoughby didn't see one damn thing funny about the whole situation. "Brubs, you know I can't swim. You know how I feel about high water and flooded rivers."

Brubs nodded solemnly. "Yes, sir, partner, I know that. And I just want you to know it takes one pure genuine Texan to ride straight up to his own booger bears and spit right in their eyes."

"A real genuine Texan," Willoughby snarled, "would have more sense than to throw himself to a sure and certain death. Why the hell don't we just wait until the water goes down?"

"Can't, Dave. Ain't got the time."

Willoughby's eyes narrowed. "So what's the rush?"

"One thing, we ain't got nothin' much to eat till we get to that Mex tradin' post. Another thing's that we done lost a bit of time already, and we gotta get these ponies to Dodge 'fore them trail herds from Texas get there. Last thing's that while you boys was ridin' along admirin' your shadows yesterday 'fore that storm hit, I rode a far piece on scout. Cut some Injun sign not more'n fifteen, twenty miles back. Kioway, most likely. Sign said they was maybe forty, fifty of 'em. I'd just as soon not hang around long enough they might find out where we're at, it's all the same to you."

The icy fist clamped tighter on Willoughby's belly.

"Don't you fret none, Dave," Brubs said. "Ain't nothin' goin' wrong, you do like I tell you. And if it did, why, you knew me and the boys'd ride our butts off tryin' to find your leftovers. We'd even say a few nice words over 'em, too."

Willoughby moaned aloud. "It never ceases to amaze me how you can bring so much comfort to a man, partner."

"Glad to," Brubs said. "Now, shuck out of them clothes."

"*What?* Strip in front of a *woman?*"

Granny Hooper spat. "Don't go gettin' all red-faced on my account, son," she said. "Your butt's too skinny to be of no never mind to me."

Tilghman chuckled aloud. Willoughby pinned

207

the big man with a hard stare, then dismounted, turned his back, and started unbuttoning his shirt. "When and if I survive this latest attempt on my life, Brubs," he said over his shoulder, "I am going to pound you into small, bloody pieces with my own bare hands."

"That's my partner," Brubs said brightly. "Sure do admire to see a man with spunk."

Fifteen minutes later Willoughby stood in his underdrawers beside Choctaw as Brubs tied the end of a thick coil of spliced lariats to the saddle horn. Willoughby's clothing and weapons were wrapped in waterproof oilskin and tied to a corner brace inside the wagon bed.

"Reckon you're all set, partner," Brubs said. "Remember what I told you, now. When old Choctaw starts swimmin', you just slip out of the saddle, grab his tail, and let 'im pull you across. Wouldn't hurt to have a hand on that there rope, neither, just in case. We'll feed the rest of the rope out to you."

"I am delighted to hear that you would take such a risk, Brubs," Willoughby said. "I certainly hope you don't suffer a rope burn in the process."

Brubs snorted. "Don't you fret none about us. Now, old Choctaw's gonna be took downstream some by the current. When you get to the other side, ride back up to that big tree yonder." He pointed toward a massive cottonwood a few feet above waterline. "Pull these here ropes across. We done got the heavy ropes tied on to 'em. Take a couple dallies of them thick ropes —"

208

"They're called hawsers," Willoughby interrupted, "and I'm going to use one to hang you with when this is over."

"And we'll let the wagon just sorta swing out and drift across to the other bank. Won't be nothin' to it."

Willoughby stood for a moment, staring at the roiling waters, trying to swallow the bile in the back of his throat and fight off the big hand squeezing his chest.

"Don't fret, amigo. We'll be here watchin' you close."

Willoughby glared at him. "Your moral support is beyond measure, Brubs. *'Suave, mari magno turbantibus aequora ventis, e terra magnum alterius spectare laborem; non quia vexari quemquamst iucunda voluptas, sed quibus ipse malis careas quia cernere suave est.'*"

"That's some mouthful of foreign lingo. That Horace feller again?"

"Lucretius. He wrote, 'Lovely it is, when the winds are churning up the waves on the great sea, to gaze out from the land on the great efforts of someone else; not because it's an enjoyable pleasure that somebody is in difficulties, but because it's lovely to realize what troubles you are yourself spared.' I think Lucretius must have ridden with a McCallan back before the time of Christ."

Brubs scratched his head. "Reckon he coulda. Don't know who my folks was back when I was borned, let alone that far back. But he sounds like a right smart feller."

Willoughby swung into the saddle, steeled himself, and stared at Brubs for a couple of heartbeats. "Yes, I suppose he does sound like a right smart feller. I obviously was mistaken in my reference to your genealogy." He touched bare heels to Choctaw's ribs and left Brubs standing with a puzzled expression on his face.

Choctaw skidded down the last three feet of mud bank, lowered his head and sniffed at the river. "Lord, it's been a long time since we talked," Willoughby muttered aloud, "but if you're not too busy at the moment —" The whispered prayer ended in a startled squawk as Choctaw leapt into the swirling red torrent.

ELEVEN

The big roan was swimming an instant after hitting the water. Dave clung to the saddle horn, transfixed in raw terror, for a few heart-pounding seconds before he remembered he was supposed to slide from the saddle.

The swirling rush of water tried to yank Willoughby from Choctaw's side as he slid from the slick saddle leather. He fought the current, keeping a firm grip on the tied-fast lariat with his right hand as he grabbed frantically for Choctaw's tail with his left. His fingers finally closed on the coarse hairs, and he hung on for dear life.

The whole scene seemed unreal to Willoughby. The far bank seemed to be speeding past from right to left; there was no sensation of movement behind the powerful rump muscles of the horse. He fought back a wave of dizziness and nausea, finally realizing that Choctaw was being carried downstream by the stiff current and that the solid ground so far away was not moving of its own accord.

They were halfway across when Willoughby heard a muted shout over the rumble of water. He glanced upstream. His heart leapt into his throat as a heavy log spun toward him, whirling in the raging waters. The log slammed into Choctaw's shoulder. The horse lost his rhythm and went under. A curtain of thick, choking red fell over Willoughby's face. He tried to raise his head above the water and panicked when he realized he did not know which direction was up. He fought against the powerful impulse to gasp air into tortured lungs, but still took in a mouthful of red, muddy water and came up spitting and choking as the big roan regained his swimming stride and popped back to the surface.

The rest of the ride was a blur in Willoughby's brain. After an eternity he felt something scratch at his belly. A stone scraped against his kneecap. The sense of movement stopped. He lay for a moment, confused and terrified, before it dawned on him that there was solid ground beneath him. He felt like hugging the muddy earth. If he had the strength.

Choctaw stood calmly, sides heaving for air, muddy water cascading from the roan hide. The horse shook himself, slinging water. The spray of Canadian water jarred Willoughby back to reality. He hauled himself to his feet by pulling against Choctaw's tail, leaned against the horse's rump, and retched violently. The spasms continued until nothing more came up, then gradually subsided. Willoughby slowly became aware of shouts from the far bank of the river, and of the heavy wet ropes dragging in the current behind him. He had to try twice before he could force his buckling knees to steady enough to mount. He shivered violently as he kneed

Choctaw up the bank toward the big tree.

Willoughby lost track of time, but suddenly Choctaw stopped. He was surprised to realize the horse had pulled up at the side of the tree, as if he knew what Willoughby was supposed to do. He began to wonder if Choctaw understood English. Willoughby reined the big roan around the tree to wrap the soggy rope around the thick trunk, then urged the horse to pull.

Choctaw leaned into the job. The ropes hissed as they dragged free of the red, rolling waters. Finally, the end of the heavy hawser line heaved into sight. Willoughby dismounted, strained to tie off the hawser line, and sank to his knees.

He heard the whoops and shouts in the distance and raised his head after a moment. The wagon, its tongue tied securely back over the seat, Granny Hooper clinging to a sideboard and two goats' heads poking over the edge, slid into the water. The wagon caught the current, lurched, and began to swing in a half circle toward the near shore, bucking under the powerful water flow.

Willoughby's breath caught as the wagon hit a submerged object and canted high. One of the goats tumbled over the side, legs flailing. The goat immediately sank beneath the churning waters. For an instant, it looked like the wagon would capsize; then it settled back down onto the water with an audible plop. Waves slapped against the wagon bed, sending spray high into the air and sloshing water over the sideboards. The wagon finally jolted to a stop against the muddy bank downstream. Willoughby kneed Choctaw toward the wagon at a run.

Granny Hooper sat wide-eyed in the wagon bed, her face the color of chalk, white knuckles still clamped firmly on wood, and stared at the water rustling against sideboards.

"Granny," Willoughby called, "are you hurt? Are you all right?"

Granny slowly raised her gaze. "I reckon." Her shoulders trembled and her voice quavered. "I ain't never been so bone-deep scared in my whole days —" She glanced around, the fear glaze beginning to fade from her eyes. "Where's . . . where's my goat?"

"Sorry, Granny," Willoughby said. "She was thrown from the wagon. I saw her go under, but she never came up."

Granny muttered a bitter oath, a quick grimace flashing across her face. Then she squared her shoulders and glared at him. "Don't just sit there, dammit! Help me outta this thing before it busts loose and heads downriver."

Willoughby slogged through the mud, wrapped an arm around Granny's thick waist as she stepped onto the hub of a wheel, and eased her to the ground. He heard her heavy sigh of relief as she sagged against him.

"Son, do me a favor?"

"Anything you want, Granny."

"Don't tell that sawed-off little runt of a hoss thief McCallan that I done peed in my pants?"

"Your secret is safe with me, Granny," he told

her solemnly. "Now, if you'll excuse me, I think I'd better get some clothes on. It's a bit drafty out here."

The sun was nearing its midway point as Willoughby leaned back against the trunk of a cottonwood, exhausted and still shivering. He couldn't seem to push the sensation of sinking into the muddy red waters from his mind.

"You okay, partner?" Brubs asked as he walked up.

"No," Willoughby said tightly, "I am not okay. And the next time you decide to drown me, why don't you just tie a couple of big rocks to my feet and throw me in a deep pool somewhere?"

Brubs grinned. "Why, Dave, you done real good out there. I told you it'd all work out, didn't I?"

"When and if I get my strength back, I am going to whip your butt."

Brubs chuckled aloud. "Now I know you're all right. I tell you, I never seen a high water crossin' go that smooth."

"Smooth! You call *that* smooth?" Willoughby snorted grains of red sand from his nostrils. "I hope to high heaven I'm never involved in a *difficult* one."

"Easy as fallin' off a bar stool," Brubs said. "We got the wagon up on high ground without bustin' so much as a single wheel spoke. Got the ponies across, didn't get but four of 'em drowned, and two of them wasn't even good horses at that.

Course, Granny's some put out over losin' another goat, but she'll get over it." He paused for a breath, then clapped Willoughby on the shoulder. "Partner, you're gettin' plumb good at these river crossin's. Might come in handy a ways north."

Willoughby glared at him. "What the hell do you mean 'might come in handy'?"

"We still got the Cimarron to cross." Brubs's tone turned solemn. "That's one bitch of a river, the Cimarron. Makes this old Canadian look like a harmless little dry creek."

Willoughby's shoulders sagged. "Thank you very much for sharing that information. You are truly a comfort."

"Pleases me to put your mind at ease, Brother Dave," Brubs said. "Let's get mounted up. We'll stop off a spell at that Mex tradin' post and restock, then point 'em toward Skull Creek. Why, we're damn near in Dodge already."

Brubs sat cross-legged, leaned back against his saddle, and watched as the other crew members finished their evening meal.

So far, so good, he thought. They hadn't lost as many horses on the drive as he had expected. The Mexican trading post hadn't exactly been chock-full of the finest groceries, but the wagon now held enough supplies to see them through to Dodge. He still wished the old Mexican storekeeper had stocked some decent whiskey. One bottle of tequila and a quart of pulque wasn't going to smooth out many days on the trail. Brubs didn't like pulque much, anyway.

At least the old Mex had plenty of chewing tobacco. Granny'd be happy the rest of the way, or at least as happy as she ever got. Brubs downed the last of his coffee, stood, and stretched. "Well, folks," he said, "won't be much longer and we'll be livin' the good life in Dodge. By my reckonin', we ought to be across the Cimarron and hit Skull Creek in five, six days. From there it ain't but a hundred and fifty more miles — and easy ones at that — to Dodge."

Tige Tilghman scrubbed a hand over the stubble of his cheek. "Been meanin' to talk to you about Skull Creek, Brubs," he said. "Got to talkin' to a vaquero down at that Mex tradin' post. He says word's out that Dutch Henry Oshman's done took over that part of the country. Vaquero says Dutch Henry's usin' Skull Creek as a permanent hideout now."

Willoughby saw Brubs stiffen. The stocky Texan's face darkened. "Who's Dutch Henry Oshman?" Willoughby asked.

Tilghman scowled. "Bad hombre. Leads a bunch of thieves, misfits, and outlaws who'd cut their own mothers' throats for five dollars. Pure poison, that bunch. Dutch Henry hisself has killed at least twenty men, most likely more. And half a dozen women, too, accordin' to the yarns I've heard."

"Brubs," Willoughby said, "why don't we just go around Skull Creek? This many horses makes a highly visible and tempting target to such men."

Brubs shook his head. "Only good water and decent grass 'tween here and Dodge is along that Skull Creek range," he said. "We *got* to go that way, Dutch Henry or no Dutch Henry." He shrugged. "Most likely, won't nothin' come of it nohow. Could be Oshman's bunch is out robbin' another bank or silver mine in Colorado."

Tilghman nodded, but the big man didn't look reassured. "Maybe so. Even if they ain't, it's a big country out here. Might not see a livin' soul for hundreds of miles."

"That's a pure enough fact, Tige," Brubs said. "Why, back in the war, two whole armies marched alongside not more'n a mile apart and neither seen the other. Besides, we got us a patron saint. Ain't nothin' gonna happen."

Willoughby sighed. "I wish you hadn't said that, Brubs. It conjures up thoughts of distant drums."

"What drums? Ain't no Injun powwows around."

"Never mind."

Dave squatted at the base of a lightning-scarred oak tree and listened to the wind moan through the charred branches overhead. It wasn't a reassuring sound.

Skull Creek was a downright spooky place.

Maybe it was only the way the wind blew down the canyon. Or the way the sunlight played shadow tricks on a man's eyes, causing him to see things move that weren't really there. Willoughby

218

was sure about one thing. There was something about this place that made his skin crawl. He would be glad to leave it behind in a few days after the horses had fleshed out for the week-long drive to Dodge.

It should have been a restful, peaceful camp. Skull Creek's waters were spring-fed and sweet, with no traces of the gypsum or salt that had tainted so many watering holes on the long drive north. The creek wandered through the Cimarron Strip breaks, nestled in a winding canyon that twisted and turned several times before ducking abruptly south to the Cimarron River itself. The grass in the canyon floor was tall, green, rich, and abundant enough to provide fodder for twice the number of horses they drove. They would follow the creek and canyon until it switched back toward the Cimarron. Then they would point the remuda northeast to Dodge.

And maybe this time, Willoughby thought, Brubs would be right. There had been no sign of other living beings for miles. In particular, no Dutch Henry Oshman. Willoughby could only hope it stayed that way.

Even the trail north from the Texas border had gone well. The Cimarron crossing had been a picnic compared to the raging waters of the flooded Canadian. The Cimarron wasn't even deep enough to float the wagon, which had bogged only twice. The quicksand had snatched at three horses, but the crew managed to pull them free before they were lost or crippled. An easy crossing, even by Willoughby's river-shy standards.

After the Cimarron, the drive settled into a welcome routine of near boredom. The trail-wise horses gave them no trouble. Even the tall clouds that billowed up in the west on occasion seemed benign, bringing rain to replenish water holes and nourish the rapid growth of grass along the Strip, but no fury of thunder and lightning to spook the remuda.

Willoughby even thought he might have put on a pound or two himself as the horses fattened up. Granny made fine corn bread, a concoction he had grown fond of since first tasting it during the war. The greens and wild onions she gathered at seeps and watering holes along the way added variety to the camp diet. There was no shortage of meat. Cal Hooper's deadly accuracy with his .38-40 and the little .22 camp gun kept them well supplied with venison, wild turkey, sage hens, rabbits, and quail from the abundant game along the Cimarron Valley.

Willoughby glanced up at the sound of approaching footsteps. Nick Chadburne strode to the tree and squatted beside him. Chadburne sported a welt on his neck, the legacy of his latest raid on a honey tree. Willoughby wondered how the dark, somber youth could spot a bee tree, climb up through a smoke cloud, and swipe the honeycombs without getting swarmed. Chadburne seldom even got stung. And the honey was a welcome addition to a diet short on sweets.

Chadburne picked up a jagged stick and poked idly at the ground for a moment.

"Something on your mind, Nick?"

"You won't laugh at me?"

"I try never to laugh at a man unless he's telling a joke," Willoughby said solemnly.

"It's . . . this place," Chadburne said. "It's kind of scary, somehow."

"I was thinking the same thing, Nick. It's almost as if there was someone watching. But when you look around, there's no one there."

Chadburne fiddled with the stick for a moment. "Mr. Willoughby, do you believe in ghosts?"

Dave pondered the question for a moment, then shrugged. "I don't know. Maybe there is something left behind when a person dies. The Plains Indians are strong believers in spirits. Presbyterians aren't. I'm not sure who's right. It's something that's been debated in religion and philosophy since ancient times, and the question still hasn't been resolved."

Chadburne sighed. "I reckon that's because only the dead people know, and they can't tell us." He fell silent for a moment, staring toward the ribbon of water that whispered past a few feet away. "Mr. Willoughby?"

"Yes?"

"What's it like, being smart like you? I mean, reading and writing and ciphering and all?" Chadburne kept his gaze downcast, as if the question embarrassed him.

221

"I don't think I'm exactly an authority on smartness," Willoughby said with a wry smile, "considering the messes I've gotten myself into over the last couple of years. But as to the reading part, it opened up whole new worlds for me, Nick. A man can go places in books, through his mind, that he could never see firsthand."

Chadburne sighed again. "I wish . . ." His voice trailed away.

"Wish what?"

"That I wasn't too dumb to learn books and things."

The statement jolted Willoughby a bit. "You're not dumb, Nick. Where in the world did you get that idea?"

"My uncle told me. Lots of times. He said there wasn't any use wasting time and money sending a dumb kid like me to school."

Willoughby nodded. "I see. And you believed him?"

"Yes, sir."

"Was your uncle a smart man?"

"No, sir."

"Did he ever lie to you?"

"Yes, sir. Lots."

"Then why should you believe him when he said you were dumb?"

Chadburne's brow furrowed for a moment. "I never thought on it that way."

Willoughby put a hand on the youth's forearm. "Nick, the only truly dumb man is the man who doesn't want to look inside himself and see the truth. Do you want to learn to read and write?"

"Yes, sir. If it isn't too late."

Willoughby dropped his hand away. "It's never too late. I can teach you."

"I wasn't talking about age, Mr. Willoughby," Chadburne said softly. "I was talking about if they're going to hang me, maybe it's too late to start now."

"Hang?" Willoughby paused, momentarily puzzled, then shrugged. "Oh. I'd forgotten about the warrant. You said back on the Pecos that you didn't kill your uncle. Is that the truth?"

"Yes, sir. I swear it. But maybe the law doesn't care, as long as they have somebody to hang."

"Give the law some credit," Willoughby said in reassurance. "They don't want to hang an innocent man. I know Tobin Jamison well enough to know that he won't quit until he finds out the truth. Nick, I didn't bring any books on this drive, but we can get started on some basics of reading and writing whenever you want."

"Is it hard?"

"Yes. It can be, at times. And it can be frustrating. But if you're willing to put out the effort, Nick, it's worth it many times over. It's something nobody can take away from you."

Chadburne frowned again. "What if I can't do it?"

"Brubs McCallan did. Sort of. And he wasn't even that much interested in learning."

"Then I suppose I could do it. But what if somebody laughs at me?"

223

"Then you do one of two things, Nick. Ignore them or punch out their front teeth." Willoughby extended a hand. "Game to give it a try?"

Chadburne took the hand. "Yes, sir, I sure am." He released Willoughby's hand. "I'll work hard." His solemn eyes suddenly took on a twinkle. "You know, Mr. Willoughby, this is just the second time in my life I've ever done something I *really* wanted to do."

"What was the first time?"

"Giving my uncle the whipping he deserved and riding the hell away from that farm." Chadburne strode away toward the wagon. It looked to Willoughby like the young man had a fresh spring in his steps.

Willoughby leaned back against the tree, feeling a warm glow of inner satisfaction that he hadn't experienced in some time.

The sensation didn't last.

Sunlight glinted from something in the shallow trench Chadburne had been idly digging. Willoughby leaned forward, levered the object from the loose soil, and then dropped it like a hot rock.

It was a human jawbone.

Willoughby was still trying to shake the crawly feeling when Brubs McCallan rode back into camp an hour before supper time.

The expression on Brubs's face didn't help Willoughby's nervousness. The Texan's normally relaxed features were drawn into a deep scowl, the twinkle missing from his brown eyes. He rode straight up to the fire where Willoughby and Tige Tilghman nursed coffee cups.

"You jackass!" Granny Hooper yelped, shaking a spoon at Brubs. "I told you to keep them damn horses away from my cook fire —"

"Shut up, Granny," Brubs snapped. "Dave, Tige — mount up. We could have a us a speck of trouble brewin'."

Granny shut up. Willoughby and Tilghman didn't stop to argue, either.

They had ridden a hundred yards from camp before Willoughby turned to Brubs. "What's going on?"

"We got company," the Texan told him. "I cut sign on top of that hill yonder." He nodded toward a flat-topped butte overlooking Skull Creek from a half mile away. "Somebody's been watchin' us. I cut the tracks at the bottom of the hill, follered 'em up."

Tilghman glanced at Brubs. "Injun or white man?"

"White man. This jasper was ridin' a shod horse. There was four cigarette butts lyin' up there, like he'd been watchin' quite a spell."

"What do you make of it, Brubs?"

"I ain't sure yet," the Texan said, his voice tight, "but I reckon a man watchin' a camp in a canyon full of horses in the Skull Creek country ain't likely lookin' for a friendly poker game."

Tilghman mouthed a soft curse. "Dutch Henry?"

"Could be." Brubs spat. "That's what we're

fixin' to find out, Tige. I follered them tracks a mile or so. Seen smoke back where Skull Creek Canyon turns north. I figgered we better have us a look-see."

The trio rode in silence for almost two miles past the butte before Brubs raised a hand. "Right up ahead's where I seen the smoke. Maybe a quarter mile." He glanced at the lowering sun. "Be sundown soon. Little after that, I reckon we'll pay a little visit on whoever's at that camp."

Willoughby's heart skipped a beat. "Brubs, we can't just ride in. If that's Oshman's gang, they'd shoot us on sight."

"You got that right, partner. That's why we ain't ridin' in just yet." Brubs glanced around, then reined his sorrel toward a rugged dry wash almost obscured by a thick stand of stunted cedar trees. "This'll do," he said as he dismounted. "We'll leave the ponies here. Dave, you watch 'em while Tige and me scouts out that camp. This here's a job for sneak —"

"I know, I know," Willoughby interrupted. "And infantry sneaks better than artillery."

"You're learnin', son," Brubs said casually, "but you artillery boys can't hold a candle to Tige and me when it comes to snuckin'." He shucked the Henry from his rifle boot, fished in a saddlebag for a spare box of ammunition, and dropped the box into a shirt pocket. "You hear shootin', Dave, don't come lookin' for us, on account it wouldn't do none of us no good. Get your butt in the saddle. Go tell Granny and the boys to forget the horses and run like hell."

"Just like that? Ride off and leave you two to face Dutch Henry's bunch alone?"

Brubs cast a wry glance at Willoughby. "Just like that. Hell, partner, you Yankees can't shoot for sour apples nohow. Wouldn't be no more help than a badger at a barn raisin'. You ready, Tige?"

Tilghman stuffed a handful of cartridges into a pocket, checked the action of the Sharps, and nodded. "Reckon so." The big man's voice was calm and cool, his hands steady. If he felt any fear or nervousness, Willoughby thought, Tige hid it well.

"One more thing, Dave," Brubs said. "Don't go gettin' spooked on us. Sure would hate to get hit by a bullet bouncin' off a rock when we're comin' back in."

"I don't have to get spooked," Willoughby said. "I'm already there."

Brubs flashed a grin. Willoughby thought it seemed a bit forced. "Aw, hell, partner. Ain't nothin' to it. Tige and me done this many a time." He glanced at the sky. "We ought to be back in a couple hours, maybe three. Let's move out, Tige."

Willoughby watched the two men stride silently into the growing twilight. He cradled his Winchester in his arms and strained his ears for any strange sounds. Only the gentle sigh of a soft breeze through the junipers and the distant hoot of an awakening owl disturbed the clear spring air. The knot in Willoughby's gut got tighter as the night got blacker and quieter. And longer.

"Dave?"

Brubs's soft call from the mouth of the wash jolted Willoughby. He started, then slowly relaxed and lowered his rifle. "Over here."

Brubs strode into view. "Like I figgered," he said. "Dutch Henry, all right. Got close enough for a good look by the light of their camp fire. Couldn't be nobody else fit that big, ugly, red-headed bastard's description."

Willoughby glanced around. "Where's Tige?"

"Be along directly. Scouted a tad further'n I did. We'll have us a little war parley when Tige gets back."

Tilghman appeared a few minutes later, giving Willoughby another start. One minute the big man wasn't there, the next minute he was. Willoughby hadn't heard a sound. Brubs and Tilghman squatted beside him.

"I made it eighteen men," Brubs said. "That tally with your count?"

"Nineteen. Eighteen in camp, cleanin' rifles and passin' a jug around. One man ridin' night watch on the cavvy a ways north of camp. No pickets out. You read 'em the same way I did?"

"Yeah. Way they was actin', I'd say they was plannin' to hit us come daylight." Brubs fell silent for a moment, thinking.

"So what do we do now?" Willoughby finally asked.

Brubs glanced up. "When you know a man's gonna slug you, the best chance you got is to throw a sneak punch and whop him first. Hard. That the way you see it, Tige?"

Tilghman grunted in agreement. "We don't grab him by the *cojones,* he grabs us by ours."

"Brubs," Willoughby said incredulously, "you aren't planning a preemptive strike, are you? Against those odds?"

"If that's what you officer boys call it. You got a better idea?"

Willoughby didn't.

"Now that's settled, let's do us some figgerin'," Brubs said. "I been thinkin' we might even could turn a profit on this deal. Tige, how many ponies we lost since we started?"

Tilghman shrugged. "Forty-one head by my count."

"Ol' Dutch Henry's got about thirty down there."

Willoughby lifted a hand. "Wait a minute! You aren't thinking about *stealing* that outlaw's horses?"

"Why not?" Brubs snorted in disgust. "It just plumb frosts my drawers that damn Dutch Henry'd even think about stealin' our horses, after we busted our butts to get 'em. I tell you, I just can't abide no dishonest horse thief."

Dave finally managed to close his mouth. "Brubs, tell me you aren't serious."

"I ain't never been seriouser."

Willoughby shook his head in dismay. "I should have stayed in that San Antonio jail," he said.

"Partner," Brubs said, "sometimes I just can't figger you, gettin' all fretted up like some ol' mama duck. Why, there won't be nothin' to it. Now, here's what we're gonna do. Tige, you know that rocky point where Skull Creek makes that bend from due west back north, about a mile this side of our camp?"

Tilghman nodded.

"You ride on back. Throw our remuda in one of them side draws off the canyon so's maybe they won't stampede too bad when the shootin' gets close. Then take that Sharps and climb up on that rocky point. That'll give you three, four hundred yards of good shootin' when them fellers take after Dave and me."

"When they *what?*"

"Hush up, Dave. I'm thinkin' here. Tige, put Nick Chadburne on the rim across from you. He's a fair enough hand with a rifle. Get Granny and her goose gun settled down in the wagon bed. Cal's our second best long gun man next to you. Station him in them trees close by the wagon. That'll put Dutch Henry in a cross fire."

"Sounds good to me," Tilghman said.

"Dave and me'll hit 'em soon's it gets light enough to see," Brubs said. "We'll run their cavvy smack-dab over 'em and back toward our camp. Time them jaspers get woke up, we'll be long gone. Oh, yeah. Tell Granny and the boys not to shoot Dave and me when we come runnin' in."

Tilghman nodded, mounted, and rode away at a leisurely trot.

"Brubs," Willoughby said, "you haven't explained this 'Dave and me' thing yet."

"Well, partner, I been feelin' mighty bad about leavin' you out of all the fun so much of the time."

"Fun." Willoughby's shoulders slumped. "Riding into an armed camp of twenty hardcase gunmen —"

"Just nineteen."

"— Is a damn strange definition of fun."

"Dave, I ain't lettin' you come along just as a favor," Brubs said solemnly. "You done got to be a first-class hoss thief, and I do somewhat admire a man works so hard at improvin' his talents. We're partners. And I got to tell you, there ain't a man livin' I'd rather have ridin' with me, times like these —"

"Thanks a hell of a lot for the vote of confidence."

"— And besides, can't neither of us shoot for squat. That won't matter much in the dark, 'cause if anybody hits anything thataway it's a pure accident. We'll need the best guns we got coverin' us when ol' Dutch Henry squalls like a painter and comes runnin' after us."

Willoughby sighed heavily. "You are a pure comfort to a man, Brubs. A pure comfort."

"Just tryin' to make sure you ain't fretted over nothin', partner," the Texan said. "Now, we best get mounted up. We got to get in position a good two hours before first light."

TWELVE

Brubs McCallan knelt behind a rockfall and squinted through the ghostly gray predawn light at the outlaw camp two hundred yards away.

Most of Dutch Henry Oshman's gang were still in their bedrolls. One man rose, stretched, knelt beside the circle of stones at the cook fire site, and struck a match. The nighthawk guarding the horses reined his mount toward the fire, his mind on his morning coffee more than the remuda. A dozen horses stood at a picket line a few yards from the fire.

"Well, partner," Brubs whispered, "looks like it's time we went to work. We ain't gonna get no better shot at 'em than right new. You all set?"

Willoughby, holding the reins of his coyote dun and Brubs's gray mustang, nodded silently. Brubs reached for the reins. "Dave, you don't look so good," he said softly. "Touch green in the gills. You spooked?"

"No, I'm not spooked," Willoughby whispered back, "I'm terrified."

"Got a little case of the crawlies myself, amigo," Brubs admitted. He didn't add that all at once his bladder felt like it needed to be emptied. He knew it didn't. It was just the brain's way of using the body to put off doing something the brain didn't want to do. "Mount up. Day's half gone and we ain't hit a lick of work yet."

Brubs winced at the creak of saddle leather and clink of curb chains and spur rowels as the two mounted. He pulled his revolver; Willoughby did the same. This would be handgun work. Rifles were all but useless in close quarters on horseback in dim light.

"Always wanted to lead a cavalry charge," Brubs said. "Troops ready?"

"Present and accounted for. And wishing otherwise," Willoughby said.

Brubs pulled his hat down, cocked the Colt, and glanced at Willoughby. "Charge, men," he said. He drove the spurs to the gray mustang. Mouse was in a dead run after two strides, Willoughby's coyote dun alongside. Brubs loosed a Rebel yell and fired into the air.

The outlaw remuda whirled in panic and stampeded toward the camp. Over the thunder of hooves and squeals of horses, Brubs heard startled squawks and shouts from the outlaws. A muzzle flash winked in the near distance; a split second later Brubs heard the buzz of a lead slug overhead. Willoughby's handgun barked twice. The scene blurred as dust thrown up from the stampeding horses all but blacked out the weak predawn light. The horses charged into the camp. Two men trying to scramble from their blankets went down under the slashing hooves.

Brubs slapped a quick, unaimed shot toward a man scrambling toward the picket line. The man staggered and fell. Yelps of surprise and pain sounded through the dense fog of dust. Something tugged at Brubs's sleeve as the flat bark of a handgun sounded. Then the horses were beyond the camp, thundering down the narrow valley toward Skull Creek.

Brubs flinched as a slug whined past his ear. He twisted in the saddle. Dutch Henry stood at the edge of the camp, barely recognizable through the cloud of dust and smoke, legs spread wide, rifle in hand. Brubs snapped a shot, missed, and mouthed a curse. Willoughby's Colt thumped twice. The big outlaw leapt aside and disappeared from view in the dust cloud. Brubs straightened in the saddle and concentrated on the run.

He could barely see the terrain before him, blinded by choking dust, putting his trust in the surefooted little gray mustang. He heard the ping of lead against stone and the whine as the slug ricocheted. He caught a quick glimpse of Willoughby through a hole in the dust cloud, riding hard, leaning low over the coyote dun's neck.

After a mile the stampede began to slow as the run took its toll on the horses. Brubs glanced back and saw dim shapes in the distance. Some of the outlaws had reached picketed mounts. They were gaining ground now but were still beyond effective rifle range. The elbow bend in the valley was less than two hundred yards ahead.

Brubs kneed Mouse closer to Willoughby's dun and whooped. "We done it, partner!" he yelled. "They're ridin' right into the trap! We got 'em right where we want 'em!"

Willoughby twisted in the saddle and glanced back toward the pursuers. "Question is who's got who!" he yelled. "They're gaining fast! I'll slow them down! Keep riding!" He abruptly reined the dun toward a rockfall at the base of the canyon wall.

"Dave! What the hell — ?"

Willoughby ignored Brubs's yell. Brubs started to rein after him, but the buzz of a rifle ball past his ear told him it was too late; the gray mustang was already twenty yards past the rockfall.

Brubs heard the distinctive crack of Willoughby's .44-40 as the first of the stolen horses made the turn around the bend of the creek. He glanced back. An outlaw's horse went down and rolled over the rider. A volley of rifle fire from the pursuing riders echoed down the narrow valley. Rock chips and dirt flew as a storm of lead slapped against Willoughby's hiding place. The pursuit slowed for a moment. No more shots came from the rocks where Willoughby had taken cover.

Brubs swallowed against the surge of bile in his throat. "Damn fool Yankee," he muttered. He fumbled his Colt back into his holster and pulled his Henry as Mouse raced into the sharp elbow of the valley.

Brubs heard the thunderous blast of Tige Tilghman's Sharps Fifty and the sharper cracks of Nick Chadburne's Winchester moments later. The winded outlaw remuda slowed rapidly, then veered away from the wagon in the Skull Creek camp. Brubs saw the barrels of Granny Hooper's ten-bore protruding over the front of the wagon. He yanked Mouse to a stop twenty yards beyond the wagon, bailed off behind a juniper tree, and squinted over the sights of the Henry.

Several men raced toward the wagon, Dutch Henry himself leading the charge. Muzzle flashes sprouted from rifles and handguns. The sound of gunfire was a constant crack and rumble along Skull Creek. Three horses ran past Brubs in panic, saddles empty and stirrups flopping. The Texan drew a bead on Dutch Henry, squeezed the trigger, and barked a curse as the slug went wide. Two men behind the leader went down, one flung from the saddle by the heavy whop of a Sharps slug, the other toppled by Cal Hooper's rifle shot. Brubs frantically racked a fresh round into the Henry's chamber. The outlaws were almost on the wagon now. The jarring whomp of Granny Hooper's shotgun came atop the billow of gray-white powder smoke from the wagon bed. The buckshot charge slammed a stocky rider over the rump of his horse. Dutch Henry twisted in the saddle, hat and handgun flying, then toppled from his horse and thumped into the sandy creek bed. Brubs heard Granny's yell above the echoes of the gunshots: "That'll learn you, you damn thievin', rapin' sons of bitches!"

The outlaw charge broke. Brubs managed to get a slug into one rider's shoulder as the remaining bandits milled for a moment, firing wildly as they fought to control plunging horses. Brubs heard the whack of lead against flesh; Granny's goat dropped straight down in its tracks. "Damn you, Dutch Henry," Brubs muttered tightly, "Granny's gonna be some put out with you now, killin' her last goat."

The outlaws whirled their mounts and spurred away. Tilghman's Sharps slammed one rider from the saddle. Only three of the attackers were left; Cal Hooper's .38-40 put one of them down. The remainong two outlaws somehow managed to make it through the storm of lead and disappeared around the bend of the creek.

Brubs lowered his rifle. He became aware for the first time that his fingers were trembling. He stood for a moment, peering through the swirl of dust and powder smoke. He heard the distant muzzle cracks as Dave Willoughby's .44-40 barked twice. Then a sudden silence fell over Skull Creek.

Brubs's ears rang from the muzzle blasts as he stepped cautiously from behind the juniper. He counted three horses and five men down within thirty yards of the wagon. Three more outlaw bodies lay on the valley floor before it bent out of sight. Two of the downed men, one of them Dutch Henry, moaned and twisted in pain on the sandy creek bed. Brubs thumbed fresh cartridges into his rifle. He never took his eyes off Dutch Henry as he strode toward the outlaw.

He kicked Dutch Henry's handgun out of reach. The red-haired bandit lifted himself to one knee, his face pale and blue eyes glazed in shock and pain. His right shoulder was a mass of torn flesh, riddled by buckshot.

"Reckon your outlawin' days is over, Dutch," Brubs said, his tone hard and cold. "You done tangled with the wrong bunch this time."

The veil over Dutch Henry's eyes seemed to lift for an instant. "Go . . . to hell . . . damn you."

"Most likely I will, Dutch," Brubs said, "if it ain't too crowded up with the likes of you."

"My . . . boys'll get you . . . for this."

"You got no boys left, Dutch. Them that got away's already headed for the high lonesome."

"Mr. McCallan?"

Brubs glanced up at Cal Hooper's soft call. The young man stood over a man writhing in pain, his boots scrabbling against the sand. "This one's still alive," Cal said.

"Fix that, son," Brubs said. Cal's rifle cracked. "Good," Brubs said coldly. "See if any of them others are still kickin'."

One was. Cal fixed that, too.

The Texas Horsetrading Company crew filtered back into camp, Willoughby the last to arrive. His face was almost black with dust and powder residue.

"You nail them last two, Dave?"

Willoughby nodded silently.

Cal Hooper stood beside the wagon and stared over the side board for several seconds before he turned to Brubs. Tears trickled down the freckled cheeks. "Mr. McCallan?"

Brubs's gut lurched. "What is it, son?"

"Granny. I think — she's dead."

Brubs was at the wagon bed in four quick strides. He stared at the body for a moment, unwilling to believe what he saw. Granny Hooper lay facedown in a pool of blood that still oozed from the ragged hole in the side of her neck. The goose gun lay at her side, the breech broken open. Two shotgun shells rested near her open hand. The sight ripped the heart from Brubs. The slug that hit her had been an accident, a fluke. A smudge of lead marked the point where the bullet had struck an iron corner brace, deflected downward, and ripped into her neck. She had probably died within seconds.

The hollow, empty hole in Brubs's belly slowly filled with the heat of growing rage and hurt. He turned from the wagon, unashamed of the tears that spilled down his cheeks. "She's dead, boys," he said solemnly.

Brubs strode to Dutch Henry, who was still hunched over, cradling his shattered shoulder and moaning in agony. "Damn your soul, Dutch," Brubs said, his voice tight with barely controlled rage. "Ever' man in this crew loved that old woman. You're gonna pay for that."

The outlaw raised pain-glazed eyes. "Then . . . go ahead. Shoot me . . . get it . . . over with."

Brubs shook his head. "You ain't gettin' out of it that easy, Dutch. Tige, tie this son of a bitch to that tree over there. He'll keep till we bury Granny."

Fear flashed in Dutch Henry's eyes. "What . . .

239

what you gonna do?"

"You'll know quick enough, Dutch." Brubs turned away as Tilghman went to work with a rope. "Cal, stay with Granny. Keep the blowflies off her. Tige, see can you dig a decent grave. Nick, you and Dave come with me. We got a cavvy to gather."

The sun was past its midway point before the immediate work at hand was done. Twenty-four of Dutch Henry's horses were now in the Texas Horsetrading Company's remuda. Brubs had counted eleven dead outlaws along the Skull Creek battlefield. He found two wounded men. There were now thirteen dead bandits.

Tilghman had Granny's grave dug above the high water line by the time Brubs rode back in, his scout completed. Dutch Henry, tightly bound to a cottonwood tree, alternately moaned in agony and shouted curses at Brubs. Chadburne finally shut him up by shoving a dirty rag in his mouth.

Brubs stood over the grave, hat in hand, as Willoughby and Tilghman gently lowered the blanket-wrapped body into the cool, sandy soil. Brubs stood in silence for a moment as the remaining crew gathered around. Then he raised his gaze to the sky.

"Lord," he said, "I ain't the one here what's good with words, but I reckon it's my job as trail boss of this outfit to say somethin'. Now, this woman here, Emeldeline Hooper, mighta been a cantankerous old bat sometimes. But she was a mighty fine woman, one of the best us boys ever met, and that counts quite a few."

He paused to catch his breath and brush the tears from his cheeks. "We all know Granny sometimes took your name in vain, Lord, but you know she didn't mean no harm by it. It was just her way of makin' her feelin's knowed." He swallowed against the lump in his throat. "Lord, you knowed her a damn sight better'n we did, I reckon, so you seen she had a good heart. We ain't gonna ask nothin' real special. Just that maybe you'll take her in, treat her for what she was and what she was worth. We reckon she'll rest mighty fine in that land of sweet water and green pastures you got up there. She was one hell of a good woman, Lord." He paused for a moment, then added, "By the way, if you got a couple extra goats up there, I reckon that'd please Granny some. Amen."

Brubs replaced his hat and nodded for Willoughby and Tilghman to start filling the grave. He turned to Cal. "Son, you know we're all hurtin', but none as bad as you. I just wish I coulda said some better words."

Cal Hooper blinked through his pain and tears. "You did just fine, Mr. McCallan. I reckon Granny was mighty pleased with what you said." He fell silent for a moment, watching the two men shovel dirt into the grave. "Mr. McCallan?"

"Yes, son?"

"What about these other dead folks? Are we going to bury them, too?"

241

Brubs snorted in disgust. "Hell, no, Cal. They ain't got no Christian burial comin'. Let the buzzards and coyotes have 'em. Critters gotta eat, too. Besides, we ain't got time to mess with 'em. We're headin' out for Dodge as soon as the boys get Granny covered up proper."

The sun was halfway down the western sky as Brubs stood beside the cottonwood tree where Dutch Henry was tied and watched the procession file past. Tilghman had the point; Cal drove the wagon; Chadburne and Willoughby rode drag behind the remuda.

Willoughby reined in and nodded toward Dutch Henry. "What are you going to do with him, Brubs?"

"You don't wanna know, partner," the Texan said, his voice tight and cold. "You all just ride on. I'll be along directly."

Willoughby looked as if he might protest, but when he saw the look in Brubs's eyes he merely nodded and moved on. Brubs waited until he figured the crew had traveled at least a mile, then stepped up to Dutch Henry. The outlaw's eyes were wide with fright and bright with pain.

"What . . . you gonna do . . . McCallan?" Dutch Henry's tone was pleading. "I'm worth money — maybe a thousand-dollar reward by now. But you got to take me in alive."

Brubs shrugged. "I ain't impressed, Dutch. I got a reward on my head, too. Twenty-five whole dollars. And for the first time in my life I ain't interested in money. You got me plumb mad. I got other plans for you."

Henry's shoulders slumped. "All right. If you're gonna kill me, do it now. Get it over with."

"No need to get in such a hurry, Dutch," Brubs said. "I said you wasn't gettin' out easy." He pulled his revolver.

Dutch Henry screamed a split second before Brubs pulled the trigger. The scream built into a thin, high screech as the slug slammed into the instep of his right foot. It ended in a whimper when another round shattered his left ankle. Dutch Henry's mouth was open, but no sound came out when Brubs's third shot slammed into the joint of his left shoulder.

Brubs ejected the empties and calmly reloaded. "Have yourself a long time dyin', Dutch. You damn well earned it."

Dutch Henry's mouth was still open in the silent scream when Brubs mounted and reined the gray mustang after the distant remuda, threading his way past the bodies along the trail. He glanced around and sighed.

"Well, Mouse," he said to the horse, "at least now, by God, we know one reason this place's called Skull Creek." He nudged the gray into a trot. "Step on out. Dodge is awaitin'."

Dave Willoughby propped a dusty boot against the lower rail of the holding pens beside the Atchison, Topeka, & Santa Fe rail line, and flexed his right hand. It was beginning to cramp from writing out bills of sale, some legitimate,

243

some forged, depending on the horses involved.

The Texas Horsetrading Company remuda had pulled into Dodge two hours after dawn, and a sizeable crowd was waiting. Brubs had ridden ahead to spread the word, and if there was one thing the man excelled at, it was spreading words. A half dozen ranchers and horse traders were waiting when the first horse trotted into the rail yard corrals. Several curious townsfolk also were on hand. Most of them had never seen that many horses in one bunch at one time.

Brubs had been right for once, Willoughby admitted. Dodge City was horse-hungry.

A rancher from the Double Bit spread in the Walnut Creek country had bought twenty head less than fifteen minutes after the remuda's arrival. Forty more were headed east, snapped up by a horse trader headquartered in Wichita. Another fifty were on the way to Colorado. Other buyers had picked out single horses or as many as ten. It wasn't noon yet, and already the remuda was less than half the size it had been at daybreak.

Bank notes, bills, and gold coins bulged the saddlebag at Willoughby's feet. He had already used up one paper tablet writing bills of sale and receipts. It was going to be a profitable day.

Brubs was in his element, Willoughby mused. If he was a top snake oil salesman when it came to talking Willoughby into some sort of outrage that usually wound up in trouble, he was even better as a horse trader dealing with strangers. The stocky Texan gestured, grinned, grunted, slapped

244

backs, cracked jokes, and spun yarns as he pointed out the merits of specific animals to potential buyers.

Cal Hooper, Nick Chadburne, and Tige Tilghman scurried about in the dusty corral, cutting out this bay or that sorrel for Mr. So-and-so at Brubs's shouted instructions.

The sun had dropped midway down the western sky before the steady run of horse buyers slowed.

Brubs gave Hooper and Tilghman twenty dollars and told them to book four rooms at the Great Western, and fetch a bottle back to the cavvy pen. He squatted at Willoughby's side, a wide grin on his stubbled, grimy cheeks. Nick Chadburne lounged against the corral fence, his swarthy face streaked by dust and sweat.

"Well, partner," Brubs said happily, "didn't I tell you Kansas'd make rich men out of us? What's the tally up to?"

Willoughby flexed aching shoulder muscles and flipped though the smart tally book. The pages were smudged with dust and his own sweat. "A little over three thousand dollars cash, two thousand more in bank notes so far."

Brubs mouthed a silent whistle and stroked the stuffed saddlebag. "Damn, I ain't never seen that much money in my whole borned days."

Willoughby rubbed a gritty knuckle across his eyes. "Let's not be celebrating too soon," he said. "We've taken in enough to cover expenses and wages, recoup what we spent on actually purchasing horses, and refit for the trip back home. By my calculations, the partnership is now showing a profit of approximately eleven hundred dollars."

Brubs chuckled. "I'll leave the cipherin' to you, partner. That's what you're best at." He rubbed his palms together eagerly, then cuffed Willoughby playfully on the shoulder. "Boy, are we gonna have us some fun the next night or two. We'll tree this here town like it ain't never been treed before. Why, I know these two girls —"

"Brubs," Willoughby interrupted, "before you start treeing Dodge and hunting up these two girls, we still have a hundred or so horses to sell."

The grin abruptly faded from Brubs's face. "Now, that's troublin' me some, I gotta admit. Word is there's two, three big trail herds not more'n a week out of Dodge, headin' up from Texas. Could be some of them trail bosses or cowboys might recognize a few of these here horses. I'd sure like to get shut of the rest of the ponies by then."

Willoughby winced. "Thank you for the comfort of that gentle reminder, friend. *'Ils commencent ici par faire pendre un homme et puis ils lui font son procès.'* "

"Talk American. That Horace feller again?"

"Molière. It translates as, 'Here they hang a man first, and try him afterwards.' "

"Aw, hell, Dave, ain't nobody gonna get

246

hanged. No need to fret yourself. You just put your money down on ol' Uncle Brubs."

"That," Willoughby said with a sigh, "is not the sort of bet I'd cover with my last dollar. . . ." His voice trailed off as a tall, broad-shouldered man with a heavy handlebar mustache stepped around the corner of the corral. He carried a double barreled shotgun. Sunlight glinted from a star on his vest.

The tall man stopped and stared in silence for a moment at the three men beside the corral. Suspicion glittered in cold brown eyes. "This the Texas Horsetrading Company outfit?"

"It is," Brubs said, warily eyeing the shotgun and badge.

"Which one of you is Nick Chadburne?"

Brubs stiffened. His right hand dropped to his side, forearm brushing against the Colt holstered at his hip. "Who's askin' and how come?"

"Nathan Holcomb, deputy marshal of Dodge City. I got a paper for Chadburne."

Willoughby's heart skipped a beat. Tobin Jamison's warrant for Nick had slipped his mind. He glanced at Brubs. The stocky Texan was about half a hiccup away from trying to pull iron on a Kansas lawman who happened to be toting a twin-bore shotgun. Willoughby grabbed Brubs's gun arm. "Easy, partner," he said urgently, "we made a promise."

"Promise, hell," Brubs snapped. "I ain't lettin' the law have this boy."

Nick solved the problem. He casually stepped

in front of Brubs. "I'm Chadburne," he said.

Holcomb stared at Chadburne for a moment, then lifted a folded yellow paper from his shirt pocket. The icy look in the brown eyes thawed. "Telegram from Texas, son," Holcomb said. "Looks like you're off the hook."

Chadburne grabbed the paper and handed it to Willoughby. The boy's fingers trembled slightly. "What's it say, Mr. Willoughby?"

Willoughby scanned the message, a slow grin spreading over his face. "The marshal's right, Nick. It's from Tobin Jamison. It says, 'Investigation death of Elton Forrest complete. Harriet Forrest confessed. Charges against Nick Chadburne dropped. Pending warrants McCallan and Willoughby aiding and abetting withdrawn. Debt cancelled but don't push your luck.' "

Brubs whooped loud enough to spook the horses. He ripped his tattered hat from his head and tossed it high into the air.

Chadburne's chest heaved in a deep sigh of relief. His shoulders slumped, and the hint of a smile touched his lips. "It's over? I'm not going to hang?"

"It's over, Nick." Willoughby put a hand on the youth's shoulder. "You are no longer a fugitive. Jamison kept his word. None of us are wanted men, now."

Nathan Holcomb raised an eyebrow at Willoughby. "Not that it's any of my business, at least officially," he said, "but what did Jamison mean, 'debt cancelled'?"

Willoughby smiled at the deputy marshal. "We helped Jamison out of some Comanche trouble a while back. I presume the sergeant means he now considers our account settled."

"By God, boys," Brubs said as he grabbed and pumped Chadburne's hand, "I reckon this calls for a double-barreled celebration tonight!"

Chadburne's face brightened, as if a heavy weight had been lifted from his mind. A slow grin spread over his face. It was the first time Willoughby could remember seeing the kid actually smile.

Holcomb turned to Brubs. "Glad to bring good news to somebody for a change," he said. "Usually, it's the other way around." He touched fingertips to his hat brim. "Just one more thing, gents. Jamison said something in that telegram about don't push your luck. Maybe he was talking about Texas, but that goes in Dodge City, too. I've been through these trail drive celebrations before. Keep it south of the deadline and away from the respectable part of town. No shooting, no brawling. I like my town quiet." He turned on a heel and strode away.

"Hot damn, boys," Brubs said after a moment, "I can near taste that whiskey and them Dodge City women —" He stopped in mid-sentence. "Well, I be switched. Would you lookee here?"

A black buggy pulled by a bay mare turned from the street toward the horse pens. Willoughby's breath caught in his throat. The buggy itself was ordinary. The mare in harness was ordinary. The girl holding the reins was anything but ordinary.

THIRTEEN

Dave Willoughby tried not to stare. He failed miserably.

The young woman on the buggy seat was tall and slender, with shoulder-length auburn hair that caught highlights of red and gold from the afternoon sun. Ripples of light and shadow flickered across the deep emerald green dress that molded itself against her body in the light breeze. But it was her eyes that held Willoughby's gaze. They were a color he had seen only in rare prairie flowers, a deep violet, and they were set wide in the oval face, with tiny crinkles of laugh lines at the corners. They were the most beautiful eyes he had ever seen.

"Damn me for a pregnant possum," Brubs McCallan muttered softly at Willoughby's side, "if that ain't the flat-out best-lookin' filly I ever seen in any remuda, and I seen a bunch of 'em."

Willoughby's cheeks reddened as he realized he had been staring at the woman for entirely too long. He forced his gaze from the haunting violet eyes to the man on the buggy seat beside her.

The man was of medium height and looked to be in his early forties, his cheeks and jowls pale as if he spent little time exposed to sun or wind. His features were rather plain, the sort of face that a man wouldn't notice in a crowd. The hint of a paunch strained the buttons of an ornately embroidered vest spanned by a heavy length of gold watch chain. He wore a freshly pressed, dark gray silk suit topped by a brushed silver beaver derby, and his low-topped black shoes sported a bright polish. He looked like money.

"Good afternoon, gentlemen," the man said as he lifted fingertips to the derby brim. "It is my understanding that you are offering a number of horses for sale."

"Yes, sir," Brubs said eagerly, the prospect of money momentarily distracting him from the woman on the buggy seat. "That's a pure fact. Fine ponies, too. Most of 'em is at least green broke, and some of 'em is done trained for ropin' and herd work. You lookin' to buy?"

The man stepped from the buggy, helped the woman down, and extended a hand to Brubs. "Jerome C. Montmorency, Boston." The voice was a cultured baritone and as smooth as the silk suit.

"Brubs McCallan, Texas Horsetradin' Company. This here's my partner, Dave Willoughby. Young feller there's Nick Chadburne, one of our top hands."

Montmorency nodded a greeting, then slipped a hand beneath the violet-eyed girl's arm. "May I present my niece, Miss Sarah Beth Thompson."

Brubs swept his hat from his head. "Mighty pleased to make your acquaintance, Miss Thompson. Seein' such a pretty critter as you sure does brighten up a man's day."

Sarah Beth Thompson's smile was almost as devastating as her eyes, Willoughby thought. The flash of even, white teeth between full lips dug dimples in her cheeks.

"Thank you for the compliment, Mr. McCallan." Her violet eyes twinkled in amusement. Her voice was a pleasant contralto with a lilt that could have been Irish.

Willoughby became aware that Sarah Beth Thompson was studying him over Brubs's shoulder. He flushed, removed his hat, and desperately tried to think of something to say. The words didn't come. The best he could manage was a simple nod. Willoughby's embarrassment deepened under the soft violet gaze. He became painfully aware of his dirty, unshaven, disheveled, grubby, and generally trail-stained state, and realized he probably smelled worse than one of Granny Hooper's nanny goats. His current appearance was not one that would impress a lady.

The man in the silk suit came to Willoughby's rescue.

"Gentlemen, I represent a rather influential and quite wealthy consortium back in Boston," Montmorency said. "The consortium has recently extended its business operations into ranching, purchasing a rather large tract of land in Wyoming and Montana. The home office has instructed me to acquire the necessary animals to stock and work the land. We are in need of horses. How many do you have left?"

"Nigh onto a hundred, give or take." Brubs turned to Willoughby. "What's the sure-enough tally, partner?"

"One hundred and four, Mr. Montmorency," Willoughby said after glancing at his notebook.

"I'll take them. All." Montmorency reached into an inside pocket of the silk suit and brought out an oversized wallet. "What's the price?"

Brubs scrubbed a hand over his whiskered chin as if in deep thought. "Normal, it'd be forty-five a head," he said, "but I reckon you want the whole cavvy, we'll toss a little slack in that rope. Forty a head."

"Done," Montmorency said. He licked a thumb. "Let's see, now . . . I believe that comes to 4,160 dollars, correct?"

Brubs lifted an eyebrow at Willoughby.

Willoughby nodded. "Correct, sir."

Montmorency thumbed through the contents of the thick wallet. "I have here," he said, "a draft drawn on the Burlington and Quincy Railroad, in which my company owns a third of the stock. The draft is in the amount of 3,500 dollars. Will you accept such a document in this transaction?"

Brubs grinned happily. "Yes, sir. The B-and-Q's a right solid outfit. I reckon their paper's good enough."

Montmorency licked a thumb and flicked through a wad of bills, then frowned. "I have only 620 dollars in cash with me at the moment. The remainder of our funds are in the safe at the Dodge House. Would it be acceptable to you if I were to deliver the remaining forty dollars to you at your place of lodging this evening?"

"Yes, sir, Mr. Montmorency," Brubs said. "We'll be stayin' at the Great Western."

Montmorency smiled and nodded. "I knew you two were gentlemen of honor and trust," he said. "I am rather eager to close this deal. I would like to get these animals on their way aboard the 4:10 freight."

Willoughby eyed Montmorency with considerably more care than before. There was something about the man that didn't feel quite right, but he couldn't figure out what. "Brubs," he said cautiously, "can I talk to you for a moment?"

Brubs waved the question aside. "It'll keep, Dave. Write up a bill of sale for Mr. Montmorency here."

Montmorency waved the offer away. "That won't be necessary, gentlemen. I pride myself on being a fine judge of character, and I recognize honest men when I see them. Your handshakes will be a sufficient contract." He handed a sheaf of greenbacks to Brubs.

The faint alarm that had been tinkling in the back of Willoughby's mind jingled louder. "Brubs, we need to talk."

Sarah Beth Thompson interrupted, gazing toward a small corner corral of the rail yard. "Is that beautiful black gelding one of the sale horses?"

"No, ma'am," Brubs said. "Them animals in the little pen's personal mounts. Black belongs to

Dave. You got a sure enough eye for hossflesh, Miss Thompson."

Sarah Beth turned to Dave. "Would you consider selling him, Mr. Willoughby? He is a magnificent animal."

Willoughby swallowed and shook his head. "Sorry, Miss Thompson. I couldn't part with him."

"I understand, sir," she said, "but if you should happen to change your mind before you leave Dodge City, will you let me know?"

Willoughby nodded lamely. "Yes, I will."

Brubs lovingly flipped the corners of the thick stack of bills before handing them to Willoughby. "Me and the boys'll load them ponies in the stock cars for you, Mr. Montmorency," he said. "Some of 'em might be a tad salty to load. They ain't seen many trains where they come from."

"That won't be necessary, Mr. McCallan. I'll hire some people to help. The horses are my responsibility now." He raised a hand in salute. "It has been a pleasure doing business with you, gentlemen," he said. "If you will excuse us, my niece and I must attend to some additional business. I'll see you this evening at the Great Western. It would be my pleasure to purchase a few rounds of drinks, if you're so inclined."

"Ain't never been inclinder," Brubs said. He watched as the stocky man in the silk suit strode away, then turned to Willoughby. "What'd you want to talk on, partner?"

Willoughby's brow wrinkled. "Something

about that man doesn't feel right," he said.

Brubs chuckled aloud. "That's a pure fact. He sure as hell ain't no horse trader. Didn't even try to talk me down on the price, and I'd a let them ponies go for thirty a head. Skinned him smooth out of ten dollars a horse."

"Brubs," Willoughby said solemnly, "the Dodge City bank has closed for the day. This happens to be Friday. The bank will not reopen until Monday. We won't know until then if Montmorency's railroad draft is in order. If it isn't, our horses will be long gone."

"Aw, hell, Dave. You just got to try and find a hailstorm under every silver-lined cloud. Don't you fret that none. The B-and-Q Railroad's got money in ever' bank from New York to San Francisco." He clapped Willoughby on the shoulder, raising a sizeable puff of dust, and pointed toward the buggy disappearing around the corner of the rail yard. "I reckon I know what's got you twitchy, partner. That leggy little gal with the big eyes." He sighed wistfully. "Damn, what I wouldn't give to snort in her flanks like a young stud."

"Brubs, trying to get your attention when there happens to be an attractive woman around is like pushing a wet rope up a muddy slope," Willoughby said in resignation.

The Texan cocked an eyebrow at Willoughby. "Way she was lookin' you over, partner, I'd say she's got her cap set for ol' Dave." He shook his head. "I swear, I don't know what it is makes prime fillies flock to you like you was the only rooster in the henhouse. And you don't even work at it smart, the way I do."

Willoughby felt a stir of irritation at his partner. "Do you think we could drop the subject of Sarah Beth Thompson?"

Brubs chuckled aloud. "Son, you got yourself a chance here most men would kill for. Play your cards right, you just might could parlay that gal's interest in that there black right into a trip under them petticoats."

Willoughby tossed his pencil stub aside in disgust. "It isn't her, dammit," he grumbled. "It's that uncle of hers. There's something about that man —"

Brubs interrupted with a wave of the hand. "Dave, you're just huntin' somethin' to booger over. Too long on the trail, I reckon. Didn't Montmorency say he'd buy us a passel of good whiskey this evenin'? That ain't somethin' a man without no ethics would say. And speakin' of which, since we're now outta the horse business, I sure could stand a couple shots of good dust-cuttin' liquor. You game?"

Willoughby shook his head. "You go on. I'll deposit most of our funds in the Great Western's safe and take our personal mounts to the public stable." He paused to brush at the caked mud, dust, and horse slobbers on his shirt and pants. "After that, I'm headed straight for the mercantile store for new clothes, inside out and top to bottom, then to the barbershop for a bath, shave, and haircut. I don't believe I have ever felt so grubby

258

in my life. I'll meet you later at the hotel. If you aren't in jail by then."

Brubs rubbed his palms together in anticipation. "Partner, we're gonna turn the wolf loose this weekend. Ain't no better place for howlin' than Dodge City. Besides, we got us a civic duty to howl. Them two green kids we brung along got to have somebody show 'em all about wine, women, and song at the end of a long trail."

Willoughby sighed. "Deal me out of any town-treeing, Brubs. The highlights of my evening will include a good steak served on a real tablecloth with honest-to-God knives and forks, topped off by a helping of deep-dish apple pie. Then I am going to conclude the day with an uninterrupted night's sleep in a soft bed with a real mattress and a roof overhead."

"You Yankees," Brubs said solemnly, "just ain't got no idea on how to have fun. Come all this way and just hole up somewhere like a badger? It ain't — it ain't *Texan,* that's what it ain't."

"I'm just a provisional Texan, remember?"

Dave Willoughby stepped into the gold wash of sunset that bathed Dodge City's main street and settled his new black beaver hat against the light westerly breeze.

The streets were busy, but not especially crowded. The Friday evening rush to restaurants, hotels, and saloons had barely started. This evening's pedestrians and horsemen appeared to be mostly local residents. The real crunch of people was still several days away, when the first of the trail herds moved in from the south. Willoughby planned to be miles away when that happened.

For now, he planned to simply relax and enjoy. It was the first time in weeks that he had felt clean.

The accumulated grubbiness of the long ride from LaQuesta was gone, soaked away in an hour-long bath in a real tub with clean hot water instead of a quick rinse in a muddy water hole. Willoughby's thick, wavy brown hair was neatly trimmed; the itchy, aggravating stubble on his cheeks and neck had been banished by an expert barber's keen razor. Soft, new, black calfskin boots cradled his feet. The crisp, clean white cotton shirt and black gabardine trousers fresh from the shelves of the general mercantile were refreshing against his skin. But despite his outward contentment, Willoughby couldn't shake the uneasy feeling in his belly as he weaved his way through the crowd to the porch of the Great Western Hotel. It was still there, a nagging worry that all was not right with the world. Maybe, he told himself, it was because Brubs was out of sight. And that often meant mischief was afoot . . .

"Mr. Willoughby!"

The contralto voice with its Irish lilt chased the nagging discomfort from his mind. His heart skipped a beat as Sarah Beth Thompson strode up.

"Good evening, Miss Thompson," Willoughby said as he touched his fingertips to hat brim.

"I almost didn't recognize you, Mr. Willoughby," she said.

He flushed. "I apologize for my appearance this afternoon. I don't relish being quite that scruffy, but I hadn't had time to rid myself of the trail dust."

She waved long, slender fingers in dismissal. "Posh. Men who work with animals don't have time to preen like town dandies. Don't give it another thought." She glanced toward the hotel door. "Are your friends inside? I have a message from my uncle for Mr. McCallan."

"I'm not sure where they are, Miss Thompson." He held the door open for her and smiled wryly. "If we don't find them here, I suppose the next logical place to look would be the jail."

Sarah Beth's laugh was throaty and lyrical. Willoughby liked it. She placed a hand on his forearm as she stepped through the door. His flesh warmed under her touch.

He was a bit surprised to find Brubs, Cal, Tilghman, and Chadburne all seated at a table in the dining room instead of standing at the bar. Even more surprising was that they were all mostly clean and still reasonably sober. That wasn't Brubs McCallan's style. All four stood as Willoughby led Sarah Beth to the table.

"Please, gentlemen, be seated," Sarah Beth said. "My uncle sends his regrets that he cannot join you. He was called from town unexpectedly on urgent business. The telegram from Boston left him barely enough time to catch the four o'clock train." She reached into her small leather bag. "He asked me to deliver these to you." She handed three gold coins to Brubs. "Two of the gold pieces are the remainder of the money owed on the horses." She smiled at Brubs. "Uncle Monty said you were to use the extra twenty dollars to buy drinks."

Brubs flashed a wide grin. "We'll be mighty happy to oblige Uncle Monty," he said. "Have a set-down, Miss Thompson. We was about to order us a big steak, soon's that pretty little waitress gal gets back over thisaway."

"No, thank you, Mr. McCallan," Sarah Beth said. "I wouldn't dream of intruding on your trail's end celebration. I'll take my leave and let Mr. Willoughby join you."

Willoughby shook his head. "Miss Thompson, I have eaten with these men all the way from Texas. I have a table reserved at the Dodge House, that I might have at least one meal in peace and quiet, a feat that is extraordinarily difficult around this group."

Brubs feigned a wounded pout. "Don't you pay no mind to this feller, Miss Thompson. We ain't rowdy sorts. Ol' Dave's a Yankee and ain't quite used to Texas ways, but he's learnin'. See you later, partner? It'll be time to hunt us up a real drinkin' spot pretty soon. We gotta get Cal and Nick here some learnin' on what railhead towns is all about. And mind our civic duty to boost the money supply in Dodge."

"I've already made my plans known, Brubs. A quiet meal and a good night's sleep, that's all."

The Texan casually shrugged, but he had a knowing glint in his brown eyes. "Sure, partner. But if you change your mind, we ain't gonna be hard to find."

"I doubt that. The barber said there were nineteen bars and saloons in Dodge City."

Brubs's face split in a beatific grin. "Yes, sir, my kind of town, Dodge. You want to come along later, just hunt up the ruckus. That's where we'll be at."

"Which," Willoughby said, "is precisely why I plan to be elsewhere." He turned to Sarah Beth. "It would be my pleasure to escort you back to your hotel, Miss Thompson."

She nodded, lamplight glistening in her rich auburn hair. "Thank you, Mr. Willoughby. I would appreciate that very much. Gentlemen, it was so nice to see you. Now, if you will please excuse us?"

Willoughby glanced back once as he led Sarah Beth toward the hotel entrance. His face flushed as Brubs closed one eye in a lecherous, knowing wink.

"Mr. Willoughby," Sarah Beth said as they stepped from the Great Western porch onto the sidewalk, "would you think it awfully brazen of me if I asked to join you for dinner?"

Willoughby's fingers suddenly went cool. His

heart rate went up. "It would be my pleasure, Miss Thompson. But I must warn you that I'm not particularly good at small talk. You might find my company most boring."

She chuckled low in her throat. "I doubt that, Mr. Willoughby. And I'm awfully interested in hearing of your long trip from Texas. It must have been most exciting."

"I suppose," he said wryly, "that it did have its moments."

Dave Willoughby lay relaxed and spent in the grassy clearing beneath a stand of cottonwood trees, listening to the cropping sounds as the buggy mare grazed a few feet away, a soothing counterpoint to the soft gurgle of water in the springfed creek two miles from Dodge City.

He was still trying to believe it had really happened.

Sarah Beth Thompson curled against his side, her auburn hair brushing against his neck, her head resting on his shoulder. Moonlight filtered through the trees, dappling light and dark swatches across her bare skin.

She sighed in contentment. Her finger traced a random pattern across his chest. Finally, she broke the lingering, comfortable silence.

"You must think I'm the most brazen hussy in the world," she said softly. "I've never done this before."

Willoughby stroked the smooth skin over her waist and hip. "I don't think you're brazen at all,

Miss Thompson, and certainly not a hussy."

She kissed him lightly on the neck. "I don't know what came over me. The wine, the moonlight buggy ride, or just being alone with you."

"Feeling regrets?"

"No. Not in the least. We're adults, Mr. Willoughby. If we perhaps exceeded the limits proscribed by society, then society can go suck a lemon. All that matters is that I don't want you to think I'm some cheap, wanton woman, like those girls in the Dodge City saloons."

Willoughby put a finger across her lips. "I don't think that at all. And I'll fight any man who says it."

She snuggled closer against his side, then suddenly giggled like a schoolgirl. "I've never had such a deliciously wicked time in my life, Mr. Willoughby. By the way, don't you think we could drop the formalities now and call each other by first name?"

"I think we're sufficiently acquainted for that now, Sarah Beth."

"And since I've already established the fact that I am totally without shame, Dave, are you free tomorrow night?"

Willoughby pulled her to him. "If I'm not," he said, "there will be a jailbreak somewhere."

"Dave, son, I'm beginnin' to get a tad fretty about you," Brubs said solemnly.

"Your sudden concern for my welfare touches me deeply, my friend," Willoughby said, cradling his coffee cup in the dining room of the Great Western. "It's a novel experience. Somewhat out of character, in fact, given your past determination to lead me into the maw of death and dismemberment at every opportunity." He sipped at his coffee. "So what is troubling you?"

"Looks to me like you're gettin' all calf-eyed over this Sarah Beth Thompson. Ever since we hit town, it was like you two was necked together on a short rope or somethin'."

Willoughby nodded. "We enjoy each other's company. Do I detect a hint of envy in your tone?"

"She's the primest filly I ever seen, at that. Reckon I can't blame you none for runnin' when she shakes the feed bucket." Brubs sighed. "I swear, I can't figger out how ever' time we get around a remuda of females, the shiniest one in the herd comes snufflin' up to you."

Willoughby finished his coffee and waved for a refill. "Just lucky, I guess. At least I have been this time." He waited until the waitress topped off their cups and moved out of earshot. "Is that what's bothering you, Brubs?"

"Some. But it ain't all. We're partners, and you ain't holdin' up your end of this partnership all of a sudden. Left me to try and drink up all the whiskey in Dodge City all by my lonesome two straight nights now. Hell, even *I* can't do that without no help."

"You look like you gave it your best try," Willoughby said. "And you weren't alone. You had

Tige, Nick and Cal to help."

"Tige was some help, I reckon," Brubs said. "But them two young'uns is just flat out amateurs at treein' a town."

"We all were, at one time. They'll learn, with you as a teacher. If they don't get shot, stabbed, lanced, or beaten to death beforehand."

Brubs rubbed his throbbing right temple, winced, and pulled a half-pint flask from his hip pocket.

"Isn't it a bit early in the day for a drink, even for you?" Willoughby asked.

Brubs downed a swallow from the flask, shuddered, and sighed. "Hair of the wolf, partner. That critter plumb bit the back of my head off last night. Feel better soon's that hits bottom. Come sundown, I won't be feelin' no pain at all." He took another nip from the flask and chased it with a swig of coffee. "You gonna come with us tonight?"

Willoughby shook his head. "I have other plans."

"That why you're sittin' here on a Sunday mornin', not even hung over, dressed up like you was preachin' somewhere?"

"Sarah Beth and I are going to church services this morning."

"Church?" Brubs's eyes widened in shock. "Dave, son, don't you know no man in his right mind don't take no woman to no place where *weddin's* happen!"

"The thought has crossed my mind, Brubs."

The Texan's shoulders slumped. "Tell me you ain't serious, Dave Willoughby."

"To borrow one of your own phrases, Brubs, I have never been seriouser." He drew in a deep breath. "I might as well drop the word on you now. Before we leave Dodge City, I'm going to ask Sarah Beth to come with me. As my wife."

Brubs's jaw dropped. "I ain't believin' this."

"Believe it, Brubs." Willoughby's tone was solemn.

"What if she won't come?"

"Then I'll stay. With her."

The stocky Texan was still sitting in stunned disbelief as Willoughby rose, paid the bill, and left.

Dave strode toward the Great Western, whistling softly and fighting back the urge to whoop in jubilation.

Sarah Beth Thompson had said yes.

Willoughby wanted to stop a drunk staggering down the street a few feet ahead, pump the man's hand, and announce the good news. He thought about hunting up Brubs and the boys, but decided against it. They would treat him to a celebratory drink, then another, and he didn't want to wake up in the Dodge City jail on the morning of his wedding day.

By noon tomorrow, he would be a married man. Sarah Beth had urged him to hurry back from the moon-dappled clearing, jabbering excitedly about the many details she had to attend to before standing at his side in the small white-washed church three blocks away.

He wondered how Brubs would take the news. It wasn't as if it were the end of the Texas Horsetrading Company. Willoughby's share of the proceeds from the horse drive would easily cover the cost of building a new house on the creek leading to LaQuesta. He would even have enough left over to buy a couple more sections of land adjoining the valley. Then he and Sarah Beth could settle in to raising horses, cattle, and kids. The thought sent a fresh wave of warmth through his chest. He had always liked being around children. He suspected he would be a good father, and Sarah Beth wanted at least three. Two boys and a girl.

Dave was still whistling and humming as he stepped onto the porch of the Great Western. He would treat himself to a solitary drink, a feast to his new bride and the future they were to share, from the as yet unopened bottle of Old Crow beneath his bed.

The distant wail of the locomotive whistle of the midnight train from Wichita sounded as Willoughby stepped through the hotel door.

"Oh, Mr. Willoughby," the aging night desk clerk called, "there's a message for you."

Willoughby strode to the desk, unashamed of the silly grin spread across his face. The clerk looked at him quizzically over half-moon spectacles as he handed him a slip of paper.

The writing was neat, crisp, and to the point.

The night deputy was holding four men — Brubs McCallan, Tige Tilghman, Cal Hooper, and Nick Chadburne — on "a variety of charges too long to list here," the deputy wrote. He added that none of the charges were felonies, but that it would be rather expensive to bail them out. Willoughby chuckled aloud.

"Good news, sir?" the clerk asked.

"You might say that," Willoughby said. "At least I know now where my friends are. And they'll keep until morning." He went up the stairs two at a time. Monday was going to be a busy day, he thought.

FOURTEEN

"Good morning, gentlemen," Willoughby said cheerfully.

Brubs groaned aloud. "It ain't good, and you don't have to be so damn chipper about it." He sat on the edge of the iron bunk and glared at Willoughby through bloodshot eyes. "And you don't have to be so damn loud, neither. Have some respect for the dyin'." His face was bruised, swollen and puffy.

The rest of the crew didn't look much better than Brubs, Willoughby thought with amusement.

Young Cal Hooper slumped in a corner, his face chalk-white except for the freckles and an impressive bruise on a cheekbone. He held both fists against his temples as if trying to keep his head from splitting in two.

Nick Chadburne's swarthy face was drawn into a pained scowl. A raw scrape ran from the middle of his forehead to his left ear. The lower part of the earlobe was missing. Blood crusted the spot where the missing chunk had been.

Tige Tilghman was the only one of the bunch who appeared unmarked — and the only one who managed a grin of greeting for Willoughby. It was a weak grin.

"You gentlemen appear to have visited the second level of Dante's tiers last night," Willoughby said.

"Don't recollect no saloon named Dontay's Tears," Brubs said. "Best I remember, it was the Alamo. Anyway, it wasn't our fault. We was just defendin' the honor of the great state of Texas. Few of these here Kansas cowboys stepped over the line 'tween joshin' and takin' the Lone Star State's name in vain."

"How many Kansas cowboys?"

" 'Bout fifteen or so, I reckon. We learnt most of 'em to mind their manners 'fore the law come runnin'."

"That was one hell of a good scrap," Tilghman said wistfully. "I ain't had that much fun in a long time. And I tell you, we're plumb proud of Cal here. Big cow chaser with the Spade outfit decided to try him on. Took two, three men to pull Cal off 'im."

Cal moaned aloud. "I can't believe I did all that. I'm going to hell for sure, now. Granny'd tan my hide, was she still alive. Drinking and fighting and taking that woman upstairs —"

"Took her up there twice, too," Brubs said, a note of admiration in his voice. "This here kid's earnin' his spurs at railhead mighty quick."

"Don't be ashamed of your actions, Cal," Willoughby said reassuringly. "Anyone can be led astray once. As Juvenal wrote, *'Nemo repente fuit turpissimus.'* "

"Talk American, dammit," Brubs grumped.

"It says, 'No one ever suddenly became de-
praved.' Of course, Juvenal wasn't riding with
Brubs McCallan at the time. You boys didn't
leave much more of this Alamo standing than
Santa Anna did the one down south, by the
way. Over two hundred dollars in damages
alone. Fines came to another hundred and
change."

Chadburne traced a finger over the ravaged
earlobe and sighed heavily. "I guess that takes
care of any wages I had coming."

"Don't fret that none, Nick," Brubs said.
"Texas Horsetradin' Company'll foot the bill.
You done good, holdin' up our reputation
thataway. You'll get full pay." He heaved himself
unsteadily to his feet. "You gonna stand there
grinnin' like a possum, Dave, or you gonna get us
outta here? I don't get some hair of that wolf that
et me pretty soon, I'll die for sure. I had me some
fair hangovers before, but this one'd take top
prize anywhere."

"I've paid you boys out already," Willoughby
said. "Come along, now. We've got a lot of work
to do. Tige, Cal, and Nick can load our supplies
in the wagon while Brubs and I settle up at the
bank. And I'd like to see you cleaned up for my
wedding."

"Weddin'!" Brubs's voice was a startled
squawk. "Don't tell me you —"

"I did," Willoughby interrupted, his chest
swollen with pride, "and she said yes. We've got
to get you some decent clothes, Brubs. I want you

to be my best man."

"Best man?"

"You're my partner and friend," Willoughby said. "Besides, I don't have time to hunt up someone a bit more respectable. We'll be married at eleven this morning. Sarah Beth's coming with us. We can be on our way home by early afternoon."

Brubs sank back onto the cot with an audible moan. "There goes a good partnership."

"Not at all, Brubs," Willoughby said. "I've got it all worked out. It will be better than ever. Now, let's get a move on, gentlemen. Time is wasting."

The tattered crew wandered outside. Brubs tagged after Willoughby to the bank, the others stumbling away to tend to business. Willoughby paused outside the bank and handed Brubs the bottle he had stashed in his room. "Some hair of the wolf, partner," he said.

Brubs lifted the bottle and downed three swallows. "Mother's milk," he said with a sigh. "I reckon I'll make it now." He didn't hand the bottle back to Willoughby. "Let's see that banker man, amigo. I'm gettin' plumb itchy to run these poor ol' sore fingers through all that money."

Willoughby stood patiently before the ornately engraved mahogany desk as the banker carefully counted out bills and gold coins as he cashed various bank drafts. Brubs licked his lips and eyed the growing stack of currency. Either the wolf hair had hit or the sight of the money had eased his hangover misery, Willoughby mused.

The banker abruptly looked up. "Gentlemen, we have a problem here," he said.

Willoughby's heart skipped a beat. "What problem?"

"This railroad draft on the Burlington and Quincy. It's a forgery."

Willoughby's face paled. "What? That can't be."

The banker wagged his head. "Sorry, Mr. Willoughby. It's a complete and total fake. And not even a good job of forgery at that." He tossed the draft onto the desk. "It appears that you men have been swindled."

Willoughby stood frozen in stunned silence for several seconds. "That can't be," he finally stammered. "There must be some mistake." He glanced at Brubs. "Wait here, Brubs. I'll go get Sarah Beth. She can straighten this out."

Willoughby strode hurriedly from the bank, darted through the light traffic to the Dodge House, and mounted the stairs leading to Sarah Beth's room two at a time. There was no response to his knock; the door stood ajar. He pushed his way into the room. The bed was unused. The drawers of the bureau stood open and the closet was empty. Willoughby strode from the room, heart pounding in his chest, and ran down the stairs to the desk.

"Where's Miss Thompson?" he said to the desk clerk. "Her room is empty."

"She checked out late last night, Mr. Willoughby," the clerk said. "She was in something of a hurry. I believe she left on the midnight train."

The empty hole in Willoughby's chest grew bigger, pushing aside his disbelief. "Train? Left? I don't understand. She and I were supposed to be . . ." His voice trailed away in bewilderment.

"She left a message for you, sir," the clerk said. He rummaged through the cubbyholes behind the desk, then handed him a paper.

Willoughby unfolded the paper with trembling fingers. The words were in feminine, flowing script. A painful lump formed in his throat as he read.

Dear Dave,
This is the most difficult letter I have ever written. By now you must suspect the awful truth. Montmorency is not my uncle's real name, nor is he my uncle. He is my husband and my partner in crime.

The ache in Willoughby's throat tightened.

By the time you read this, dear Dave, I will be far away, going to join my husband. My heart weeps to have done such a terrible, awful thing to such a fine and wonderful man as you. I truly felt something special for you, Dave. I was not acting a role during the buggy rides, the memory of which I will cherish throughout my life. My job was to merely distract you from your suspicions. This time, however, I became personally in-

volved to an extent I never thought possible. I will not be so presumptuous as to ask your forgiveness; I know that would be impossible. I can only remember what might have been, had we met under different circumstances.

The note was signed simply, *I'm sorry. Sarah Beth.*

Willoughby blinked against the sting in his eyes and the cold, icy fist of betrayal and loss that clamped around his heart. He strode deliberately from the Dodge House, stopped midway across the street, tore the message into a dozen pieces, and tossed it away.

Brubs was waiting outside the bank, a saddlebag draped casually across his shoulder.

"Well, partner?" he said. "Get it straightened out?"

"I got it straight, all right," Willoughby said, his tone cold and tight. "We were had, Brubs. Skinned like a couple of greenhorns. Montmorency is a crook. Sarah Beth was his associate." He sighed heavily. The ache didn't go away. "Brubs," he said, "I've been nine kinds of a fool."

"I reckon this means there won't be no weddin'?"

"No. There won't be no weddin'. Let's get the hell out of Dodge."

The Texas Horsetrading Company caravan was camped three nights out of Dodge City, heading south. There was none of the usual good-natured banter of the trail.

Tige Tilghman wasn't with them. He had stopped his horse at the outskirts of Dodge City and offered handshakes all around. "I'll be leavin' you boys here," he said. "There's still a few states and territories I ain't been run out of yet." With that, he reined his horse toward the northwest and rode away.

Willoughby turned the cleanup chores over to Cal Hooper and strode to Brubs's side as the reddish-gold wash of sunset began to fade from the western sky.

"Brubs," Willoughby said softly, "I've been a complete idiot. You have every right to dissolve our partnership, maybe even shoot me, and I wouldn't blame you one bit if you did."

"Now, why in the blue-eyed hell would I go and do somethin' like that for, Dave? We're partners. Have been since I sprung you from that San 'Tone jail. Ain't nothin' happened to change that."

"Losing my head over a woman is nothing? Costing us 3,500 dollars is nothing? Dammit, Brubs, I should have known. I even suspected something was wrong, but I ignored the warning my gut was trying to sound."

Brubs fell silent for a moment. "I seem to recall you was tryin' to tell me somethin' back there at them railhead pens. I reckon I wasn't in the listenin' mood. Hell, son, if that's all that's botherin' you — losin' the money, I mean — we ain't got no worries. I thought you was still hurtin' over that gal."

Willoughby sighed. "I am. I thought I had the whole world in my hands for three days. It's hard to put into words, but I was really in love with that woman."

Brubs pursed his lips in thought. "Thought I was in love once myself," he said after a moment, "but when she kept chargin' me for it, I figgered I was wastin' my time. Now I ain't tellin' you to forget that Sarah Beth, 'cause that'd be a damn sight easier said than did. But you can quit frettin' over the money. Hell, a few dollars don't mean nothin'. Money ain't no good without it brings a man fun, not hurt. You squat down here and think on it a minute, partner. I'll be right back."

Willoughby was still thinking on it when Brubs returned, a quart of Kentucky sour mash in hand. Brubs twisted the cork free, tossed it aside, and handed the bottle to him. "This maybe won't make the hurt go 'way, partner, but it'll cut the sting some."

Willoughby tilted the bottle, swallowed twice, winced and handed it to Brubs, who lifted it in a toast. "Here's to our future, partner." He knocked back a couple of slugs of the liquor.

"Future?"

"Sure." Brubs waved the bottle toward camp. "Cal there, he's got him a herd of goats waitin' back in LaQuesta. He gets a little more seasonin' on him, I reckon he'll see the light, sell them damn goats, and get into a real ranchin' business like cattle or horses."

Willoughby reached for the jug.

"Nick's made a right fair hand. I been thinkin' about us maybe takin' him on as hired help, at least for a spell while you learn him readin' and writin' and cipherin'. He ain't got nowhere else to go, anyhow. Pass me that jug while there's still some left."

Willoughby surrendered the bottle. "You're riding around the herd again, my friend. Take the point."

Brubs lowered the level of the jug another inch. "Look at it thisaway, Dave. I don't reckon there's a man livin' ain't been took advantage of by a woman. I figger it's best you found out now what that Sarah Beth really was, 'stead of after she had the hobbles on you."

Willoughby reached for the jug. Brubs took another swallow before handing it back.

"Ain't it a fact you left home on account of somebody was always tellin' you what to do and when to do it?"

Willoughby nodded.

"Woulda been the same thing, had you two married up. Why, you wouldn't a been able to go to the outhouse without askin' her permission and tellin' her what you planned to do and what time you was comin' back." He snorted in disgust. "Seen many a good man ruined by gettin' hisself hitched in double yoke. Gimme the jug."

Willoughby handed it over.

"Now, partner," Brubs said, "look on the sunshine side of this here rock. We made us a fair to middlin' profit on this trip. Had us a little fun along the way, most times."

"You have an odd definition of fun," Willoughby said.

"We made enough money we don't have to hit a lick of work for a year, we don't want to," Brubs said earnestly. "And we got us a good business. We got us a warm cabin. We got us a good whore back home. Couldn't be nothin' but rosy times ahead for the Texas Horsetradin' Company, way I see it. Texas and Mexico's still full of horses that ain't been stole, whiskey that ain't been drunk, and women that we ain't had yet." Brubs hoisted the battle again. "Hell, Dave, I can't handle all that entertainment by my lonesome. You gotta lend me a hand. That's what partners is for."

Willoughby fell silent for a moment, staring into the darkness that had settled over the campsite. Finally, he sighed. "Thanks, Brubs."

"What for? I bought that there bottle out of your share of the hoss money."

"Not for the whiskey. For being my partner."

The Texan cuffed him lightly on the shoulder. "Now you're talkin'." He downed another shot and handed the jug back to Willoughby. It was a meaningful gesture. Even if the bottle was empty. "Poor bastard."

"I am not asking for sympathy, Brubs," Willoughby said.

"What? Oh. Wasn't talkin' about you. I was feelin' sorry for that Colorado cowman bought that damn coyote dun. How many times we sell that plug, anyway?"

Willoughby's brows bunched in thought. "Five, I think. Maybe six."

"Gonna miss that jughead some," Brubs said wistfully. "We made us a passel of money on ol' Ugly." He leaned back on his elbows and stared at the stars above. "Tell you what, amigo — I been wonderin' if maybe we couldn't make us a little detour on the way home. I seem to recall that little redhead down in Denton had a mighty fine-lookin' cousin."

"Brubs McCallan," Willoughby said, his words beginning to slur, "you are absolutely incorrigible, totally without morals, and otherwise generally beyond redemption. You are a complete and total hell-raiser, a disaster waiting to happen —"

"Why, thanks, partner. I was afeared you mighta been gettin' bored."

"And I can't think of anybody I'd rather be hanged alongside," Willoughby said, smiling. "Let's go home."

The employees of G.K. Hall hope you have enjoyed this Large Print book. All our Large Print titles are designed for easy reading, and all our books are made to last. Other G.K. Hall books are available at your library, through selected bookstores, or directly from us.

For information about titles, please call:

(800) 257-5157

To share your comments, please write:

Publisher
G.K. Hall & Co.
P.O. Box 159
Thorndike, ME 04986